THE ACQUITTAL

By the Author

Veritas

Runaway

The Acquittal

Visit us at www.boldstrokesbooks.com

THE ACQUITTAL

by
Anne Laughlin

2014

Credits
Editors: Greg Herren and Stacia Seaman
Production Design: Stacia Seaman
Cover Design by Sheri (graphicartist2020@hotmail.com)

Acknowledgments

For valuable first reads: Joan Larkin, Patricia Barber, Beth Brandt, Ann Farlee, and Liz Laughlin.

For help understanding bipolar disorder: Maureen Fayen, M.D., Kathleen Baldwin, M.D., and James van Bavel, M.D. Any misrepresentations of the condition are solely my doing.

For help on a few gun and car questions: Paul Braasch.

To Greg Herren for his encouragement and for clever help on plot points. As is often said of a good editor, he made this a better book.

And, finally, Linda Braasch, who's read *The Acquittal* almost as many times as I have. Her unfailing encouragement kept me going during the long haul of writing a novel. I'm thankful every day that she's in my life.

For Linda

CHAPTER ONE

Friday, February 15

Lauren flipped on the kitchen lights and saw the body of her lover sprawled at her feet, a bullet hole centered on her forehead. She knelt and felt for Kelly's pulse. There was no need, really, since half of her head appeared to be stuck to the breakfast room wall. The body was still warm, the smell of the gunshot still fresh in the air. Kelly's glorious hair was fanned out and drenched in blood. Her arms and legs were shooting out at curious angles, so at odds with the graceful woman she'd been. Lauren had to turn away. She saw her own revolver on the floor a few feet from the body. When she touched it she could feel it was still warm as well.

A tremendous clatter came from the hallway behind her, booming in the dead quiet. Lauren grabbed the revolver and shot blindly, splintering a kitchen cabinet. All was quiet for a moment before her cat came rocketing out of the doorway, galloped across the family room, and flew onto the fireplace mantel. She licked herself furiously. Lauren dropped the gun where she found it.

She sat next to the body and watched a small rivulet of blood make its way toward her, heedless of the ridiculously expensive business suit she wore. Kelly had given it to her as a gift. She was quite generous that way, as long as she was using Lauren's credit card. She felt guilty thinking ill of Kelly. The things she complained about were the very things she'd found charming about her when they first got together. The gift buying, the elaborate care she took of herself, the relentless cheerfulness morphed over time into reckless spending, shallowness, and inability to take anything seriously. They'd had a bad fight about her spending that morning.

But Lauren felt real sorrow. They'd been together a number of years. There'd been many good times. She stood and reached into her bag for her phone. She dialed 911 and then went to see if the cat was okay.

Chapter Two

Friday, September 6

The paint was barely dry on the walls when Josie Harper's first client walked through her office door. Josie sat cross-legged on the floor of the reception room, trying to put together an Ikea chair. She hadn't expected any business her first day, but now an exceedingly tall woman was standing with one hand on her door, reading the words stenciled on the glass—Josie Harper, Private Investigations.

Josie got up from the floor. She was shoeless and wore a tattered Led Zeppelin T-shirt and blue jeans. She was dressed for back-room assembly, not front-room sales.

"Can I help you?" Josie said. She could feel a flush of color move up her face.

"I'm Sarah DeAngeles. I have an appointment with Stan Waterman. I think his office is past yours."

Sarah appeared to be in her thirties, good-looking, if your preferences ran to cheerleader faces and ponytails. Josie's did not. She watched Sarah's eyes as they traveled from her ancient ball cap, past her old 501s, down to her polka-dot socks. They might as well have been different species.

"Sure, I know Stan," Josie said. He ran Shield Detectives down the hall.

"When I saw your name on the door I decided to come in," Sarah said. "I'd much rather work with a woman on this matter."

"Naturally," Josie said. She had no idea what the matter was, but was happy to take advantage over a PI with more experience than her—a group that included every PI in Chicago.

"Is this a good time to talk?" Sarah said.

"Of course. Let's go into my office."

Sarah took a minute to cancel her appointment with Stan Waterman before following Josie through the Ikea detritus and into her office. The window faced east toward Lake Michigan. The light streamed over the desk and visitor chairs that were fortunately assembled and ready for business. The rest of the room was a mess. Josie's laminated wood desk would be peeling in a year's time. It was littered with office supplies still in shrink wrap. Josie could see the wary look in Sarah's eye as she took the chair in front of her desk.

"I'm sorry things are such a mess. Setting up an office is a real pain," Josie said.

"But you've been in business for a while?"

"I was a cop for over ten years. I've been doing investigations for a long time." Josie felt that was true, depending on what definition of "long" was being used. Or "investigations," for that matter. She'd been a property crimes detective for a couple of years before leaving the department. "Why don't you tell me what brings you here?"

"I'm a member of the board of directors for Wade-Fellows Publishing. Our president and editor-in-chief was recently acquitted of murdering her partner. We need help clearing her name and I've been put in charge of that effort," Sarah said.

It took a moment for the words to sink in and Josie felt a twinge of panic. Murder? It didn't seem possible her first case would involve murder. And Sarah hadn't delivered the statement with the right amount of gravitas. She sounded like she was inquiring about getting new carpet for her home.

"What did you say?" Josie said. She'd placed her hands flat on her desk and leaned slightly forward.

"You sound surprised. Haven't you handled murder cases before?" Sarah said.

"Not as a private investigator. You won't find many of us who have." Josie didn't want to tell Sarah that Stan Waterman was one of the few PIs with actual homicide experience. Hell, he was a former homicide detective.

"Then you have at least two things in your favor," Sarah said. "You're female and you have police experience. Should I tell you the story now?"

"Please."

Sarah got herself settled in her chair. Apparently she was one of those women who constantly drink water. She'd already taken several long pulls from the bottle she'd walked in with. She dropped her bag to the floor and took another swig before shrugging out of an expensive high-tech climbing jacket Josie doubted would ever brush up against a mountain.

"Are you familiar with the Lauren Wade case?" she began.

"Not really. I've heard her name on the news once or twice."

"It's unusual for a woman to be accused of murdering her female lover. I'd have thought it would grab your attention."

"Why would you say that?" Josie asked.

Sarah cocked her head to one side. "Am I getting this wrong? I read you as lesbian. I was thinking that I'd gotten very lucky when I walked through your door."

Was she that obvious? Josie thought of herself as average. Average height and weight, average face. Not average lesbian. Simply average.

"For the record," Sarah said. "I am too. But you probably guessed that."

No, she hadn't. She would have lost a lot of money on that bet. "So your company is concerned?" Josie prompted.

"Yes, of course. Having our top executive arrested for anything would be of concern to the board, especially a murder charge. But Wades have always been at the head of the company; Lauren Wade is naturally given a lot of leeway before action would be taken against her by the board."

"But she was acquitted," Josie said.

"The board thinks that still leaves the question of whether she committed the murder hanging in the air. There was no evidence that she didn't do it. The jury simply felt the prosecution didn't meet their burden of proof. There are plenty of people in the business world who think she may be guilty." Sarah looked hurt at that opinion, as if it reflected on her personally.

"Why is that a concern?" Josie asked. "The system says she's not guilty."

Sarah looked at Josie as if she'd just said something odd. Or stupid. "Obviously there are authors and companies who will refuse to do business with us."

Josie shrugged. "What about the police? Won't they be trying to catch the real killer?" Josie knew that was unlikely. Once someone's acquitted, the file's unofficially closed. The police always think they got it right the first time.

"I'm sure they think they already have. We're not counting on further action from the police. We want you to identify the killer."

Josie pulled a notebook out of her bag and wrote Lauren Wade's name on a fresh page. The pages before it were filled with notes from when she was a police detective. "What's your relationship with Lauren Wade?"

She'd been reading books on how to be a private investigator. One stressed the importance of knowing your client's true motivation. Sarah, however, seemed taken aback by the question.

"Why do you need to know that?"

"It's pretty basic information. Is there some reason you don't want to tell me?" Josie said.

Out came the bottle of water again. Sarah appeared to be buying some time by taking a long drink. Finally she capped the bottle.

"Initially, Lauren and I had a strictly business relationship, which goes back a few years now. In addition to sitting on the board, I also publish books with Wade-Fellows. We're not best friends or anything, but we've had enough meals together to say the relationship goes beyond business."

"Did you urge the board to fund this investigation?" Josie said.

"I don't know why you're questioning my motives," Sarah said, sounding a little annoyed. "I'm trying to help her, not harm her."

Josie didn't want to lose her first client before she even got started, so she backed off.

"Why don't you tell me the story and we can figure out where to go from there."

Sarah relaxed and sat back in her chair. "I know a little about Lauren's relationship with Kelly. They'd been together for five years when Kelly was murdered, and from what Lauren told me they were happy."

"When did she tell you this?" Josie had zero experience in happy relationships.

"It was several weeks before Kelly was killed. They'd just finished redoing their house. I don't think you do a renovation when your relationship's on the rocks."

"Why not?" Josie said. "People have babies to try to save relationships."

"True, but Lauren seemed genuinely excited. I got the impression they were a pretty solid couple. It turns out there was trouble. But I'll get to that."

She didn't think Sarah had been unhappy to hear Lauren and Kelly's relationship was shaky.

"Tell me about the murder," Josie said.

"You'll find all this in the trial transcript, which I'll give you, but the bare facts are Lauren came home around eight thirty on February fifteenth and found Kelly dead on the kitchen floor. She'd been shot through the head. When the police arrived they discovered Lauren's own revolver next to the body and no sign of forced entry anywhere in the house. The gun had been recently fired and they found powder residue on Lauren's hands. They took her in for questioning and then charged her with the murder."

"How did Lauren explain the gun and the residue?"

Sarah leaned forward. "That's what's so weird about this whole thing. Lauren wouldn't say anything at all to the police."

"You mean she requested a lawyer?"

"No, she refused a lawyer. She wouldn't say anything to defend herself. The detectives and their lieutenant took her refusal to answer questions as tantamount to a confession. They felt they had enough to charge her."

Josie was drawing question marks in her notebook. "Tell me more about Lauren's work."

"Wade-Fellowes Publishing is an old family company. They produce hobby and lifestyle books," Sarah said. She sounded very formal. "I write crafts books and publish with them, which is how I first knew Lauren. I joined the board only recently. I was scheduled to have a business lunch with her the day after her arrest and I had to call her office several times to find out why it was canceled. None of her staff would say anything, but one referred me to the *Tribune*'s website, where the story was breaking. Everyone was stunned, of course," Sarah made this sound like she spoke for the nation.

"I left Lauren's assistant a message with the name of the criminal defense attorney recommended by our general counsel, but I didn't know at the time she was refusing counsel. Lauren eventually ended up using that lawyer. I was touched she took my advice."

Josie looked up from her notebook. She saw Sarah had a little color on her cheeks. Even a PI with Josie's limited experience could see she had a thing for Lauren, and the crush, or whatever it was, was probably enough to convince Sarah of Lauren's innocence.

"The trial only took a few days," Sarah continued, "and most of that was jury selection. Lauren didn't take the stand. All her lawyer could do was argue the evidence was insufficient to meet the beyond-a-reasonable-doubt standard."

"Why do you think Lauren didn't testify?" Josie found Lauren's silence the most disturbing thing about the story. How could she help someone who didn't want to be helped?

"I really don't know," Sarah said. "I haven't had any contact with her other than sending her the attorney's name. She refused to see me when I went to Cook County Jail for a visit."

"So far I don't see how Lauren got acquitted."

"I think it was due to Nancy Prewitt, Lauren's lawyer, who gave an amazing closing. She pointed out what I think the jury already thought—the prosecution had done a half-assed job and the police investigation may have been worse. The jury couldn't see past the fact Lauren was unlikely to be stupid enough to shoot Kelly with her own gun and then leave it next to the body before calling the police."

"The prosecution didn't offer anything else at trial?"

Sarah looked uncomfortable. "The only other thing that came out was Kelly was having an affair with another woman and Lauren had recently found out about it. That's what I meant about Kelly and Lauren not being as happy as I thought they were."

It also gave Lauren a whopping motive. Josie contemplated what to say next. The case seemed tremendously fucked up and probably nothing but trouble. But it was a paying case—if she could manage to get hired.

"Have you considered the possibility my investigation may prove Lauren did murder Kelly?" Josie asked.

Sarah looked unconcerned. "There's no downside. Lauren can't be retried for the same crime. And after all, that's the information the company wants an investigator to find."

"True, but perhaps it's something you'd rather not know."

Sarah waved that away. "I'm not worried about it. I don't believe for a minute she'd hurt anyone. But you can see how murky the whole thing is and why it's important to remove that doubt."

Josie couldn't, really. She'd think Sarah would thank her lucky stars for the acquittal and leave it at that. It seemed Lauren had.

"I can check on the status of the police investigation," Josie said. "I have contacts in homicide." She thought that should impress Sarah. "What does Lauren think of this effort of yours? She doesn't seem very interested in keeping her name untarnished."

Sarah fiddled with her water bottle. "She doesn't know anything about it."

Josie stopped writing and looked up, careful to take the sarcasm out of her voice.

"You want me to find the person who killed Lauren's girlfriend, presuming it's not Lauren herself, without her knowledge? Won't she know the board hired an investigator?"

"We're not volunteering the information, but we're aware she'll find out as soon as the investigator starts interviewing people." She paused. "You sound like you may believe she's guilty. I need you to be on board."

Josie didn't believe in causes. She believed in paychecks and getting the job done. She stole a look at her watch. She was going to be late for her therapy appointment.

"I have an appointment I need to get to, so we'll have to stop here. I have to think about this before I can agree to take your case."

"Of course. And I've not yet decided whether to hire you," Sarah said. She pulled a thick file out of her bag and pushed it across the desk. "You'd find most of this on the Internet, I imagine, but I'll save you the time of looking it up. These are the media reports and trial transcript. Maybe you could read them and we'll meet again tomorrow morning."

Josie looked at the file skeptically. She wasn't a particularly fast reader. She'd just finished the Lord of the Rings trilogy and that took forever. This was a very thick file. "I could meet you back here at four tomorrow afternoon. That'll have to do."

Sarah rose and put on her jacket. "Fine. I assume all this will remain confidential?"

"Of course."

There was a hint of a smile on Sarah's lips as she turned away and left the office. Josie took a moment to whisper a thank-you for the possibility of a paycheck and another thank-you for all the medications that made it possible for her to take on this case. She grabbed the Lauren Wade file, found her shoes, and hurried to her fifty minutes of torture.

CHAPTER THREE

Josie's office was on the second floor of an old brick two-story building, similar to most of the buildings that lined the commercial streets of Chicago's Lakeview neighborhood. Many had shops on the ground floor and a long hallway of offices on the second. She headed toward the rear stairway, passing the doors of two dentists, a Reiki practitioner, and Stan Waterman's Shield Detectives. The lights were off in Stan's office. He must've left after Sarah canceled her appointment. Shield Detectives was a bit of a hobby for Stan, something to do after he retired from the CPD and broke up his long partnership with Josie's father, who still worked as a homicide detective.

Stan Waterman's presence was a drawback to signing a lease in the building, but the rent was as cheap as she could find in the area. The location was great, and best of all, it came with parking out back. As she approached her ancient Toyota Corolla she could see the car next to it parked way over the line, forcing Josie to climb through the passenger side to get in. She could practically hear the switch click on in her brain, instantly catapulting her into outrage. She didn't know if it was despair or anger she felt whenever people acted as if they were the only ones who lived in the world. Whatever it was, her reaction was much bigger than the thing itself. She'd been told enough times to try not to let these things get to her. She wasn't built to handle it. Her desire to take a tire iron to the offending car nearly overwhelmed her for a few seconds, and then she calmed down.

Since one of the reasons she was in therapy was to deal with her irritability, if that's what they wanted to call it, she supposed she'd have a victory to report to Greta. She could feel the anger leaving her, and it did so much quicker than it would have in the past. She turned her thoughts to the Lauren Wade case and how it might make her feel good for the first time in ages.

She drove as fast as she could up to Andersonville, buzzed at the ground floor of Greta's office building, and took the stairs two at a time. She was a half an hour late. Greta was waiting at the far end of the hallway, holding her door open as she watched Josie trot toward her. She was a tiny woman, somewhere in her sixties, dressed in elegant clothes that didn't seem the least bit fussy. Josie had spent months studying Greta's wardrobe, wondering if she'd ever be capable of putting herself together as well and surprised to find she was even thinking about it. Perhaps better clothes would make people take her more seriously.

"There's no need to run, Josie," Greta said.

Josie stopped in front of her. "You're not mad? I'm really late."

"Let's say I'm curious. It's not like you to be late."

They walked into Greta's office and took their usual chairs, facing each other from a few feet apart. Greta's side table was equipped with a clock, a box of tissues, and her ever-present cup of tea. She was Austrian, her accent thick, though she'd lived in the States many years. Josie had never known an Austrian. There were no Austrian neighborhoods in Chicago, no cultural festivals. The only things she knew about Austria were from *The Sound of Music*.

"What's going on?" Greta asked.

"My first client walked through the door, that's what. I couldn't believe it. Sorry I'm late, but the whole thing was pretty involved. I couldn't break away."

"Congratulations." Greta looked genuinely pleased. Josie hated how much that meant to her, how a kind word from Greta sometimes made her want to cry. It was ridiculous.

"It's a huge case, too. This woman was acquitted of a murder charge and my client wants me to find the real murderer." Josie bounced on the edge of her seat.

"What?" Greta looked incredulous.

"I know. It's not your run-of-the-mill PI case. I can't wait to get started."

"I don't understand. Isn't that something the police should be doing?"

"I have to look into all that," Josie said. "There's a lot I don't know." Now Josie's leg was swinging back and forth.

"Is it even wise to take this on?" Greta leaned forward in her chair. Josie leaned back in hers.

"What's that supposed to mean?" Josie asked.

"You've been doing very well for some months now," Greta said. "Your mood's stabilized, your sleep's good, even your diet's improved. I don't want to see the stress of a case like this set you back."

Whatever elation Josie felt about her new career sank below sea level. Greta's obsession with stress drove her crazy. She glared back at her.

"I don't think you'd be satisfied unless I worked as a janitor in a funeral home," Josie said. "I can handle stress, and more importantly, I can't avoid it. Why can't you be happy for me?" She could hear the agitation in her own voice.

Greta smiled and Josie knew it was meant to placate her. "I am happy. I know success is important to you. I also know long periods of stress can trigger episodes."

Josie stared furiously at the clasped hands on her lap.

"This is still very new to you," Greta said. "I understand how much you hate it. But we're still discovering how well you do with your medication, what supports your stability and what upsets it. When we talked about this before, you seemed certain you could run the business by working regular hours."

Josie reluctantly looked at her. "I still think that's true ninety percent of the time. I got my ten percent dropped on me the first day. What are the chances?"

Greta stared.

"There's no way I can turn this case away," Josie said.

Greta looked disappointed. "I can't sign off on this, Josie. You're sabotaging your recovery."

"That's a little dramatic, don't you think?"

"A year ago you were in the hospital with an uncontrolled bipolar I manic episode. You could end up there again," Greta said, her stern expression setting Josie on edge.

She stood, unable to stay a moment longer. She had an amazing opportunity to start her new career with a huge success and ease the memory of her humiliating exit from the police department. She couldn't listen to Greta's rationale. She'd never get anywhere if she did.

"I'm going. I'll be here on time next week."

Josie left the office and clambered down the stairs, her face hot with shame. She was a coward to flee Greta's office, and God knew it wasn't the first time she'd done it. But she had to make a living and have some purpose in her life. Her symptoms were under control. It was time to get on with things.

She crossed through the stalled traffic on Clark Street. It was late Friday afternoon and everything was busy. People poured into Cheetah's Gym for their pre-partying workouts, while others went straight to the restaurants and bars that lined the street. The September air was still warm and the sidewalk tables were filled. It felt like a village instead of a single street in an enormous city. Before her breakdown, this strip had been home, as much so as her nearby apartment. Now she avoided almost every place on it.

One exception was Kopi Café, her hangout during the long months after she left her job. Going there kept her from being completely isolated in her apartment. She'd always have a book open on her table, next to her coffee cup, and the wait staff never mentioned that she rarely turned a page.

Now she set up in the rear of the café and dug out a fistful of paper on Lauren Wade. Her coffee and scone appeared without her ordering, much like her brand of beer used to appear on the bar before she'd settled onto a stool.

"You look busy today." It was Casey, the guy who usually waited on her. "Or industrious, at least."

"Busy." Josie smiled as she looked up at him. "I've got my first case."

"Case? Case of what?"

"Client, I should say. You know—for my new PI firm."

Casey put the coffeepot on the table. "Josie, I don't know what you're talking about. Are you a private eye now?"

"Yeah. I'm sure I told you about it. What's so surprising?"

Casey shrugged. "It's not every day someone tells you they've become a private eye. What happened—did you wake up one day and say, 'I know, I'll be a private eye!' It seems a little out of the blue."

"It's not out of the blue," Josie said, trying to not sound defensive. "Lots of ex-cops become PIs."

He pointed at the top page in front of Josie. "Kudos if your first case has to do with Lauren Wade."

Josie looked down at a photo of a dark-haired woman surrounded by reporters pointing their microphones and cameras at her. She covered the paper with her arms.

"That's confidential." She felt her cheeks flame red.

"Honey, I won't say a word. Your barista is like your priest, only safer. I will say if your new case puts you in contact with Lauren Wade, you're a lucky girl. She's hot. Not as in sizzling hot. More like gorgeous and mysterious hot. And she may have killed her lover. How much more mysterious can you get?"

Josie didn't know what to say. She slipped the papers back into the file.

"I'm glad she was acquitted," Casey continued. "I never thought she did it. So what if her girlfriend cheated on her. It's not like Lauren couldn't have someone new in an instant."

"Right. The conveyor belt of love. Maybe they used that as a defense," Josie said.

"No, that's where the mystery comes in. Maybe that's where you come in. According to the papers, Lauren Wade wouldn't defend herself at all." Casey turned his head as someone called him to a table. "I have to fly. Don't be a stranger."

Josie gulped her coffee, stuffed the scone in her bag, and left the café as quickly as she could. After a long afternoon of surprises and irritants, she needed to get home. She also felt strangely at peace for the first time in months. She finally had something to focus on other than her illness. She longed for involvement in anything outside her own head, work that would help her forget those god-awful weeks of manic behavior that landed her in the hospital; the behavior so mortifying she couldn't bear to think about it. Greta constantly urged her to forgive herself, but Josie was realistic. There wasn't a chance she'd forgive herself.

When she got home to her third-floor apartment she opened the blinds on every window in the place. She'd been living like a mole for months, in the classic pose of the depressive, curled up on the sofa in her dark living room. Now she was in action and it felt great. She washed down some leftover Thai food with the one beer a day she allowed herself, though Greta said she shouldn't even have that. Josie thought that restriction a bit much and didn't she prove to herself every day that she wasn't an alcoholic? One beer would not be enough for an alcoholic but it wasn't a problem for her. So the hell with Greta. She was still mad at her anyway for not recognizing a fucking miracle: a murder case on her first day on the job!

Josie put on her favorite sweats and her go-to Lucinda Williams CD and spread the Lauren Wade file over her dining room table. Sarah appeared to have searched deep into the Internet to find everything she could about Lauren Wade; she seemed obsessed with her. There were the expected Wikipedia and local newspaper reports about Lauren and her company, along with business articles and interviews found only through paid research services. She'd also used an online background-checking service to look for any evidence of hinkiness in Lauren's past, but there was none. Interestingly, the report was printed before Kelly Moore's murder. The other news stories about her business and civic life were also printed before Sarah should have had an interest in seeing how she could help Lauren.

Sarah had been building her file on Lauren for quite some time.

Josie read through the background material. What emerged was a profile of a forty-year-old businesswoman who ran a successful publishing company and was active in a number of civic organizations, including LGBTQ. An interview in the local gay press covered her involvement with a lesbian cancer organization. It also touched on Lauren's private life, the only reference to it Josie could find in the file. The interview was dated a year before her arrest, and Lauren spoke warmly about her partner and their tentative plans to have children together. She sounded happy.

The photos of Lauren at various banquets and galas showed a slender woman with dark eyes and prominent eyebrows. Her hair was black and perfectly straight, parted off-center and often partially hiding her face. She wore well-tailored pantsuits. Josie couldn't find Lauren smiling in a single photo. The two of Kelly and Lauren together showed Kelly's light to Lauren's dark. In one shot, Kelly wore a short dress and impressive heels, clinging to Lauren's arm with a big smile on her face as they posed on what looked like the red carpet for a film opening.

Lauren's face was a blank. Another photo was a candid shot at a fundraiser held on a boat. With other couples around them, Kelly could be seen sitting on Lauren's lap, throwing her head back and laughing, hiding Lauren's face from the camera. Josie wondered if Lauren was smiling while holding a beautiful, laughing woman on her lap. She somehow doubted it.

She read through some articles found in the trade press about Wade-Fellows. It was known for publishing high-quality design, craft, and fine art books. Lauren's parents ran the company from the early 1970s until their early retirement in 2009. A press release issued at that time reported Lauren would lead the company, while her brother Tim was promoted to vice president of operations. Josie couldn't find any indication Wade-Fellowes was in financial distress, but it was a privately held company and information on its finances was limited.

Josie moved these papers into a new pile, which she referred to as the "good to know but doesn't get me anywhere" pile. Like a snowdrift, it grew steadily higher as the evening wore on. Her running list of questions was over two pages long. Some of the questions she hoped Sarah DeAngeles could answer, but most were the questions she was being hired to answer herself. At least she hoped she was being hired. She needed to develop some plan of attack that would impress Sarah, a woman who didn't come off as easily impressed.

At nine she pushed back from the table and looked inside her refrigerator. There were the beers, lined up like soldiers, ready to march into her hand. And that was it. An assortment of frozen foods from Trader Joe's were stacked in the freezer, covered in a burr of ice. Her cell phone rang. There were only a few people that called Josie; she wasn't surprised to see her mother's name on the screen.

"Hi, Mom. Kind of late for you to be calling, isn't it?" Josie said.

"True, but I've been thinking of you and finally got a chance to pick up the phone," she said, as if she'd been seeing patients all day instead of sitting at home watching the clock.

Josie sat back down and took a breath. "Lucky me."

"Don't be that way, Josie. Tell me how you are."

"Do you mean how am I in the general sense, like 'what's new?' or 'how was your day?'"

"Josie." Her mother's voice had a warning tone to it.

"Or do you mean 'did you take your medication today?'" Josie didn't hide her impatience. She was staring at her left biceps where a colorful tattoo said "Wish I Were Me," surrounded by roses. She had no memory whatsoever of getting the tattoo.

"Can't it be both?" her mother went on. "I'm a worrier, you know that. It's only natural I want you to take care of yourself."

Josie held her tongue. It was more likely the case that Elaine wanted to avoid another embarrassing episode of crazy from Josie. She was sick of being asked about her medication. It made her not want to take it.

"Yes, I took my medication. I haven't missed once, Mom."

"I know, sweetheart. It's just that all the literature says bipolar people resist taking their medication. That scares me."

"Bipolar people?" Josie said. "That sounds like some indigenous group. 'The bipolar people of the Amazon rainforest'…'"

She heard her mother laugh, followed, as night follows day, by the sound of ice hitting the bottom of a rocks glass. It was remarkable, really, that Elaine sounded as sober as she did. She would have had her first drink no later than four fifty-nine that afternoon and been steadily drinking since. Yet she sounded like she could preach a sermon without a single eyebrow lifting in the congregation.

"I'm glad you haven't lost your sense of humor after all this," her mother said.

"I think it's the only thing that keeps me relatively sane, at least according to Greta."

"Did she actually say that?" Elaine didn't particularly like Greta.

"She didn't use the word 'sane.' She said a sense of humor helps keep me moving forward, whatever that means."

"Because you were never insane, Josie. You were only ill for a little while," Elaine said adamantly. "I think it's a dangerous word to use."

Josie wasn't going to argue semantics with her mother when she was three sheets to the wind. Elaine might not be slurring her words, but Josie knew the signs of her mother's inebriation. The most obvious was how loudly she spoke. The difference between her morning voice and her evening voice was like a softly played etude and Metallica. Josie wondered what mechanism of the brain made drunks believe the whole world had become hard of hearing. Then there was the way she repeated things. She prefaced most sentences with "Did I tell you…?" Chances were good she had.

"Did I tell you I'm having lunch with Aunt Mary tomorrow?" Elaine said. "I really wish you'd come."

"Yes, you did, and no, I can't." Josie was intent on escaping a meal with cranky Aunt Mary.

"Well, I won't press you," Elaine said.

"Thanks." Josie needed to get off the phone. "I'm beat. I'm going to turn in now."

She could practically hear her mother scrambling to come up with something to prolong the conversation. "Josie, did you take your medication today?"

It was impossible to not find this maddening. "I told you I did. Do you want me to sign an affidavit?"

There was silence on the line. Josie heard the click of a Bic lighter and more clanking of ice cubes.

"There's no reason to get nasty, Josephine. I'm so afraid you'll have another episode like last fall."

Josie sighed loud enough for her mother to hear. "I've got to go, Mom. I can't have a conversation with you when you've been drinking. I'll see you Sunday at brunch."

That earned Josie a slammed phone in her ear, which she was expecting. Anytime she poked through the veil of her mother's denial about her drinking, she got the phone slammed in her ear. It was a sure fire way to cut a conversation short.

Josie left the dining room. Her apartment was a vintage one-bedroom, large by most standards with its separate dining room and eat-in kitchen. She'd lived in it for over ten years and never given much thought to decorating. She kept it clean and in good repair, but it was furnished as if for a graduate student in off-campus housing. One girlfriend had actually moved in and put framed posters on the walls and colorful placemats on the dining room table. But the girlfriend and her accouterment were gone after the night Josie brought a woman home for a three-way. In her amped-up state, the idea seemed not only reasonable, but brilliant. The girlfriend could not have disagreed more.

Josie flopped onto her old sofa and tried not to cringe at this or a thousand other fuzzy memories like it. That was then. Now she had a way to climb back into life. She knew the shortest route to finding the inside dope on the Lauren Wade case was to call her former partner, Beverly Morton. Bev had been transferred to Major Crimes shortly before Josie left the CPD. Her connection with Bev could be key in getting Sarah to hire her, and she wanted the job. Being able to pay her bills and work on an interesting case seemed like a dream come true. She fell asleep thinking about how to approach Bev after all she'd put her through.

Chapter Four

Saturday, September 7

Bev and Josie sat in Bev's unmarked sedan near Foster Beach, their eyes fixed on Lake Michigan in front of them. The wind whipped up a steady stream of whitecaps on the lake that broke apart as they hit the cement wall at the water's edge. A long line of empty parking spots was on either side of the sedan, the gloomy weather leaving only a few cars parked within sight. They were all driven by men looking for other men, stubbornly using a long-standing system of signaling each other through headlights, a sort of urban sexual semaphoring. It was made completely outdated by the new phone apps designed for cruising. Who needs headlights?

Bev and Josie had often eaten their lunch here. Bev bit into one of the sandwiches she'd picked up on her way over, but Josie could barely eat a bite. Being with Bev, being in a police car again, the sound of the staticky radio—all sharp reminders to Josie of what she'd lost. She kept her eyes firmly on the dark and turbulent lake, knowing she should break the silence and start talking, but she felt bound at the chest, breathless.

When their partnership had been broken up by Bev's promotion to homicide, Josie thought she'd simply break apart. One minute she'd felt like there wasn't anything she couldn't do, and the next she felt the universe had ripped away the one person she couldn't do anything without. Bev was closer to her than any one of the depressingly small number of people in her life. She understood her, had patience with her. She had Josie's back. But truthfully, Bev didn't seem as devastated as

Josie when she learned they'd be parting. She could see the relief in Bev's eyes as she hugged Josie and moved her gear three rooms over to the homicide division.

"You know," Josie said, breaking the silence in the car. "I may have gotten my first clue something wasn't right when I saw you skedaddle away from property crimes."

"It was a promotion, Josie. You would have skedaddled too, especially from property crimes."

"Maybe," Josie conceded. "Was I really that bad?"

Bev turned to look as her. "You weren't bad. But you were ill, which I didn't know, and it was getting worse. I admit I'd taken about all I could."

Josie looked down at the food in her lap—a barely touched roast beef, with melted provolone and some peppers that about took the top of her head off.

"I never knew I was ill. I felt invincible and then more invincible still. I was bored with tracking down missing property; I kept trying to make it more exciting."

"Well, you certainly did that," Bev said, her mouth full of tuna salad.

Josie took a deep breath. "It turns out I have something called bipolar I disorder, which makes me slightly crazier than bipolar II disorder. But on the overall scale of BPI craziness, I come in somewhere toward the lower end. I wanted you to know that."

"I'm glad you're better, Josie. I'm not here to rehash how annoying you were while you were sick."

"Why are you here, then?" Josie asked.

"You tell me. You're the one who called."

Bev was about the coolest person Josie'd ever met. She could tell her anything and she wouldn't raise an eyebrow.

"I need your help in a case my new agency caught."

"New agency? What's that mean?"

"My PI agency. I just opened it, as in yesterday, and I already have a murder case."

Bev looked stunned. Maybe she could still be surprised.

"Didn't I tell you that?" Josie said. "It seems like I would have told you that. This medication makes me a little spacey."

"How're you doing with that? I understand a lot of people go off their meds pretty regularly."

At least she didn't say "bipolar people," like her mother.

"The medication sucks but yes, I take it every day. I'm ten pounds heavier than I was a year ago, and I'm sure you've noticed the spots on my face. Exactly what every thirty-five-year-old wants—weight gain and acne. Now we're onto treating the side effects. It's a lot of fun."

Bev laughed. "I'm sorry. I know it's not funny. It's that you're funny. I miss that. This guy they have me teamed with is the least energetic person I know, and as much fun as a migraine."

Josie relaxed a little. She'd always been able to make Bev laugh, even when she couldn't stop talking or stay remotely on topic. Thoughts used to blow through her mind like a high-speed chase on a crowded highway, weaving in and out, dangerously wild, dangerous to others and herself.

"So, I caught this case and I think you might know something about it. Did you work on the Kelly Moore case? The murder Lauren Wade was acquitted for?"

Bev stared at her for a moment. "Yeah, I worked on it. At least for a little bit. My partner, Bill Nicholson, was primary on the case when I joined up with him. Of course he thought I couldn't do anything more than log files, so that's mostly what I did. I put together all the reports and statements and that sort of thing."

"That guy's a complete asshole. Even my father hates him."

"Well, you can see why you in a manic state is preferable," Bev said.

"He's probably one of the buttheads at the station who talked about me," Josie said.

Bev looked puzzled. "What do you mean?"

"You know, after I did all that stupid stuff at the FOP dance and ended up in the hospital." Josie had a petulant look on her face, waiting to hear how people ridiculed her behind her back.

"Josie, no one talked about you at all, except to say it sucked you were sick and had to resign."

It had never occurred to Josie that people weren't talking about the embarrassing pass she'd made at a superior officer or any of the other brazenly insane things she'd done. Greta once mentioned part of her disease was being grandiose, thinking the world revolved around her, that everyone noticed and cared about everything she did.

She kept forgetting that.

"I wasn't going to take a fucking desk job," Josie said. "Apparently, there's some nutty rule about not allowing crazy cops armed on the streets."

"Are you carrying a weapon?"

"Hell, yes. Wouldn't you be if you were working on a murder case? I mean, you are. But if you were me is what I meant."

Bev smiled. "Tell me what you want from me."

Josie leaned forward and with as much sincerity as she could muster said, "I want a copy of the official file on Kelly Moore's death, along with the detective notes."

Bev stared at Josie as if she were, well, crazy. But then she shrugged. "I can get you the official file, but no way on the other. You know Nicholson's not going to put his notes in the official file, and we're nowhere near close enough for me to ask for them."

Josie sucked on her bottom lip for a moment. "How about this? Since no one is pursuing an alternative killer since Lauren Wade was acquitted, why don't you say you want to look into it in your spare time and you'd like to see his notes."

"Spare time?"

"That's what you could tell him," Josie said. "It might work."

Bev nodded. "Okay, I'll try. But don't count on it. He's not going to want his investigation to look weak."

Bev looked disgusted, a good cop frustrated by a bad one. Josie felt an overwhelming sense of loss. She'd always counted on the two of them eventually being homicide partners, a contemporary Cagney & Lacy, where Josie was the butch, hard-drinking Cagney and Bev was Lacy, complete with husband and kids, as she had in real life. They would have kicked ass.

"I'll get you what I can," Bev said. "I need to head back to work. Maybe I can send it over today."

"Whatever you can do, Bev. I'll owe you."

Bev snorted as she pulled out of the parking space. "Yeah. I'll put it on your tab."

CHAPTER FIVE

Lauren Wade wondered how a day at liberty could feel as long as a day in Cook County Jail. She'd been home for a week, but the six months of unimaginable tedium, bad food, and occasional bouts of terror had thrown her into a deep depression. She'd thought anything in contrast to jail would make her happier. Instead, she found herself unable to feel anything at all.

She sat on the deep sectional sofa in the family room of the house she'd shared with Kelly. The room was part of a recent addition she'd put on, mainly to please Kelly. The huge family room and kitchen on the first floor and master suite on the second were appended to the old brick house Lauren had owned for ten years. Kelly picked out the furniture and finishes with obsessive attention to detail and total disregard to price. That Lauren would be paying for everything was never discussed, simply assumed. Kelly made a decent salary at her marketing job, but she deposited her paycheck in a private account, from which she paid for clothes and meals out with friends. Their joint account was funded by Lauren.

She chastised herself for dwelling on the negative. Kelly was dead. The troublesome parts of their life together were now moot, but she couldn't help wonder how she could have been so blind to Kelly's true nature. The first years of their life together had been so happy. Sexy, fun, energizing. Realizing Kelly was essentially a gold digger was disappointing, but she'd adjusted to it. The harder discovery was Kelly's affair with Ann-Marie, a member of Lauren's own book club. Kelly had begun to sit in when the club met in their house, which was most of the time. Lauren guessed it was the month they discussed *Tipping the Velvet* when she'd begun her affair with Ann-Marie, if that's what you'd call it. It seemed too casual to be classified as an affair. Kelly had given more thought to the selection of the sofa Lauren now sat on than she did to the consequences of cheating on her lover. When Lauren confronted her about Ann-Marie, Kelly admitted, with only the mildest apology in her tone, to sleeping with her, as if she were confessing to bringing a puppy home unannounced. Lauren retreated to her study and avoided Kelly. One week later, Kelly was shot dead in the kitchen she'd so carefully designed.

Lauren hauled herself up from the sofa. Her body was soft from the months of inactivity, but she was loath to do a thing about it. The depression that had begun long before Kelly's death was now cloaking her in lead. She felt underwater. She understood Virginia Woolf and the rocks in her pocket.

She put a pot of coffee on and started to unpack the groceries she'd brought into the house an hour ago. Every small task felt monumental, another thing added to the list of reasons she'd grown to despise herself. Can't complete simple tasks, can't stand up for herself, can't win this fight against her brother. She felt her whole personality had changed.

Her thumb sank into the side of a pint of ice cream as she put it in the freezer. When the doorbell rang, she dropped a cantaloupe and watched it roll across the floor, not bothering to pick it up or to answer the door. She knew who it was. Her brother Tim strolled into the kitchen, pocketing the key he'd used to let himself in and swooping up the cantaloupe, bringing the end to his nose and giving it a sniff.

"I hope I'm not interrupting anything," he said. They both knew he didn't care at all whether he interrupted her. He tossed the fruit onto the island. "That's not ripe yet, by the way."

"What do you want?" Lauren said.

"I want to see how you are, of course." He dropped a small duffel bag on the counter and moved to the refrigerator. "Cook County Jail has broken stronger women than you. Did anyone make you her bitch? Is that how you survived?"

Lauren didn't respond.

"That's what I thought," he said. "Well, you've got to do the hard things to survive sometimes. Isn't that right?" He pulled a beer out and took a long swallow. He was tall and rangy, dressed in a flannel shirt and jeans and clunky hiking boots. Lauren knew this was one of the many looks he adopted. He had a multiple sartorial disorder. A Seattle grunge band musician one day, a Brooks Brothers executive the next, a J.Crew yacht club member the day after that. But his demeanor toward Lauren was consistent—a conversationalist who refused to listen, a cheery sadist who never seemed to tire of his elaborate games.

"Tell me how Mom and Dad are. You better not have hurt them," Lauren said.

"Better not, or what? I don't see you have much leverage here, little sis." His eyes sparkled. Eyes that were so blue they almost didn't look like eyes. They had mesmerized a lot of people.

"Tell me how they are." Lauren sat on a stool at the kitchen counter, staring at him with all the loathing she could muster, which was plenty. Tim leaned against the counter, the coffee brewing behind him.

"I haven't done a damn thing to them. Relax. They're safe in their little hideaway, plenty relieved you were acquitted, I can tell you that. If you'd gone down for murder, they were going to go down too and they knew it. What's the point in keeping them? They're fucking expensive to maintain," he said, as if they were stabled horses. "Without our arrangement in place, it's bye-bye John and Helen."

Lauren needed no reminder of what was at stake. As long as she agreed to publicly humiliate herself in a seemingly endless series of scenarios Tim designed for her, he would keep her parents alive. If she were to refuse an assignment or fail in some way, they would die. He'd kidnapped them a few months before she was arrested for Kelly's murder. It seemed like a hundred years.

"Was that supposed to be your endgame, Tim? You'd kill my lover and frame me for it, then get rid of our parents after I was convicted? Did you get off watching me led in by the sheriff's deputies every day and returned to jail every night? I don't see where this is going or how long you think we can keep it up."

He shrugged. "It was surprising you were acquitted. Cook County has some shitty prosecutors. Having you put away for good would have changed some things at Wade-Fellowes, which had interesting possibilities. But to answer your question, I really don't have an endgame in mind. It ends when I get tired of it, that's all. And I'm having way too much fun right now. Which brings me to the point of this visit—your next assignment."

Lauren could feel the bile working in her throat. "I can't do it anymore. I can't."

"That's one way to end this, I suppose. But you know the deal. If you fail to comply, I'll kill them. It's as simple as that."

"How do I know you haven't killed them already? Maybe you did while I was in jail."

"You want proof of life?" Tim said. "I could send you another one of Dad's fingers."

"No!" Lauren took a couple of breaths and tried to focus on navigating the impossible. Her father lost a finger shortly after Tim found Lauren rummaging through his house, trying to find some clue to her parents' whereabouts. "I think it's reasonable to ask for a photo, something that lets me know they're okay. Better yet, a phone call or a visit."

"A visit is out of the question, but I'll think about a call or video. First you'll complete this assignment or I'll send you a photo of them dead." Tim finished his beer as he leaned against the counter, next to the gleaming knives.

Lauren put her fingers to her temples. "Let me hear it."

"Oh, how I've missed this! It was the worst part of you being in jail. But we'll make up for lost time with this one."

Tim rubbed his hands in glee and reached for the duffel bag. Lauren recognized that look from their childhood. It was the way he looked right before doing something awful to her like bullying her school friends. It had taken her years to figure out why it was her friends would suddenly stop liking her. She and Tim were largely left alone by their parents, who worked constantly and spent their free time sleeping or having the occasional night out, just the two of them. Lauren often thought if she had a brother she was close to, her childhood wouldn't have felt so lonely and scary. Her parents believed in a sort of "throw the baby in the deep end" philosophy of child rearing. Tim and Lauren were left to fend for themselves, and Lauren had to always be on guard with Tim.

Tim seemed to despise her from the time she was aware of such things. There was something about her that made him want to torment her. If he saw she was making friends with anyone, he'd act as obnoxiously as it took to drive them away. If her parents occasionally praised her for something she'd done, Tim would retaliate. One time he set fire to her science fair project, which she'd spent weeks working on. There was no safety. Their parents expected them to get along or work it out when they didn't. They felt this was a better preparation for the real world than coddling them, solving their problems. It never occurred to Lauren the actions of an unpleasant older brother were the precursor to those of a sociopath.

She stared in dismay as Tim pulled women's clothing out of the bag. A spangly tube top, a black stretch skirt that looked no bigger than a headband, fishnet stockings, and four-inch stiletto heels. He tossed a small bag of cosmetics on top, followed by a blond shoulder-length wig.

"Your mission," Tim grinned, "is to infiltrate a queer bar in the role of a desperate, forty-year-old tart. You'll hook up with whoever is drunk or desperate enough to want to bed you. You'll stay at the bar until you're successful, and if no one agrees to leave with you tonight, then you'll return each night until someone does."

Lauren was speechless. Since Tim's campaign began, the things he demanded she do had steadily escalated in degrees of humiliation. At first the tasks seemed disproportionate to the kidnapping and imprisonment of her parents. She'd been forced to enter an elevator in her office building and push the buttons for every floor after people crowded in to start the workday. Since most of those in the elevator were her own employees going to the top two floors of the building, she had to endure the embarrassment of the doors opening uselessly on each floor along the way. Tim was in the elevator, disguised as a flower deliveryman, his face hidden behind a bouquet of lilies. He loved to see Lauren squirm.

It was well known by the staff of Wade-Fellowes that Lauren and Tim's parents were smart enough to leave the company in Lauren's hands when they retired but soft enough to keep Tim on despite his disruptive presence. John and Helen hoped by passing Tim over, he would get the message he needed to knuckle down and get serious about the welfare of the company. Everyone knew it was a great embarrassment for him, and it was compounded later by being fired by his sister after many warnings to improve his performance. Lauren knew he was furious, but she hadn't anticipated him holding his parents hostage for a ransom that seemed to solely consist of Lauren making a repeated fool of herself.

He had her dress like a homeless woman and strum lamely on a ukulele, singing the same song over and over while sitting at a busy corner near their offices. He forced her to sing at a karaoke bar, an exquisite hell for Lauren, especially with members of her staff in the audience. She was ordered to spit on the floor while talking to the celebrity guest at an HRC gala. Kelly had witnessed that one and she didn't talk to Lauren for a week. Lauren couldn't offer up any plausible reason for spitting three inches away from the open-toed shoes of the star of some recently canceled sitcom.

But now she was being asked to sexually engage with someone, a new frontier for Tim. How much did she want to keep her parents alive? Enough for this?

"Tonight?" she said.

"Why not? It's Saturday night, baby, and the lezzies will be out in force. Of course, they'll be much younger than you and undoubtedly not dressed like a street whore, but what's the fun if there's no challenge?" He picked up one of the shoes and looked appreciatively at the impossible stiletto heel.

Lauren started to cry, something she never wanted Tim to see. But she was exhausted, hopeless. He was committed to his game and he would kill her parents if she refused to play. But she was so tired she didn't know if she could continue to keep them safe.

"I'll be right there watching," he continued. "I thought about how to determine your success, given I probably can't be right in the room while you're having sex. That would be gross. So I'll go easy on you. All you have to do is leave the bar with someone and go to their home. If you want to play Scrabble all night, that's your business. Now, quit your blubbering and get dressed. We're going out at nine."

Lauren picked up the pile of clothes and headed upstairs, unable to imagine her acting skills were good enough to lure interest from anyone while she was dressed in this pathetic costume. She considered killing herself, but that would mean the death of her parents. It would also mean Tim would inherit full ownership and control of the company. It seemed worthwhile to stay alive to prevent both things, but she felt parts of herself killed off every day. She wasn't sure she could keep it up much longer.

She couldn't think of a way to save her parents that wasn't unacceptably dangerous. Her first attempt had been a simple plan to find out where Tim was hiding them. She'd broken into his house and worked her way through every paper in his office, looking for a lease, a map, anything that might point her to them. There was nothing. Five minutes after she got back in her own house, Tim called her.

"Do you consider yourself an intelligent woman?" He had a patronizing tone that drove her mad. She suspected something behind the question, something not good.

"I suppose I'm intelligent enough," she said.

"I used to think so. You showed off enough in school—it was kind of hard to miss. Waving those trophies and certificates, as if anyone cared."

"What are you talking about?" She was alarmed. Tim never talked about their childhood.

"Oh, please. Every other fucking day you trotted home from school with a prize for this, an award for that. Mom would pat you on the head. I'd come home with my report cards and all I'd see is disappointment in their eyes."

Lauren didn't know where he was going with this and she was afraid of sparking his anger.

"That didn't have anything to do with intelligence, Tim. I was a geek. All I did was study, while you were out playing with your endless number of friends."

Tim seemed to consider this for a while.

"Let's leave it at that for now. The fact is you weren't quite smart enough today to get away with your adventure in breaking and entering."

Lauren remained silent, her heart thumping a steady beat.

"Through the wonders of technology I was able to film you the moment you entered my house. CCTV cameras are the rage in England, and you know what an Anglophile I am. It took you twenty-two minutes to get through the load of crap on my desk. Were you disappointed to find you're not the beneficiary of my will?"

"I didn't expect to be," Lauren said.

"Anyway, as you know, you didn't find a single clue as to where Mom and Dad are. I'm sure it's driving you crazy. But I'll let them know about your bravery. I'm sure they'll want to send you a present."

Two days later her assistant had brought in a small box marked "personal and confidential." The postmark was Chicago, the return address Tim's house in the city. She slowly removed the wrapping and found a long black box, one that might once have held a bracelet, but now held her father's right index finger. She recognized a mole above the second knuckle. A note in the box said "Keep trying. There're thirty-nine fingers and toes left."

CHAPTER SIX

By the time Sarah DeAngeles arrived at four on Saturday afternoon, Josie had managed to put her office in order and read her way through most of the Lauren Wade file. She felt prepared for the meeting, dressed in black jeans—new ones that were a dressy jet black—topped with a charcoal wool blazer and a button-down white shirt. It was still too warm for the wool, but Josie wanted to look professional, and to cover the holster at her back.

They faced each other again across Josie's desk. Sarah was also dressed in jeans, but hers clung to her long legs and cost considerably more than the pair Josie bought at Target. Sarah's shirt was a plunging V-neck that clung tightly to her breasts. She leaned forward to put her bag on the floor and Josie got a good look at her cleavage. She was relieved to feel something in response. She'd feared her medication had killed her libido, which had swung from wildly overactive during the months before her hospitalization to its current moribund state.

"Did you have a chance to read the materials I gave you?" Sarah said, settling back in her chair.

"I did. All but the trial transcript, which I'll get to soon." Josie assumed a relaxed posture in her new chair, her notebook perched on her knee.

Sarah looked around the room. "You've been busy. I see you got things squared away in here." Sarah flashed a smile at Josie. She seemed more relaxed and friendly than she'd been the day before. Josie hoped that meant she'd decided to go ahead and hire her. "What are your thoughts on what you know so far?"

"There wasn't much I read that added to what you told me yesterday," Josie said. "It's not much to go on."

Sarah looked surprised, as if she expected more of a sales pitch than that. Josie wanted the job, but wouldn't promise more than she knew she could deliver.

"I got in touch with a CPD contact of mine, someone who worked on the Kelly Moore murder. She pointed me in a few directions. Whether any of those leads will produce a suspect is impossible to say."

Bingo. How could she resist a contact like that?

"Of course. I can accept whatever the outcome is as long as I know the best effort's been made."

"Good. I can promise you I'll do that," Josie said. "I'm curious about your business relationship with Lauren. What books do you publish with her?"

Sarah smiled. "I have lots of them. Books on knitting, embroidery, scrapbooking. Things like that."

These were skills as mysterious to Josie as flying a rocket ship. "Do you make a living writing those books?"

"Yes, I do. A very good living. My first concern is Lauren herself, but I also want to make sure her company stays healthy. It's been a very good relationship for me."

It looked like Sarah was comfortable with her and it was time to lock it down. Josie sat up straight in her chair. "Would you like to move forward?" she asked. This was called closing the deal, something she did quite successfully when the deal involved getting a woman into bed. Maybe she was a natural salesperson. The thought was disturbing.

Sarah looked at her for a few moments before nodding. "I think I would. It seems like you've got the most time available of anyone I've talked to and maybe the best contacts."

They negotiated a rate and a schedule of how often she would report to Sarah with her progress. Josie pulled a contract out of her file drawer, a replica of one Stan Waterman gave her to use as an example. She watched with a perfectly still face as Sarah wrote out the $5,000 retainer check and pushed it across the desk toward her.

"I know some friends of Kelly's. It might be a place to start."

"If your friendship with Lauren stemmed primarily from your business relationship, how did you get to know Kelly's friends?"

"I don't know them well," Sarah said. "I was out to dinner with Lauren and my agent one night after we signed a book deal. I was a little surprised Lauren agreed to meet us for dinner, since normally she turned down evening invitations. I'd asked her to dinner a number of times. It was one of the reasons I felt we were developing a real friendship. She must have wanted to spend time with me if she agreed to join us for dinner."

Josie thought it sounded unlikely. She suspected when Sarah talked about her relationship with Lauren, she was operating in a slightly different reality. Lauren probably had dinner with her because she was a board member. But with a $5,000 check in hand, she didn't care.

"Was Kelly with you at this dinner?" Josie said.

"No, she wasn't. But she was at the same restaurant we were, having dinner with three of her friends. It was simply coincidence. She came over to our table and convinced Lauren and me to go to a bar with them after dinner. I think Lauren wanted to get us somewhere away from my agent." Sarah had the look of someone thinking of a fond memory.

"When was this? Do you know whether Kelly was having her affair at this point?" The affair was a big problem for Lauren. Jealousy was hard to disprove.

"No, it was before that. At least a year ago, maybe longer. Kelly loved going out. When we got to Tillie's she acted like she lived in the place. She knew the bartenders, the owner, and a lot of the guys sitting at the bar. Lauren stayed for one drink and left. She said she had a headache, but I think she couldn't stand seeing what a flirt Kelly was. I stayed and hung out with Kelly and her friends."

Josie tried to place Kelly among the faces she'd seen regularly at Tillie's, wondering if she'd picked her up. Kelly didn't sound like a person averse to such a thing. But it was all a blur; she had no memory of Kelly at all.

Sarah wrote out a list of Kelly's friends and identified one of them, Denise Traieger, as Kelly's closest friend.

"I only have one more question for you," Josie said. "At least for now."

Sarah smiled. "Whatever I can do. I'm excited to get started on this."

"I'm confused about Lauren's silence. What's that about?"

Josie watched Sarah carefully, looking for any signs she was lying. She couldn't see any.

"I said yesterday I don't know why Lauren wouldn't testify on her own behalf, wouldn't offer anything at all, according to the police. It doesn't make any sense to me either, and I know it makes Lauren look guilty. She seemed resigned to being convicted of a crime I'm sure she didn't commit. I have no idea why."

"This is really an investigation to answer two questions, isn't it?" Josie said. "Who killed Lauren's girlfriend and why Lauren was taking the fall for it."

"I guess it is." Sarah nodded, pleased with the idea. "She'll know the board is behind the investigation. I'm not sure if she'll open up because of it; I know she'll be mad about it."

"And you don't want that," Josie said.

Sarah looked down at her lap and spoke quietly. "No. I really don't."

"Are you in love with Lauren?" It seemed obvious to Josie. Maybe it wasn't to Sarah.

"In love with her?" Sarah said. "That's the reason you think I'm doing this?" Sarah seemed more surprised than angry.

"It did occur to me," Josie said.

"I don't think you have the right context for this. We're paying for this investigation because we have to decide Lauren's future with the company. Personally, I want to do what I can to help her."

Josie thought about that for a moment, not sure whether to believe Sarah or not. Whether or not Sarah was in love with Lauren didn't really matter. She said good-bye to Sarah and got to work.

❖

The file Bev emailed her was thin. It contained crime scene photos, various dry and unhelpful reports. A lab analysis confirmed the gun found at the scene was the murder weapon and the prints on it were Lauren's, and the residue on her hands was from gunpowder. The time of death was established between 8:00 and 8:30.

She set these aside and read through Bev's notes. Bev's partner took a statement from Kelly's sister, Nikki, who let the police know about the affair Kelly was having with Ann-Marie Hessen. It was the first the cops had heard of it and probably shut down any thought of other possible suspects. Bev also had a list of Kelly's friends, most of whom Josie recognized from the one Sarah had given her. The only signed statements in the file were from Nikki, Ann-Marie, and Lauren's assistant, Eva, who could not establish an alibi for Lauren. There were brief interview notes on a few others. Josie added the new names to her own interview list. Bev's notes also mentioned her inability to find Lauren's parents and brother, who Nicholson, the senior detectie, wanted to interview. Josie would follow up on that as well. It looked to her like the investigation ended there. The file wasn't going to be much help. Lauren owned the murder weapon, she had the motive of Kelly's recent affair, and she had no alibi. Josie had to start somewhere, so she called Kelly's friend Denise.

It was seven o'clock on a Saturday evening and Denise was on her way out for the night. She agreed to talk with her later at Tillie's. Josie hung up and felt something all too familiar buzzing through her. It was excitement and fear combining in a potent brew. In different times she might take it as a warning she was feeling a little manic, but she was well stabilized now on her medication. She was jazzed to start work again and scared she'd screw it up. Her nerves rumbled beneath her like a motorboat.

CHAPTER SEVEN

Josie walked through the door of Tillie's for the first time in a year. She hoped she looked all right—dark jeans, a gray sweater that hadn't lost all its shape, her trusty Frye boots. It should be fine unless Tillie's had undergone a radical change from neighborhood tavern into a wine bar. She hadn't been in any bar since her hospital stay. In the months before her breakdown there'd hardly been a night she wasn't hunkered down in one. She was drinking so much in those days, she thought she'd join the rest of the alcoholic Harpers. But instead she got a bipolar diagnosis. Lucky her.

At nine o'clock on a Saturday night, the bar was starting to get crowded. Tillie's hybrid clientele of gays and lesbians and everyone not neatly gender labeled were spread out from the front bar, across a small dance floor, over two pool tables and into a back "quiet" room. Josie didn't know what Denise looked like, but based on the photos she'd seen of Kelly, she guessed her to be in her thirties and very feminine. Denise said she'd be at Tillie's with friends and Josie instantly imagined a pack of females like the ones that terrified her in high school and college.

Her first pass through the bar didn't turn up any likely candidates. The men far outnumbered the women and half of the women were at the pool tables. Some nodded at Josie as she walked through and one actually snarled. She hated to think what was behind that. When she returned to the front room she saw four women come through the door and she knew Denise was one of them. They were laughing, probably a little drunk, and peering around for somewhere to sit. She waited for them to settle at one end of the bar before she approached. She felt nervous and wondered how she could be the same person who'd questioned hundreds of witnesses while on the job, who'd easily picked up women with a babble of bullshit. Passing a calculus test would be easier than approaching these women.

One of the four women eyed her as she drew near.

"Are you Josie Harper?" she said, turning her bar stool fully around to face Josie. The woman's friends all swiveled to take a look at her. They wore dresses and more accessories than Josie could comprehend. They whooshed and clacked with every move.

"I am," Josie said. "You must be Denise."

"Sarah said you were cute, and for once I agree with her."

One of the friends started laughing and Josie glanced at her before returning her gaze to Denise. She'd need to separate Denise from this herd if she wanted to have anything resembling an interview.

"Can we go in the back to talk?" Josie said.

Denise slid off the stool and waggled her eyebrows suggestively at her girlfriends, who exploded in laughter. Charming. Depressingly, Josie knew a year ago she would have been hitting on Denise, probably successfully. Now nothing could have interested her less.

They walked through the pool room to get to the back bar, which was small and noticeably subdued. A few couples sat at high-top tables, leaning toward each other on wobbly bar stools. The back bar was tended by a large woman with ornate tattoos and a huge nose ring. You could hitch a rope to it and lead her out to the back forty.

They found a table and Josie got a good look at Denise. She was pretty and wore an elegant mauve dress and matching heels. Mauve? It wasn't pink and it wasn't purple. It wasn't typical Tillie's attire, which tended toward funk or indifference. Denise also had a prominent scar across her cheek, which Josie found the most attractive thing about her.

"I'm sorry to interrupt you on a Saturday night," Josie said.

"It's no problem. I told my friends I'd be meeting you."

"Were any of them friends of Kelly's?"

"No, different crowd," Denise said.

Josie tried to imagine having so many friends they were sorted into different crowds.

"I've been hired to try to identify the person who killed your friend Kelly."

Denise rested one butt cheek on the bar stool, not quite committing to the conversation. "Yes, and I'm really glad someone's doing that."

"Why?" Josie asked.

Denise looked confused, as if she'd been asked to solve a math problem. "Why? Because of Kelly, of course. I'm not entirely sure Lauren didn't kill Kelly, but either way, Kelly's killer is walking around scot-free. That's not right."

"I'm trying to get a handle on Lauren and Kelly's social life and I'm hoping you can fill me in."

Denise smiled. "I'd be happy to. I mean, I can tell you about Kelly. I was about as close to her as anyone was. I didn't know Lauren well. She didn't come out with Kelly all that often."

"Why was that?"

"She and Kelly were very different people. Kelly was much more social than Lauren. But Lauren sometimes made an effort. I've double-dated with them, been to their house for dinner. Lauren even lasted a couple hours here at Tillie's one night."

"Was Kelly unhappy about their differences? It sounds like they were incompatible," Josie said.

Denise shrugged. "Kelly mentioned it a couple of times. She thought Lauren was a bit too tightly wound. But Lauren didn't complain about her going out, so Kelly didn't complain about Lauren staying home or working late at the office. It seemed to work for them, though it wouldn't have worked for me. They seemed more like roommates than lovers." Denise looked at Josie with an eyebrow raised. "Do you know what I mean?"

"I think I've got the picture."

Josie brought up Kelly's infidelity and Denise sighed. She looked down at the table before looking back at Josie. "Do you want a drink? I could use one."

Josie stepped over to the back bar and ordered a beer and a glass of wine. While she waited for her change she saw a woman at the end of the bar glance at her. Twice. Josie felt a flicker of recognition and then nothing, like a firefly—a little flash of light that blinks and then moves out of reach. She knew it was entirely likely she'd either slept with her or otherwise made a complete ass of herself. When she saw her glance at her again, Josie gave a quick, thin-lipped smile and nodded. She hoped the woman, whoever she was, didn't hate her. She was cute.

Denise was fiddling with her phone when Josie returned with the drinks. She picked up her wine and an impossible number of thin silver bracelets slid down her arm.

"You were going to tell me about Kelly's new girlfriend," Josie said.

"I wouldn't say girlfriend at all. Kelly and Ann-Marie slept together a number of times. But Kelly didn't intend to turn that into a relationship."

"How do you know that?"

"We're best friends, remember? I asked her about it. I didn't think it was right. Lauren didn't deserve that, and Ann-Marie had a partner, too."

She was surprised by Denise's reaction. She'd assumed Denise would be cheering Kelly on. Denise took a drink of wine before continuing. "Lauren found out, of course."

Josie saw the woman from the bar leave the room, turning before she reached the door and giving her an enigmatic look. It was halfway between an invitation to follow her and a look of pity. Christ. She turned back to Denise.

"Did Kelly tell you how Lauren took the news?"

"Screaming and throwing things wouldn't be Lauren's style. She wasn't a very demonstrative person and certainly not volatile like Kelly, who said their fights usually consisted of Kelly yelling and Lauren asking her to calm down. She said when Lauren heard about Ann-Marie, she simply left the room and went into her study. Kelly was murdered before I heard whether they were going to try to stay together or break up over it."

"Do you think Lauren was capable of killing Kelly over this?"

Denise thought for a moment. "I think it's possible. I don't know Lauren well enough to guess what she's capable of. I still think her silence at the trial doesn't look good for her."

"So you lean toward Lauren being guilty."

"Let's say I'm neutral."

Josie was about to ask her another question when Denise touched her hand. "Can we call it quits now?" she said. "I need to get back to my friends."

"Would you meet with me again?" Josie asked. She fumbled in her wallet for one of the new business cards she'd had made up at Kinko's.

Denise's smile widened. "I'd like that. Give me a call. Or I'll reach out to you." Denise sounded like Josie had asked her on a date. She slid off her stool and went back to her friends and Josie stayed where she was, finishing her beer. The thought of dating had been out of mind for so long, even the hint of it felt startling. Denise didn't tempt her, but maybe someone would. She was beginning to think it was possible.

Then she thought of the woman who seemed to know her. Josie wondered if she was still in the bar. She hoped she could sneak past her; it was unlikely Josie would hear anything good from her. She was halfway through the front room before she saw her. There was nothing enigmatic about the look on her face. Her smile was inviting, her eyes friendly. She got up from her table and walked over to her.

"Josie. I didn't know if I'd ever run into you again. It's been a while."

Nearly every social interaction Josie had since her diagnosis was difficult in some way, and usually embarrassing. But she saw warmth in this woman's eyes. Maybe she hadn't messed up with her. "I'm really sorry. I don't remember your name."

"It's Lucy. We met here a few times last year." Lucy was looking up at Josie's face. She was short and slender, with a shock of thick, curly red hair and expensive horn-rimmed glasses; she'd be easy to draw as a cartoon. She was distinctive enough looking that Josie should have recognized her, but she didn't. There were times Josie wondered how she'd lived through those months of mania and heavy drinking. She seemed to have been in one long blackout.

"Come on. Sit for a minute," Lucy said, pulling her toward a table. Josie saw Denise and her friends still gathered together, laughing their heads off. She wondered if they were laughing about her. She turned a chair around and straddled it, facing Lucy from behind a barrier.

"Are you here alone?" Josie asked.

"For the moment. I'm supposed to meet a friend in a little while," Lucy said. Josie didn't say anything in response. "Can I get you a beer?"

"No thanks. I've had my one."

"One?" Lucy looked curious.

"I've changed my drinking habits quite a bit from last year."

Lucy looked at her for a long moment. "You seem really uncomfortable, Josie. Different than before."

Josie looked restlessly around the bar, avoiding Lucy's eyes. "I have to be honest, I don't even remember you. I'm sorry."

Lucy smiled. "I should be honest, too. I heard what happened to you, or at least the bar version. Is it true you ended up in the hospital for bipolar disorder?"

Jesus. How'd that become news at the bar? Josie frowned and kept scanning the room. She saw a woman she hadn't seen before sitting at the end of the bar opposite Denise. She looked like a street prostitute who was none too picky about her customers. Tillie's wasn't upscale, but tiny tube tops and micro skirts weren't usually seen outside the annual drag show.

"You don't have to answer that," Lucy said, continuing the conversation Josie had checked out of. "I want you to know I understand more about it than most people. My mother and my brother are bipolar."

Josie looked at her. "I'm sorry to hear that." She truly was. She wouldn't wish it on anyone.

"If you ever want to talk, I'm here for you. No judgment."

Lucy seemed earnest, at ease, welcoming. She smelled like herbal tea. Greta would love it if Josie opened up to someone like Lucy. Josie smeared on some Chapstick and scraped her chair back.

"Thanks, but I'm fine now. And I should go." She tried to smile at Lucy. "I guess I wasn't a complete ass when we spent time together. You're being too nice for that."

"You were great, Josie. I really enjoyed our time together." Lucy looked perfectly relaxed as she gazed back at Josie.

Josie was horrified to feel a lump in her throat, a physiological reaction to someone being nice to her. She had to fight to not cry, something that was happening more frequently. She reached for her Chapstick again, as if it were a drink.

"I'm very glad to hear that," she said, her voice thin with strain.

"Though I know a couple of women who aren't thrilled with you," Lucy said, easing Josie's tension considerably.

"There are a surprising number of women in that club," Josie said with a laugh. She couldn't remember the last time she'd actually laughed.

Lucy laughed also. "I'm serious, though. I'd like to hang out. I loved our conversations and I didn't even think you seemed particularly manic."

"I was busy self-medicating. Maybe the worst of my symptoms were tamped down."

Lucy reached into her bag and brought out a card. "Call me," she said, standing up and pressing the card in Josie's hand.

Josie walked away, heading to the bathroom in the back before going home. She felt almost buoyant, lighter than she had before. She entered the bathroom and found three empty stalls; when she finished in one of them and went to the sink, the woman she'd seen at the bar dressed in slutty clothes walked in. She was teetering on ridiculous high heels and her wig was listing to starboard. She stopped when she saw Josie and for a brief moment they stared at each other. Then she careened toward an open stall. Josie was embarrassed for her and tried not to look her way as she held her hands under the old, noisy dryer. She heard something fall to the floor and turned to look. The contents of the poor woman's purse were scattered at her feet.

"Oh, no," she said. Josie thought that sounded odd. She would have said "Oh, fuck," herself, so she presumed a prostitute, or someone who doesn't mind looking like one, would swear with the same vigor. Without thinking, Josie dropped to her knees and started gathering the things together.

"You don't have to do that," the woman said. She was standing over Josie holding her hand over her mouth, as if she were hiding bad teeth.

"Frankly, the way you're dressed and with those shoes? This maneuver may be beyond you," Josie said. The woman now covered her entire face with her hands.

Josie looked at the items as she dropped them into a gold sequin clutch purse. House keys, Lexus key fob, an iPhone, a slim billfold, and a small Moleskine notebook. What any modern prostitute would carry on a working night. Josie had been a street cop for a long time. All she knew was this woman looked like a pro, but not the sort who did well enough to drive a Lexus or own an iPhone.

Josie rose and handed the purse to her. She had a hard time looking at her with her lopsided wig.

"Thank you," said the woman. She looked down and Josie could see the tears fall down her cheeks.

"Are you okay? You don't seem like you're okay," Josie asked.

"I'm fine. Thank you for your help."

Apparently she was also a very polite, Lexus-driving street whore who kept track of her business in her Moleskine notebook and checked in with her pimp on the latest model iPhone.

The woman glanced at Josie and tried out a seductive smile. "Maybe there's a way I can thank you. Would you like to take me to your place?"

Josie felt her mouth drop open. "You're kidding, right?"

The woman grabbed onto Josie's collar as she leaned in to whisper in her ear. "I can make you very happy. You won't regret it." Her voice was more strangled than husky.

Josie took her wrist and gently pushed the woman away. "I'm sorry. I don't know what your story is, but I'm not interested."

Someone walked into the bathroom and Josie took the opportunity to scoot out the door. She walked to her car, confused as hell by the woman in the bathroom and trying to think who she reminded her of. There was something about the face that was familiar.

CHAPTER EIGHT

Lauren finished off her second Cosmo and quickly ordered another. Her only chance of completing Tim's assignment was to be drunk enough to go through with it. The alcohol blunted the sting of the bartender's smirk, of the people next to her shifting as far away from her as possible. It was going to be hard to seduce anyone when she was repelling more people than attracting them.

She yanked again on the stretchy fabric of her skirt, trying in vain for it to cover another inch of thigh. She caught sight of Tim sitting at a table, nursing a drink and staring at her. His eyes were hazy, as if he were on drugs or sexually stimulated. He wore a shirt straining across his surprisingly muscular chest, with skinny mustard-colored pants. Lauren could see every man in the bar give him the once-over. As the bar grew more crowded, he lost his ability to clearly see Lauren. She tried to think of some way she could use that to her advantage, but no clever plan came to mind. She knew he'd start moving around the second she did, always to keep an eye on her. That seemed to be the whole purpose of these exercises, the pleasure Tim took in watching Lauren do humiliating things. He didn't seem to be tiring of it, and like an addict he kept needing more to get the same effect. Even the clothes he wore were part of the game. He somehow managed to dress like a gay man without over- or under-doing it. He was a genius with clothing.

She looked down the bar and around the room in search of a likely target. She recognized a friend of Kelly's at the other end of the bar and quickly turned away. It was unlikely Denise would recognize Lauren if they stood nose to nose, but it would be disastrous if she did. Her makeup was dramatic enough to serve as a mask, and her clothes were the opposite of what Lauren would normally wear. Everything was opposite of what she'd normally do.

After her third Cosmo she knew it was pointless to wait for anyone to come to her at the bar. She grabbed her purse and maneuvered off the bar stool. She looked ridiculous wobbling on her heels and she could see heads turning to follow her, Tim's among them. It was as if she'd dressed outrageously for a costume party, only to find out at the door it was a formal affair. That's how much she stood out. She figured the pool room was her best bet at this point. Hopefully, the butches gathered around the tables were well on their way to being blind drunk and none too picky about whose skirt they got up at the end of the night. It was possibly still too early for that. She'd already been turned down by one woman during her last trip to the bathroom. It was too bad. She was attractive and kind, maybe even someone she would have enjoyed talking to before Tim hijacked her life.

She leaned against a wall next to the cue rack and inventoried the room. The only lighting came from the two fixtures hanging over the pool tables, which were placed end to end in the long, narrow space. The semi-darkness could only help her, she assumed. The spectators lined the wood-paneled walls like they were at a cockfight. They were all women and trans men, some standing by themselves, some with friends. Tim came in and took up position across the room from Lauren. Two women next to him pointed at her and laughed. Tim leaned toward them and said something, and the women laughed even harder.

She thought by now she would have become inured to other people's judgments of her. She'd been embarrassed and humiliated so often over the past year she didn't think she had any shame left in her. But apparently she had an inexhaustible supply. She was standing in a place with perhaps the most accepting of all people, yet even they couldn't overlook her jarring appearance or the desperation that was written plainly on her face.

Staring at her from one corner of the room was a tall, perfectly androgynous woman. She didn't look at Lauren with the derision she saw in everyone else's face. She seemed impassive, perhaps a little curious, and she wasn't looking away. When Lauren met and held her gaze, the woman pushed off the wall and made her way over, taking the empty space along the wall next to her. Lauren didn't look at her. She kept her eyes on the pool table. Beyond it she could see Tim straighten up from his slouch, a smile on his face. They both knew it was show time.

"I haven't seen you here before. My name's Cory." She turned to Lauren and stuck out her hand. "What should I call you?"

Good question, Lauren thought. She took Cory's hand and scrambled for a name. Why hadn't she thought about this before?

"Helen," she said, using her mother's name because it was the only one that came to mind. It made her slightly ill, but so did everything else about her situation.

Cory looked amused. "What's your story, Helen?"

"My story?"

Cory still faced her, trying to catch Lauren's eye. "I know you've got one." When Lauren still didn't respond, cursing herself for not knowing how to flirt, Cory said, "You look really uncomfortable."

"It's the shoes," Lauren said, finally raising her eyes to meet Cory's and trying out a seductive smile. She was sure her face would crack open.

"That wig can't feel very good either. It must be hot." Cory looked sympathetic. "You might want to straighten it a bit, though. It's dipping to the left."

Lauren's hands shot up to the wig. She realized she had no idea how to adjust it without making things worse. Cory gently took hold of her arms and lowered them.

"Let's go in the bathroom where you can see what you're doing," she said.

Lauren looked at Tim, who was watching intently, before following Cory into the bathroom. All of the stalls were occupied. One of them had two sets of legs showing below the door. She could hear the moans the couple was trying to muffle.

"Sounds like true love," Cory said. "In a bathroom stall kind of way."

Someone was throwing up in another. The door to the third stall opened and a woman stalked out. "I was just peeing," she said.

"What's the matter, Betty? No one willing to take you on in the bathroom?" Cory said. Lauren watched as the two women looked at each other in the mirror and laughed.

Betty dried her hands and headed for the door. "Well, fuck off, Cory. I'm sure I'll see you around."

"I'll look forward to it." Cory was smiling when she looked back at Lauren. "An ex," she said. "We're only on slightly friendly terms."

"You don't have to explain."

Cory watched as she straightened her wig. The moans were getting louder from the middle stall and Lauren looked more embarrassed than ever.

"Come on," Cory said. "Let's get out of here."

Lauren was beginning to hope she'd complete her assignment with the help of this very kind woman. She felt like a homeless person, saved by a kindhearted stranger who feeds her a big meal and points her to the nearest shelter. Cory wasn't the thoroughly drunk and sleazy person Lauren thought she'd end up with.

Cory took her hand and led her into the back bar, seating her at one of the small tables and getting them both drinks.

"I'll be real honest with you," Cory said. "I don't believe this is the way you normally are. You don't pull it off. In fact, you're really terrible at it. So what's your story?"

Lauren saw Tim enter the back bar and take a seat at the next table. She was certain he'd be able to hear their conversation. She looked back at Cory.

"I'll forgive the insult since you seem like such a nice person," Lauren said.

"It wasn't an insult," Cory said. "But I don't get it. You don't even talk like someone who would dress like…that."

"Aren't you stereotyping a bit? Are my vowels not flat enough? Should I be chewing gum?"

Cory looked uncomfortable for the first time. "I'm sorry if I misunderstood."

Lauren leaned forward and took Cory's hand. "It's forgotten," she said. "And besides, I agree with you about one thing."

Cory raised an eyebrow. "What's that?"

"I'd look better out of these clothes than in them."

Cory took a moment before speaking.

"I may need empirical evidence of that. I'm naturally a skeptical person." She had a slight smile on her face. "Do you have any suggestions?"

"Do you have a car and a place of your own?"

"I do."

"Then let's go. I'm dying to get out of this wig."

Relief washed over her as Cory took her hand and led her out of the bar. She tossed Tim a triumphant look. As soon as they hit the open air she began shivering in her tiny clothes. She would not be considered overdressed in a sauna. Cory took off her jacket and wrapped it around Lauren's shoulders as Tim came out and lit up a cigarette, waiting to see which way they'd go. As soon as they headed north, Tim scrambled to get to his car. Cory seemed to have no awareness of him. She unlocked the door of her beat-up Mazda and closed it behind Lauren. She was very old-school butch, but couldn't be over thirty. She eased into the Saturday-night traffic on Halsted and headed north.

"Where do you live?" Lauren said.

"Uptown. And not a particularly nice part of it. But the rents are cheap."

Cory turned onto Broadway and flipped on her windshield wipers as it began to rain. Lauren stared out the window at the people moving quickly up and down the slick sidewalk, past shops with hand-painted signage, most of it misspelled. The streets were filled with foreign shopkeepers trying to make a living selling used bikes and native clothing, hookahs and wholesale gewgaws. In the middle of it all was a giant, brand-new Target, looking as out of place as a skyscraper in the desert.

She snuck a look out the back window and saw Tim's car right behind theirs. He was forced to drive on when Cory pulled into a private lot behind an apartment building. She didn't know if he'd be watching to see if she left the building right away, but she assumed he would. He saw all these stunts through to the end.

Cory's apartment was small and extremely clean and neat. The main room was furnished sparingly, but each piece was of good quality. The place looked pristine enough to have real estate photos taken. Cory led her to a love seat in the living room and sat down beside her after grabbing a couple of beers. Lauren realized she had more control of the situation than she thought she would. All she had to do was cajole Cory into letting her spend the night.

"Would you do me a favor?" Cory said.

"Of course."

"Go into the bathroom and take off your wig and makeup and put on the robe that's hanging on the door. Then come back in and introduce yourself."

Lauren did as she was asked, thrilled to scrub her face and rip the wig from her head. She took her clothes off as well and returned to the living room naked under the robe. Cory stood when she entered the room, smiling broadly. Lauren thought of how Kelly once smiled at her. It wasn't half as genuine as Cory's smile was.

"I knew it," Cory said. "I knew underneath all that crap was a woman I'd ask out in an instant."

"Does that make this a date?" Lauren asked.

Cory pulled her down beside her. "It is if you want it to be. I believe on a first date, two people are supposed to get to know each other. So tell me your story. Please."

Which story? That she was Lauren Wade, recently acquitted of murder and out for the night dressed as a prostitute? Cory didn't seem to recognize her, but she would have heard about the trial and known the name. Or she could tell her she was being blackmailed by her brother, but Cory seemed the sort who'd want to save her, no doubt getting her parents killed in the process. It was easiest to do what she didn't half mind doing with this attractive woman. She pulled Cory to her and whispered an inch away from her lips.

"Let's make up our own story."

CHAPTER NINE

Sunday, September 8

"Where's Dad?" Josie said. She sat in the dining room with her mother, where the oval table was covered with a wine-stained cloth and set with her wedding china. Elaine had brought in the last of the brunch food. There wasn't a warm dish on the table. Mornings weren't the best of times for Elaine, and cooking brunch was well beyond her capabilities. Josie was used to the bagels and lox, Danish and fruit. The food wasn't a hardship. What was a hardship was simply being at the monthly Sunday brunches her mother insisted she attend.

They didn't seem any easier on her mom. She looked bilious, but Elaine still made the effort to dress up for the occasion. Josie had recycled her socks that morning, hoping things would go well enough at brunch that she could bring her dirty clothes in and avoid the Laundromat.

"Your father had poker last night," Elaine said. "He should be up anytime."

It was a little after noon. Josie sipped her coffee as she watched her mother drink her suspiciously thin orange juice. Even in her most manic, beer-soaked time, Josie never drank in the morning. It always seemed the line you couldn't cross without becoming an alcoholic. Her mother had crossed it ages ago.

"I know your father's anxious to see you," Elaine said. "He talks about you all the time."

More news from Elaine's fantasyland. Josie hadn't seen her father in months; he always seemed to have something going on that prevented him from being home for brunch. She was a little nervous because it seemed he was here today. She'd only seen him a few times since she got out of the hospital, and none of those visits had gone well. Early on in her recovery Greta wanted to have a family session about Josie's illness, but Jack sent word through Elaine he didn't want anything to do with shrinks. Her mother thought there was little point in her attending if her father didn't, so she excused herself as well. Josie was relieved. Greta was concerned.

Josie was pouring more coffee when she heard the sound of football coming from the basement rec room. All the bungalows in the neighborhood had additional living space in the basement. Nearly all were finished with knotty pine paneling. Most had bars set up in a corner, sometimes elaborate structures with beer taps, liquor wells, TVs mounted on the wall, mirrors on the back bar. Josie's father had transformed his into a tiki bar, complete with faux shack, brightly colored bulbs, and battery-operated hula dancers.

"I guess he's up," Elaine said as she slathered cream cheese on a bagel and then put it on her plate in favor of more orange juice.

Josie looked at her blankly. "I thought you said he was anxious to see me."

"Oh, he is. But the Bears are playing. I think you'll need to go downstairs."

Josie fumed. Greta said anger was the way Josie covered up how hurt she was, and maybe that was true. But right now she was sure what she was feeling was anger. She considered leaving without seeing him at all, but realized that was exactly what he wanted her to do. She'd inflict herself on him instead, the bastard.

The basement smelled of cigarettes and cigars and last night's beer. The large card table in the middle of the room was littered with overflowing ashtrays and empty bottles and cans. On one side of the room was the tiki bar and the other held a single reclining chair in front of an enormous flat screen TV. Her father was sprawled in the chair, reclined to nearly horizontal. He turned his head when she kicked a beer can across the room. Then he turned back to the game. Josie dragged a chair from the poker table and sat down next to the recliner.

A minute or so went by with neither saying anything. You'd think as a homicide detective he'd have mastered waiting out a silence; it's a classic interview technique. But he'd always been unable to tolerate uncomfortable silences.

"Stan tells me you've set up shop as a PI," her dad said. "I thought he was joking."

He lit a cigarette and didn't take his eyes from the Bears grinding out their yardage. His beer sat in a cup holder built into the recliner.

"I've never known Stan to be much of a kidder," Josie said. She had her eye on the fridge next to the tiki bar. If she brought over a beer and talked about nothing but the Bears, things would be tolerable. But she didn't. She sat on the stiff-backed chair with her arms crossed, determined to not let him get to her.

"I don't understand you. Are you determined to embarrass yourself again? What do you know about being a PI?" He didn't look at her as he spoke. There was an ad for Pabst Blue Ribbon beer on the screen.

Josie took in a couple of long breaths. She'd harbored some hope her father's first words might have been to ask how she was or what was new in her life. She was in as much a fantasyland as her mother. She sat quietly, trying to decide whether to stay or go.

"Well, what do you have to say for yourself? Your mother and I aren't going to keep supporting you. You've got another month, maybe two."

"Good to know how much rope I have, Dad. But you can keep your money. My new business is doing fine."

He turned to look at her. "Is that right? Did you get all the lesbian infidelity cases? That's not going to keep you in paper clips for long." He laughed his nasty, derisive laugh that was like nails on a chalkboard to her.

It hadn't taken him long to touch on the first reason their relationship had disintegrated over the past years. When Josie had joined the police department and started her rookie year working out of the same district as her father, he was ready to burst. He was a bragging, hugging, back-slapping proud daddy. Then word got around the district that Josie had been seeing another female patrol officer and they'd had a messy breakup. He didn't speak to her for six months, though Stan Waterman told her no one else in the district really gave a shit about her and her girlfriend.

Josie felt anger starting to churn in her gut; left untended it could cause her to do almost anything, like throw a stale beer in his face or stomp on his remote control. The thoughts started to tumble around in her brain, so she closed her eyes and took a few deep breaths.

"If I was handling cases involving your infidelity, I'd be the richest PI in town," she said.

Jack looked amused, as if he approved of her anger. "Whatever drips and drabs come your way, you'll end up fucking them up. That's how you're built. The crazy in you will slap down anything you try to do." He turned his attention back to the game.

And there was the second reason. When word got out Josie had tried to seduce Commander O'Neil and then ended up in a psych ward, Jack essentially disowned her. She hadn't heard a kind word from him since.

"It so happens I already have my first case. A big one."

"Yeah? How big can it be?"

"Big. As in murder big. I can't say more than that."

He laughed out loud. "Of course you can't. You made that up. Who would hire a brand-new private dick to investigate a murder case, especially you." He laughed again.

"Oh, fuck you." Josie got up and kicked her way through the basement, her father chuckling behind her. She found her mother still at the table, her plate full of untouched food and a full glass of orange juice in her hand.

"Did you have a nice chat?" Elaine said.

Josie walked past her and out the door.

CHAPTER TEN

Lauren dropped the plastic grocery bag on her kitchen counter. It held her skirt and top, stuffed into her stiletto shoes with room to spare. She wore painters pants and an old T-shirt Cory dug out of her dresser, with flip-flops on her feet. She was chilly, but not in comparison to how cold she'd been in the bar the night before. Being home again felt like a warm bath, which she intended to take first thing.

It was noon; the church bells started ringing as Cory dropped her off. Lauren should have given her a decoy address; her Lincoln Park house set off another round of questions from Cory about who she was and what she'd been playing at in the bar. They'd made love far into the night and again when they woke up, and talk was minimal, but Cory's curiosity couldn't be held off much longer. Their lovemaking had surprised Lauren. She'd had the best twelve hours she'd had in a year. She almost felt sad she wouldn't be seeing Cory again.

She went up to the master suite and started to draw a bubble bath in the enormous tub Kelly had picked out. The humiliation of the night before felt quite real, while everything else in her life felt abstract. Her life as a business executive was all she had, and these stupid games of Tim's were ruining her reputation. She'd lost all contact with the few people she counted as friends because they'd abandoned her after her arrest or Lauren never returned their calls. She had no one to reflect anything back to her, no one but Tim with his wildly distorted lens.

The fact her parents were being held somewhere, terrified and dependent on her for their lives, felt increasingly like a novel she might find engrossing and suspenseful, but with no real ability to affect her. The more time that passed without seeing or talking to them, the less she found herself willing to do whatever it took to keep them alive. They no longer felt real. This last assignment from Tim had required her to dig deeper than she thought possible. She might simply crack if he asked her to do much more.

Yet the few hours of sex with Cory reminded her of what feeling good was like. Cory was a gentle but thorough lover and Lauren had abandoned herself to the pleasure. She felt momentarily victorious— the very thing Tim thought would make her the most uncomfortable turned out to be the only pleasurable thing she'd done in months.

She was in her bath when the door flew open and slammed against the wall. Tim strolled into the bathroom and looked down at her. Lauren kept washing.

"I thought that would get a scream out of you," he said. "I'm a little disappointed."

Lauren lay back in the tub and closed her eyes while Tim sat on the toilet on the other side of the room and pulled out his phone. He was dressed as a hipster, the first time Lauren felt he'd misfired on his choice of clothing. He was far too old for the skinny jeans, the wool cap pulled down to his eyes. His shirt coordinated with his pants and the scarf bunched around his neck. Each piece of his ensemble looked brand new. He was the hipster you'd bring home to Mom and Dad.

"I see your trick for the night dropped you home," he said. "I got some photos of her. Him? Her, I guess. Very handsome all the same and I have to say, well done you. I really expected you were going to flee her place as soon as you could, but you stuck it out."

Lauren turned her head toward him. "Does that get me anything?" There were still remnants of makeup rimming her eyes.

"Huh. I hadn't thought about that. But fair's fair. Let me consider it." He was sitting with his legs crossed and his chin on his fist. Rodin's *The Thinker* on the toilet.

Lauren finished cleaning herself and rose from the tub. She was beyond any modesty with him. Tim stared at her with a critical eye.

"You're looking a little thin, sis. That prison diet didn't agree with you? I've heard about the bologna sandwiches at Cook County Jail. Nasty."

She pulled on a robe and headed downstairs. Tim didn't immediately follow. She was trying to pretend he wasn't there, like a small child squeezing her eyes shut to make the bad thing go away. She put on a pot of coffee and pulled one mug from the cabinet. Tim came in a few minutes later. She'd have to sweep for bugs again. He liked to put them in her bedroom, as if anything happened in there but tossing and turning and a little bit of sleep.

"I've thought this over," he said. He put his phone on the kitchen counter. "I'm going to show you a video I took of Mom and Dad yesterday. I was going to use it as a motivator, but what the hell. I can be generous. Consider it a reward."

He clicked his way to the photo function and brought up a video. Lauren stared at it from a few feet away. When Tim started it, she walked over and took the phone from him.

John and Helen sat at a small Formica table, their hands clasped together. She could see the stub of her father's index finger. Behind her parents there was an old, round-top refrigerator and some dingy cabinets, but not much else. There was no window in sight, no way to place them anywhere other than in a run-down house.

A newspaper lay in front of them and John picked it up so it faced the camera, while Tim zoomed in to show the date on the *Tribune*'s front page.

"It's been a while now since we've been able to talk to you," John said. "The days and months run into each other. Everything seems long."

Lauren saw her mother grip John's hand tighter, trying to hold herself together. They were always hanging on to each other, as far back as she could remember.

"I know you're doing what Tim says to keep us alive," Helen said. "We've talked to him. He doesn't listen to reason. You'll have to figure something out." Lauren was shocked to hear her mother plead. "You can't let us die, Lauren." She could hear Tim laugh in the background. "He's told us some of the things he's been making you do while he has us captive here…"

The video shut off and then started up again. Helen picked up where she left off. "I've just been reminded to not give you any hints as to where he's keeping us. Unfortunately, I'm not clever enough to think of any.

"He's not hurting us," she went on, "as long as you do as he says. I simply don't know how it will end."

The video ended. Lauren saw Tim studying her. "You do know

if you don't keep up, I'll kill them. I don't think I've given you any reason to doubt that. And if anything happens to me, they'll die from starvation. I'm the only one who knows where they are, and there aren't any neighbors. I've given you your proof of life. Let's go on from here."

The part of Tim that chilled Lauren the most was he didn't seem the least bit crazy. What he was doing was crazy, but his manner was completely calm and measured. After years of aimlessness, he'd finally gotten serious about something, and this was the work he'd chosen. There was no exit strategy she could come up with that didn't involve getting her parents killed.

"So, now we've exchanged all this goodwill, I think I'll leave you alone for a few days. I need to think up your next assignment. This is very creative work, don't you think?"

Lauren held tight to her mug and swung it as fast as she could at Tim's face. He caught her wrist just before it reached him and then gave her a backhand slap, nearly in one motion. Lauren staggered back, her bare feet slipping in the spilled coffee. She crashed against the counter before she dropped to the floor.

"Oh, my God," Tim said, staring down at Lauren. "What possessed you to do that? Did you think you'd kill me with a coffee mug? I'm embarrassed for you." He watched her sitting slightly dazed in a puddle of coffee. "And you know this has consequences."

Lauren scrambled up to face Tim. "No. Do not take this out on them." She tried to hide the desperation in her voice and sound contrite. "I'm sorry I tried to hit you. I must have snapped." She saw Tim's face settle into stone. "It was wrong."

"Nice try, Lauren. Don't give up your day job for an acting career. You'll starve."

He shoved his phone into his pocket and turned to leave.

"What are you doing?" Lauren said.

Tim turned back with a big smile. "I'm going to see Mom and Dad, of course. I'll be sure to tell them you were thinking about them before you tried to cave in my pretty face."

Lauren froze. "Tim, please don't hurt them. They can't take much more." Lauren was pleading now, and Tim watched her, enjoying her groveling. "Hurt me if you have to hurt someone."

"No, no, no. Your guilt is the whole point of this. It's delicious to watch. It practically oozes from your pores," he said, heading for the door. "Keep a lookout for a package. I'll have Mom wrap the gift up nice and pretty."

She couldn't believe she'd put them in so much jeopardy. She wouldn't win any points with her parents for this. In a moment of selfish anger she'd put them in even more danger.

CHAPTER ELEVEN

Josie met with Kelly's younger sister on Sunday afternoon at the Starbucks in Nikki's condo building. Josie was on time; Nikki was a half hour late. Josie had time to review Nikki's police statement, which wasn't long and centered on Nikki telling the police about Kelly's affair with Ann-Marie. That was the most damning evidence against Lauren, as far as Josie was concerned.

Josie identified Nikki as soon as she walked through the door. Based on the photos of Kelly she'd seen, Nikki looked like Kelly's twin. She had the same long, silky hair, carefully made-up face, and stylish clothes. The only distinguishing feature seemed to be Nikki wasn't dead.

"Sorry, sorry," Nikki said. She sat down across the small table from Josie and thrust out her hand. "I overslept! God, I hate being late."

She didn't look like she was sorry in the least, the mark of the chronically late. Sleeping until two in the afternoon usually meant one of two things, insomnia or hangover. Nikki wore the mask of the deeply hungover. Josie knew the look intimately.

"Thanks for meeting," Josie said, returning the handshake. "I'm sorry for your loss. You must have been close to your sister."

"Yeah, we were close. But it's been a few months since she passed. I'm doing a lot better." She plucked her wallet from her purse and went to the counter to order a drink. Apparently the drink required every ingredient available in the coffee shop. It took ages before Nikki returned carrying an enormous cup with a mountain of whipped cream on top.

"So tell me again why you're investigating Kelly's death." Nikki took a sip and slowly licked the whipped cream from her top lip. Josie found it curiously unappealing. A year ago she would have taken it as an invitation to leap over the table at her.

"There are people who feel Kelly's real killer is still out there."

"Who hired you?" Nikki said. She was now reducing the mound of whipped cream through a direct assault with her tongue. She seemed only vaguely interested in the murder.

"I can't say, I'm afraid. But I can say they want to know justice is being done for Kelly."

Nikki considered this for a moment and then shrugged. She was starting to remind Josie of Bev's teenage daughter. "I don't know what I can do, but if you want to ask me questions I'm cool with that."

"As I understand it, you're the one who first told the police Kelly was having an affair. How did that come about?"

Nikki was simultaneously drinking, fiddling with her phone, and absentmindedly listening to Josie. "The detective who told my folks Kelly had been murdered came back to their house the day after. I was there with them. My parents were kind of in shock, so the police asked me most of the questions. They asked a lot about Kelly and Lauren's relationship, and I could tell they didn't know about Kelly's affair with Ann-Marie. So I told them."

"I imagine they found that interesting," Josie said.

"Oh, yeah. I hadn't really thought about whether Lauren had killed Kelly. I didn't know she'd been arrested. But when I thought about it later I could see where people would think she had. It happens all the time in the movies, right?"

"Do you think Lauren did it?" Josie asked.

She shrugged again. "I don't know. There are some things that make it seem obvious, but from what I know about Lauren, I can't really see it."

"What do you mean?"

"You'd think there'd be more heat in their relationship. You know, crime of passion. I didn't see much passion between Kelly and Lauren."

"Tell me about them."

Josie got her notebook out, which seemed to wake Nikki up. "Honestly, I didn't know them as a couple very well. I mean, they're the only gay couple I know, so I'm not sure what's normal. Kelly wasn't close to my folks, so they didn't come around for family stuff. And they had a totally different set of friends from mine. But Kelly and I talked on the phone a lot and she seemed happy." She peered at the notebook.

"What did you think when you saw them together?" Josie said.

"I went over to their house occasionally, but most of the time Lauren was working when I was there. When she was at home she left Kelly and me to ourselves, but she was always nice to me, and she was sweet to Kelly. She always kissed her hello or good-bye, and she pampered her a lot."

"You mean she gave Kelly lots of things."

"Pretty much whatever she wanted." Nikki looked a little peeved about that.

"Did Kelly talk about Lauren's money?"

"I'd say she bragged about it. To me, anyway. I'm sure Kelly loved Lauren, but I think she loved her money more."

Nikki slurped down the rest of her drink and looked at the time on her phone. "I'm going to be late meeting a friend," she said. Josie didn't think being late was really much of a concern for her.

"How did you find out about Kelly's affair?" Josie asked.

"She called me the morning after Lauren found out about it. It was really early, like the middle of the night early, and I was pissed she woke me up. But she was frantic. She told me she'd come home the night before and Lauren could tell she'd been with someone. How is that, by the way? Is that a lesbian thing?"

Josie didn't respond.

"Oh. I thought you were gay. Sorry." Nikki looked chagrined, like she'd just told Josie she thought she had herpes and was apologizing for thinking so. Josie thought of the hundreds of things she could say in response but kept her mouth shut instead.

"What else did she say?" Josie said.

"She said she was a little drunk and kind of a bitch about it when she admitted the truth to Lauren. Then she was angry Lauren didn't act mad about it. But Lauren never acted mad about anything, and that drove Kelly a little crazy. I think Kelly had the affair to see if Lauren cared, but then she panicked about the money. She didn't know if Lauren was going to kick her out or not."

"Did Kelly tell you before she died what Lauren decided?" Josie said.

"No. I talked to her the day before and she was still walking on eggshells. Lauren was keeping to herself. All she would tell Kelly is she needed time to think about things. That was the last time I talked to her."

Josie was struck by how blasé Nikki was about her sister's death. "Can you think of anyone else who might have wanted Kelly dead?"

Nikki put her purse on the table, ready to go. "I really can't. I thought about Lauren's parents, that they might be really pissed at the way Kelly was going through Lauren's money. It's really a guess. I can't think of anyone who'd want her dead."

"Where were you the day she died, say from the afternoon through evening?" Josie said.

"I get it. You have to ask everyone this, right?"

"Right."

"Well, this is easy. I left work at five and went out for cocktails with friends and then on to dinner. They can vouch for me."

Josie wrote down Nicki's parent's names and phone numbers. Then she asked Nikki where she worked.

"I work in marketing at Jones Bell."

"Same sort of work as Kelly," Josie said.

Nikki shrugged. "I guess," she said. "Different companies, but I might not be there much longer. I'm applying for Kelly's job, which is much cooler than mine. The person they hired after Kelly didn't work out. It's looking like I'll get it. Isn't that awesome?"

Nikki rose and stuck out her hand again. "I've gotta go. Let me know if I can be of any help." She walked away, leaving her sticky cup on the table. Josie dutifully bussed it and walked out after her, thinking Nikki's desire for Kelly's job was a possible motive for killing her sister, though a weak one. Josie hated to think anyone could be that venal, though she knew some were.

The streets and sidewalks were busy on the beautiful Sunday afternoon. Josie headed back up to Andersonville to meet Ann-Marie. She'd have liked nothing better than to sit at a sidewalk café with a book, or maybe stop into Alamo Shoes to pick out a replacement for her fifteen-year-old Frye boots. She wanted to spend some of that $5,000. Instead, she walked into the dark of Kopi Café, fully expecting to be there before Ann-Marie. Casey intercepted her near the front, balancing a tray full of panini and leaning down to whisper.

"There's a hot one waiting for you."

"A panini?"

He looked at her sternly. "You're in worse shape than I thought. It's a woman, Josie. Remember those?"

Josie tapped her forehead with her finger. "I'm crazy, not dead. Where is she?"

"The two-top over by the travel books. I'll be by in a few to get your orders." He winked at her before rushing off with his deliveries. Josie walked across the length of the café and approached Ann-Marie's table. She also had the long shiny dark hair that seemed to be characteristic of this tribe of women, but hers was piled on top of her head, held there by an invisible device that was doing a miserable job of keeping everything in place. Tendrils fell haphazardly, as if she'd been interrupted on moving day and was about to blow the hair out of her eyes. She turned her head as Josie approached, watching her warily.

"Ann-Marie?" Josie said.

Ann-Marie rose from the table and kept rising until she towered over Josie by a head. She was six feet, at least, and model thin. As they shook hands, Josie saw the bony wrist, the fingers with the prominent knuckles. She also saw the blue jeans Ann-Marie wore were covered in smears of paint.

"Are you an artist?" Josie asked, settling into her chair. She brought her notebook out, which only increased the spooked look in Ann-Marie's eyes.

"I'm sorry," she said, ignoring the question. "I really don't understand what we're doing here. I've already talked to the police."

"I'm not with the police. I've been hired to find out if the police arrested the right person."

She looked surprised at this. "Why would anyone want to keep this mess alive? It's been horrifying enough." She swept the hair off her face and squinted at Josie.

Casey appeared at their table with a big smile on his face. He turned to Ann-Marie. "Welcome to Kopi. Any friend of Josie's and all that. Can I get you some wine? Something sweet? Something warm?"

Ann-Marie seemed to relax a little. "I'll have a green tea, please."

"Usual for you, Josie?"

"I think only the coffee this time, Casey." Ridiculously, she thought she'd be judged by Ann-Marie if a giant scone was dropped in front of her. It looked like Ann-Marie disapproved of eating in general.

"As I was saying," Josie said, "I've been hired to see if the murderer was someone other than Lauren, or whether the evidence continues to point to Lauren. She can't be retried for the same crime, as you probably know."

"Yes." Ann-Marie was studying the scratches in the old wooden table, running her thumb along them. "I don't see what I can add to the investigation."

"Maybe it would be best for you to tell me what happened with you and Kelly, and then I can get your opinion on whether Lauren did it or not," Josie said, prodding the conversation along.

Casey delivered their drinks and Ann-Marie spent time dipping her tea bag up and down, up and down into her cup. If Josie watched too much longer she'd be hypnotized.

"I hate telling this story. I feel a lot of shame about it," Ann-Marie said.

Josie leaned forward and lowered her voice. "A year ago I was on a marathon of mortifying behavior. I could be an exhibit in the Shame Museum. There's nothing you can say that will make me judge you."

Ann-Marie returned Josie's steady gaze and gave her the smallest of smiles. "I doubt that, but I'll tell you what I can. Gabby, my partner, joined a book club Lauren was in, and she wanted me to be in it with her. We often met at Lauren and Kelly's house, and that's where it started.

"It was quickly apparent Kelly was not a big reader," Ann-Marie continued. "She never contributed to the discussion. She kept bouncing out of her seat to leave the room. When she returned she looked like she'd never been so bored in her life. I started to notice she was giving me the eye. You know, sweeping me top to bottom, very slowly, with the touch of a smile on her lips. At first I felt a little excited about it. Who doesn't want to be admired? But I was nervous Gabby and Lauren would see what she was doing. I think it was Kelly's brazenness that partly attracted me."

"So how did it move out of the book club?" Josie listened closely. Being with all of these women over the past few days was starting to wake the sleeping giant—her libido—which in the past had known no settings other than absent and superhuman. She was getting hints of something in between.

Ann-Marie took a sip of tea. "I was at Tillie's one night with my friend Anya, and Kelly was there with a group of her friends. Lauren wasn't there and Gabby was working that night. Kelly kept checking me out from the other end of the bar. Eventually she came over to me, and Anya left to talk to some other people. And there it was. We talked for a bit about our partners. I complained about Gabby working evenings and never being around to do things together. Kelly said Lauren always worked a lot, but she didn't mind. It was what made her family's business successful and you could tell Kelly was all for that. She did complain Lauren had recently been acting very oddly. She seemed very distracted and uncomfortable and Kelly was beginning to wonder if Lauren was having an affair."

Ann-Marie shifted in her seat. "It didn't take long before I agreed to leave the bar with her, though the story doesn't sound like much of a seduction. Let's say Kelly has a way of drawing you in, and I was clearly game for it. We had to go to a hotel because both of us were living with our partners. Even now I can't quite believe I did it. I'd been with Gabby for ten years, and I slept with another woman as if it were nothing."

"Why Kelly?"

Ann-Marie laughed, which surprised Josie. "Probably because she was the only one who'd ever propositioned me in those ten years. I think what the fling with Kelly taught me was my relationship with Gabby was in trouble. I hadn't been happy with her for some time."

Josie thought this would all have made a terrific lesbian soap opera if there weren't a real murder involved.

"How many times were you with Kelly?"

Ann-Marie winced at the question. "Maybe eight? We had fun and the sex was great and all the while I felt terrible about it. I got into that mentality of 'one more time can't hurt.' It was Kelly who put a stop to it. She called not long before she was murdered to tell me we wouldn't be seeing each other again."

Ann-Marie concentrated on her tea. "I don't know if I would have put a stop to it myself. Gabby was clueless, which shouldn't have surprised me. Still, it was wrong to betray her like that. I told her about it after Lauren was arrested, since I knew the story would come out before long. Either in the news or at Tillie's. She was bound to hear."

"And what was her reaction?" Josie said.

"Unequivocal. I was told to pack and get out." Ann-Marie made it sound like she'd gotten exactly what she'd deserved.

"Where did you go?"

"I grabbed a few things and went to my sister's in the West Loop."

Josie wrote a few notes while Casey came by to warm up their drinks. "You girls look like you're discussing famine in Africa. How can I cheer you up?"

They both looked blankly at him until he walked away, with a small smile aimed at Josie.

Josie turned to Ann-Marie. "I have a few more questions for you now, but I may have more later. First, how did you feel about Kelly's death?"

"Shocked, of course. The murder of someone you know is the last thing you expect to happen. Kelly and I'd been intimate, at least physically. I can't say I really knew her at all. I guess I'd say I was surprised and saddened, but not grief stricken. And part of me—the old Catholic schoolgirl part—couldn't help think God had delivered punishment for our sin. But why her and not me, I couldn't say."

"How likely do you think it is Lauren murdered Kelly?" Josie said.

"I honestly have no idea. When Kelly called me late to end the affair, she said Lauren had found out about us a few days before and had just that day decided to try to make their relationship work. Kelly sounded hugely relieved and said she wouldn't jeopardize it again by being unfaithful. Who knows if she would've held to that, but she sure meant it that night. Why would Lauren murder Kelly when she'd decided to make a go of it? On the other hand, it wasn't the first time Kelly had cheated. Maybe Lauren snapped."

"Where were you the evening Kelly was murdered?"

Ann-Marie looked startled. "The police asked me the same thing, which I assume is standard. Do you have reason for suspecting me?"

"It's standard for private investigators also. Where were you, let's say from late afternoon through late evening that day?"

"I was teaching in the afternoon. I'm on the adjunct faculty at the Art Institute. Then I went to my sister's and spent the evening there. I don't remember if she or her husband were there when I arrived."

"What time did you leave work and what time did you get home?" Josie had her pen poised over her notebook.

"I left after four, I'm not sure exactly when, and I stopped at a grocery before getting home."

"Which grocery?"

Ann-Marie looked flustered. "The police didn't ask me all these questions."

"Well, I'm not here to comment on the police investigation. Which grocery?"

"The Mariano's on South Halsted."

"Did you charge the groceries or keep a receipt?" Josie said.

"Jesus." Ann-Marie scrubbed at her face. "I'm sure I charged them. Do I need to dig up the information online?"

"It might be helpful. What'd you do after the grocery?"

"I cooked dinner for my sister's family and spent the rest of the evening there." She stood to leave and Josie asked for her sister's phone number as well as Gabby's. She hesitated before giving it.

"Did you go out at any point?"

"I said I was there for the evening." She didn't hide how impatient she was to leave.

Josie wrote the information down and closed her notebook. "Please don't take any of this personally," she said. "I'm doing my job."

Ann-Marie looked down at her. "I suppose."

With that she walked away. Josie signaled Casey and ordered her scone. She was going to have to start tacking things up on a murder board in her office.

CHAPTER TWELVE

Lauren picked her book up and set it down again. She went to the kitchen and started unloading the dishwasher and stopped halfway. She walked to the sliding glass door leading to her backyard and stared out. The twilight was darkening its edges. Her perennials needed attention. The garden used to be the part of the house where she was able to relax and be active at the same time. Digging and weeding had been welcome tasks; now she couldn't care less. She sat back on the sofa and picked up the book.

Her thoughts drifted to Cory. Her mind had been blank during their few hours together. Was that what made people sex addicts—arousal and orgasm being a sort of oblivion? She was entirely willing to become a sex addict if it would keep her from crawling out of her skin, or worse, giving up altogether on her parents. She picked up the stilettos that still lay where she had tossed them that morning and pulled out the stockings in the left shoe. A note fell to the floor, with Cory's name and number on it. She called the number.

"I found your number in my shoe," Lauren said. "At least I'm hoping it's yours."

"Helen?" Cory said.

Lauren blanched at hearing her mother's name. Using it in pursuit of sex seemed entirely wrong.

"Yes. I wanted to thank you for taking such good care of me last night."

Cory talked over the noise in the background. It sounded like she was in a bar. "It was my pleasure, honestly. Are you okay today?"

Lauren paused. "I'm a little lonely."

Cory had moved somewhere quieter. She was probably at Tillie's. "Are you at the house I dropped you at this morning?"

"Yes, it's my home."

"I can be there in fifteen minutes," Cory said. She sounded eager, excited. Young.

"No, it's better at your place." Lauren imagined Tim bursting through her bedroom door or, worse, monitoring the action from his CCTV command post. "But, Cory? Same rules apply. No questions about what I was doing last night or anything else. Think of it like *Last Tango in Paris*."

"What?"

She wasn't surprised Cory didn't get the reference. She was much younger and probably no film buff. "It's a film about two lovers who don't exchange names. They're completely anonymous to each other."

Cory hesitated. "Well, we already know each other's names, but I think I catch your drift. I'd still like you to come over."

"See you in a bit."

She dressed and brushed her hair. In the mirror she saw her pallid complexion and the bags under her eyes, but she didn't put makeup on. This was all about her, not how anyone else perceived her. The need to claim some small bit of control over her life was driving her, and her sharp arousal was a surprise. Within a minute of walking through Cory's door, Lauren led her to the bedroom and pushed her down on the bed. She stripped out of her pants and before even kissing her she straddled Cory's face and lowered herself, holding onto the headboard.

"Make me come," Lauren said, her eyes closed as she moved against Cory's tongue. She'd never done anything as bold, as lewd. She felt she would explode in an instant, so she slowed down, moving evenly as Cory tried to match her pace. She looked down and saw Cory's startled eyes looking back at her, turning hungry as their gaze held. She brought her hands to Lauren's hips and held her in place as she used her tongue with focus and speed and considerable skill. Soon Lauren grabbed the headboard with both hands as she came and came and came.

She lay next to Cory, stunned by the intensity of her orgasm. Perhaps if she'd gathered together all of the orgasms she'd experienced with Kelly and turned them into one, it would have been half as powerful as the orgasm she'd just had. Maybe. She watched impassively as Cory pulled her T-shirt over her head, yanked off her pants, and then turned to Lauren to unbutton her shirt and unhook her bra. She started to lie on top of her.

"Hold on a sec," Lauren said, blocking Cory with her arm. "That about crippled me."

Cory looked her in the eye. "I remembered who you are," Cory said.

"What?" Lauren didn't approve of the choice of pillow talk.

"All last night I kept thinking you were familiar, especially after your makeup was off, and it came to me this morning. You're the chick who was accused of murdering her girlfriend."

Lauren stared at her for a long moment, trying to imagine what Cory thought about a possibly murderous publishing heiress who dresses like a whore to pick up women in bars. She started laughing.

Cory looked at her warily. "Should I be worried?"

"Do you really think I could get the advantage of you? You look like much more of a threat than I do."

"I can take care of myself," Cory said evenly.

"See? And don't forget our rules. The anonymity thing is blown, but I don't want any questions. I have much bigger plans for our time together."

Cory leaned over to kiss Lauren, draping herself over Lauren's long thigh and starting to move against her. Lauren could feel moisture spread over her skin and she lifted her thigh to give Cory more traction. As Cory started pushing faster, Lauren stared at the ceiling, plotting exactly how she'd have Cory bring her to at least two more orgasms and then how she'd slip away home. She felt like a chess player, three steps ahead of her opponent and in total control. It was thrilling.

Chapter Thirteen

Of the many gaping holes in Kelly Moore's skimpy police file, the absence of any interviews with Lauren Wade's family seemed the most curious. The detective's interview with Lauren after her arrest was there, so Josie knew what Lauren had said, or, more accurately, not said at the time of her arrest. But nothing from the parents or brother. Bev's notes indicated Lauren and Tim's parents were sailing around the world, according to people in their Gold Coast high-rise. A neighbor there said he hadn't seen them for months, the doorman said he'd been collecting their mail for a long time, and the property manager said their monthly assessments were being paid so she really didn't care where they were.

Apparently the parents were incommunicado. Bev's notes indicated the detectives couldn't find the brother either. Kelly's parents had told them Lauren had a brother, but they didn't know him. Clearly no extensive effort had been made to find him. Once the case was in the hands of the state's attorney, the motivation seemed to drain right out of the detectives assigned to the case, except for Bev, who had very little influence as the junior member on the team. And she was kept too busy to poke around on a case that had at least unofficially been closed.

Josie found Tim Wade with a simple search on Google. Digging a little deeper, she was able to come up with his home address. She was beginning to think homicide detectives were not the stars she always thought they were.

She didn't bother calling for an appointment with him. She showed up at Tim's Lincoln Park house late on Sunday afternoon and he answered the door without hesitation. He didn't even ask who she was before he started talking to her about the Bears and how humiliating their loss that afternoon had been. He was dressed in cut-off khaki Dockers, a huge Bears jersey, orange tube socks, and navy blue sneakers. It wasn't what she expected the scion of a publishing company to look like. Even more confusing was his expensive haircut and sharply handsome face. None of it integrated in any way. He seemed to see the confusion on her face.

"I always dress like this during a game. It's a lucky-charm thing." Josie listened for other people in the house, maybe other nerdy guys he was watching the game with. All was silent. "I suppose I should ask who you are," he said.

Josie explained what she'd been hired to do and asked if she could talk with him about his sister.

"Of course," he said. "Let me get changed and we'll have some coffee." She perched on a stool at the breakfast bar to wait. Josie didn't know much about high end anything, but she knew that refrigerators wide enough to hold a baby elephant were owned by the wealthy, not by the bungalow class. The range looked like the kind they used on the cooking shows on TV. Everything was sparkling clean.

When he entered the kitchen, Josie turned to see a completely different man striding toward her. Now he was wearing tennis whites, including a cable-knit sweater and long pants, as if he were Bill Tilden playing in the '20s.

"Are you playing tennis today?" Josie asked.

Tim looked down at himself, as if considering the question an odd one. "Ah, no. I dressed to watch a match later." He went to an incredibly complex coffee machine and started fiddling around. It looked like it could manufacture widgets or launch a missile, but soon the smell of strong coffee filled the air. Josie was wondering if he was crazy, a term she no longer used lightly, given her own diagnosis.

He turned to her with a brilliant smile. "Do you like your espresso neat or with some milk?"

"I'm not sure," she said. "I've never had espresso."

"Oh, darling. That is sad. Let's start you off with a latte so we don't blow a hole through your head." Josie wondered why he put it that way. Had he recently blown a hole through Kelly's head?

More fiddling as he blended some milk into a froth. He finally placed their drinks on the counter and settled on a stool next to her. "What would you like to ask me about my sister?"

"I discovered you hadn't been interviewed when Lauren was arrested, and I thought that was odd. Your parents weren't either."

Tim somberly took a sip of his coffee in its tiny cup. She watched for his pinkie finger to extend, and there it went. She was no stranger to weirdness when it came to interviewing people, but this guy was impossible to tag as one thing or the other.

"Well, my parents are sailing around the world in their own boat, so they're impossible to reach. They've been gone for ages. I tried to reach them when Kelly was murdered but couldn't find a way to get a radio or satellite message to them. They didn't leave any of that information for us. I don't think the police even tried. My parents still don't know Lauren was arrested and tried for murder. And as for me, the police never got in touch. I was a little insulted, to tell you the truth."

"You could have gone to them," Josie said. "Wouldn't you want to say something to them to support your sister?"

He looked at Josie as if she'd asked him to roll in the mud with his tennis whites on.

"It's understandable you wouldn't know any of the family history, but rest assured, I wouldn't support my sister. It was too bad for her my parents weren't in town when this happened. They would have done anything to make the situation go away. Bad for business, you know," he said bitterly, before falling silent, staring into his espresso cup. "You'll have to excuse me, but I really can't talk any further about my family."

"I'm sorry if I brought up a tough subject, Mr. Wade. But I have to ask whether you believe Lauren was capable of murdering her partner?"

He returned to his relaxed demeanor. "Absolutely. I think my sister's capable of anything. She's proved that over and over again. If something infuriated her, I could see her pulling the trigger." He sprang off his stool and looked at Josie. "I wish I could invite you for some dinner, but I'm off to Midtown Tennis Club. There's a tournament starting tonight and I like to watch."

Josie stopped at the door. "Can we meet again when you have more time? Maybe for coffee somewhere?"

"I'm not sure I see the point, but I'd be delighted. I'd love to hear how you're getting on." He reached for a stack of cards on an antique table in the foyer. "Feel free to give me a call. I think you're on a wild goose chase. Lauren's the murderer, I'm sure of that. You won't find anyone else."

"Why didn't you tell the police that?" Josie asked.

"She's still family. I'm loyal to family."

That didn't make much sense. How could he be loyal to and hate his sister at the same time? Greta would say something about "enmeshment," a state of family fucked-upness Josie's family suffered from as well. Or so Greta said.

Tim opened the door. "One last question, then," Josie said. "Where were you between seven and ten o'clock on the evening of Kelly Moore's murder?"

Tim grinned as he pulled out his iPhone. "This is great. I'm a big fan of the TV crime shows. Did you know in France they call them 'Les Policiers'? I love that." He tapped at his phone for a moment. "What day was that, again?"

"February fifteenth," Josie said, curious he hadn't already considered his alibi. Or maybe this was another act, which was more likely.

"Hmm. Unfortunately my phone says I had no events that day. Kind of sad. Also, pretty inconvenient in terms of an alibi. At this point I have no idea what I was doing that day."

"Do you keep any kind of personal journal? That might jog your memory."

"God, no. I don't want to go noodling around in my brain. It's best to keep things as they are."

Josie was quite sure there was room for improvement there. She took one of his cards and left the house. Once in her car, she jotted down what had happened before she forgot any details. Tim was definitely weird, but crazy might be a stretch. Clearly the Wade family had strained relationships, particularly between Lauren and Tim. All she knew was there was an extremely odd son and a possibly murderous daughter, and neither could be trusted in what they said about the other.

She'd start all over in the morning, trying again for an appointment with Lauren, who was guarded more fervently than the pope. She'd tried all day on Friday, but Lauren's assistant said no each time and there was no getting beyond that. She'd keep trying.

❖

A few hours later, Josie strolled into Tillie's to meet Lucy. In two minutes of conversation the day before, Lucy had made Josie feel as safe with someone as she'd remembered ever feeling. Maybe Greta did, too, but Greta felt more like a mother figure, whatever it was that was supposed to feel like. Lucy was someone she would date, a word as foreign to her as "relax." She'd called to ask her to meet her at Tillie's, and Lucy had eagerly agreed.

They sat at the bar, nearly empty as the Bears game was over and its result no cause for celebration. The stereotype that queers didn't like sports was simply crap. You couldn't move in this place on game day. Josie hated stereotypes. She grew up hearing them every day from her father, who seemed encyclopedic in his knowledge of how to lump a group of people together in the most unflattering way possible. She remembered how red her face turned during the time she was in uniform, on-site at a murder her father was the lead detective on. The victim was an Orthodox Jew, the blood from a gut shot turning his white tzitzis dark red. Every stereotype about Jews came tumbling out of her father's mouth, as if they were standing in 1939 Munich rather than West Rogers Park. Josie could hear the other uniforms nervously laughing around her.

She realized she was brooding, so she turned toward Lucy, glass in hand.

"Cheers," she said, watching as Lucy's eyes locked onto hers. "I better drink this while it's cold, since I only get the one a day."

They drank, and Lucy put her mug down first. "I was pretty certain you were alcoholic before…"

"My hospitalization," Josie finished. "Don't dance around it for my sake."

"Okay. But you must not be an alcoholic if you can stop at one a day."

"What if I was an alkie then but not now?" Josie was teasing, but Lucy looked at her earnestly. She was adorable.

"You can't be alcoholic and then not an alcoholic. It's like unringing a bell," Lucy said.

"Yeah, I know that actually. My mom is a stone alcoholic. My dad, too. That probably tells you a lot, doesn't it?" Still, Josie started to find the focus on it a bit irritating.

"I can't imagine you escaped the disease with the background you have," Lucy said.

"What difference does it make to you whether I'm alcoholic or not?"

Lucy watched as Josie pushed her beer away from her. "It matters a great deal. I make it a policy to never date an alcoholic."

They were sitting on bar stools facing each other, knees touching. There was that word "date" again.

"You look apoplectic," Lucy said. "If this isn't a date, say so. You made it sound like one when you called."

"I did?" Josie looked perplexed.

"Yes, you absolutely did. You had a flirty tone to your voice,"

Maybe she hadn't lost her swagger after all.

"I can't say it's not a date," Josie said.

Lucy laughed and picked up her beer. "Pardon me while I swoon. A sentence with two negatives in it makes my heart soar."

Josie shrugged. "Stopping by Tillie's for a beer isn't a proper date. I planned to ask you out while we were here."

Lucy's smile was brilliant, transforming her plain face into something entirely desirable. "That would be great. I was hoping you felt that way."

"It's only a date," Josie said, turning her head away from Lucy. "Don't order the U-Haul yet." Talk about stereotyping. Lucy laughed.

The bartender came over to clear away their empty mugs and wipe the counter. Josie knew bartenders were usually fonts of information.

"Kris, you must know a bit about the Kelly Moore murder. What do you think about it?"

Kris was a big woman who played on the offensive line for the Chicago women's professional football team. You wouldn't want to be in her way once she had a head of steam behind her. But she was a popular bartender and people told her things.

"What do I think? I don't think about it, is what I think. I only know one of my regular customers got shot and killed."

"Kelly came in here a lot?" Josie prodded.

"Yeah. Over the last year or so. Hell, I saw you putting the moves on her soon after she started hanging here."

Josie blushed, which was all shame and nothing about flattery.

"I have a terrible memory, you know that," Josie said. Lucy looked empathetic.

"Well, you struck out, Ace. I remember the look on your face when she walked out the door," Kris said.

"It must have been an off night for you," Lucy said.

"I also saw what was going on with Kelly and that tall girl she cheated with," Kris said. "I think her name's Ann-Marie. I kept my eye on that because Gabby and me are friends. She's a medic for the football team."

Lucy looked like she was settling around a campfire for a good story.

"When did you start noticing that?" Josie said.

"Hell, I don't know. Not long before Kelly was murdered."

"Did you tell Gabby you thought Ann-Marie and Kelly were sleeping together?"

"Honey, there was no sleep involved where they were concerned," Kris said. "They both lived with their girlfriends and had to get in before curfew. But no, I wasn't gonna get in the middle of that. I seen the way Gabby treated Ann-Marie, well before she found out she was cheating on her. Looked like there were some issues to work out."

Kris wiped down the bar, an autonomic action for a bartender, like breathing.

"How did Gabby treat Ann-Marie?" Josie asked. "Was she abusive?"

"I don't think many people noticed, but I notice a lot. One night Gabby grabbed onto Ann-Marie's arm and held it hard. There were a few times she pulled on her hand and led her out of the bar."

"And she's a friend of yours?"

Kris gave her a sharp eye. "I don't judge."

"Do you think she was aware of Kelly and Ann-Marie having a thing going?"

Kris shrugged again. "Don't know. I'd guess no, since they were still coming to the bar together, and Gabby would have gone ballistic hearing about Ann-Marie and Kelly. She was hard on Ann-Marie, you could tell. I didn't like that much. But I think Gabby was too dense to pick up on anything going on.

"Like I said," Kris continued, "it seems like both Gabby and

Lauren Wade had cause to be upset. I don't know Lauren, so I can't tell you whether I think she'd murder Kelly. But I can't see Gabby doing something like that either."

Kris got called down to the end of the bar. "Why couldn't she see Gabby doing that?" Lucy asked. "She just got done telling us how Gabby was abusive."

Josie looked at Lucy. It almost felt like Lucy was a partner, helping her sort through a case, having her back, caring. Maybe it was something more than a partner? She'd never flirted or had sex sober that she could remember, never knew whether desire was real or the result of the mass quantities of alcohol she'd been drinking. She wondered if it was desire she was starting to feel with Lucy, who winked at her as she looked her way.

"Definitely something to look into," Josie said. She was excited to have any kind of lead. She'd seen in the police file there'd been a brief interview of Gabby, who didn't have an alibi for the time of the murder.

The bar was filling up again and Josie and Lucy moved their stools closer to one another. Josie ordered a couple of Diet Cokes and they got down to the business of getting to know each other. Most of what she learned about Lucy was delightful, with the possible exception that she was a social worker. That meant another set of knowing eyes and ears on her, keeping tabs on how she was managing her disease. She liked to have options, to hide her moods, to lie about them if it suited her. She had a feeling Lucy would be able to see through all that. Still, she allowed herself to be charmed by Lucy's openness, her red hair, her brilliant smile, and the simple fact she seemed to like Josie for who she was.

CHAPTER FOURTEEN

Monday, September 9

Josie walked toward the exit of Acme Insurance Company, thinking the name was about as old-fashioned as the people who worked there and the equipment they used. She was sure she saw a secretary typing on a Selectric. Perhaps the company was founded by Road Runner. But her first freelance contract was clutched in her hand, so she didn't concern herself with the office's decrepitude. They paid in US tender. She'd already called on three insurance companies that morning and hadn't gotten any contracts; by the time she hit Acme she wasn't picky about who she'd work for.

The man who'd given her the contract, a paunchy, humorless middle manager named Fredrick, looked like an Obersturmfürher in WWII. Josie's rates beat anyone else's and Acme had plenty of insurance fraud cases to investigate; he didn't care about her inexperience and she didn't care how mean he was. The case she'd been assigned was a typical worker's compensation matter. Acme felt steel worker Bill Swanson was faking a lower back injury and wanted Josie to film him doing something that showed his back was perfectly fine. How hard could that be? She'd stake him out and catch him mowing the lawn or something. Then Mr. Swanson would be back on the second shift.

She went back to her office to pick up her camcorder and head out to the Swansons'. She wanted to get that check cashed. After she finished there she needed to interview Gabby and Lauren Wade. She also needed to give the whole case a good think, which she could do while staking out the Swansons'.

As she stepped into the hallway of her office building, she saw Stan Waterman locking his door. He turned when he heard her and a big smile creased his face.

"Josie! I expected we'd be running into each other. I haven't seen you since you opened up." He walked toward her as she put her key in the door of her office. She'd been expecting this chat.

"Hey, Stan," she said, walking into the outer office. "I've been pretty busy. In fact, I'm only stopping by to pick something up before I'm out on the job again." She walked into her private office, not surprised to hear him follow, uninvited. The trouble was, Stan was such a sweet man she always found it impossible to ignore him, as much as she'd like to. Stan took a seat in front of her desk.

"Hold up a sec," he said. "Don't you have time to say hello to an old friend?"

Stan was in his late fifties, same as her dad. He had a saggy face and nearly white hair, which made him look older. He was still nimble as hell, though. It wasn't much more than a year ago that Josie heard about him tackling some perp who'd slipped past her father. Stan saving Jack's reputation once again. His longtime association with her father made her wary of him. But thankful, too. She knew Stan had tried to temper Jack's Neanderthal beliefs, a Sisyphean task if ever there was one.

Josie sat behind her desk and tried not to sigh. She pulled her camcorder out of a desk drawer and fiddled with it to remind Stan how busy she was.

"Sure, I can take a minute. Then I have to go out on a bad-back case. It's very hard to stand the excitement." She didn't know if Stan would catch the sarcasm.

"It looks like you've gotten off to a good start," he said. "Those bad-back cases are bread and butter. Infidelity, too. That's a huge part of what we do."

Josie looked up at him. "What's with the 'we'? I thought you were on your own."

"For the most part, I am," Stan said, looking as comfortable in her cheap visitors chair as he would on a chaise lounge. "I hired a young ex-cop to pick up my overflow work, but he's worthless. I took his word he left the job because he didn't like the chain of command. Found out later he'd washed out."

Silence. Josie was reasonably sure Stan hadn't purposely steered the conversation to her own departure from the police. But there they were.

"I'm sorry," he said, leaning forward. "I wasn't thinking how leaving the job would be a sore spot."

Josie smiled wanly. "It's not so much how I left. I could've stayed if I accepted a desk job. I'm more sensitive about all the stupid shit I did before that."

Stan waved it away, as if Josie drunkenly trying to seduce a commander in a banquet hall women's room was merely a blip on the screen. But Josie knew it was a big fucking blip.

"Look at your dad. He's done more embarrassing things than I can count and it doesn't follow him around."

"He has you for cover, like I had Bev. Both you and Bev were enablers."

"So what? We were partners. And partners do for each other. Your father was a pain in my ass, but he was my partner."

Josie didn't know what to say to that. She stood and picked up her camcorder. "I really have to go, Stan."

"Of course," he said, standing with her. "If there's anything you need, any help I can offer, please call me or knock on my door." He put his arm around her as they walked into the outer office. "I mean that, Josie. I've always had my eye out for you."

Here was another of those goddamned moments when she felt a tear springing forth because someone genuinely cared for her. Wasn't it supposed to be pain that brought on tears? Her feelings were upside down.

They said their good-byes and Josie scrambled down the back steps, anxious to get to her paying job, desperate to get away from Stan.

CHAPTER FIFTEEN

Josie loaded up her Corolla with the camcorder, binoculars, water, a sandwich, and two cups of coffee from Starbucks and headed out to her assignment. Bill Swanson lived in one of the northwest suburbs, on a street filled with identical trilevel houses from the '60s. The challenge in staking out a location like this was to avoid being noticed by the owners of the others houses on the street, all of whom parked their cars in their driveways or garages. Since Josie hadn't gone so far as renting the proverbial white paneled van with a "Bubba and Wayne's Sewer and Drain" sign on the side, she hoped most people would be at work. Sitting in her Corolla for hours would draw attention.

She pulled up and parked across the street, slightly angled away from the giant picture window in the front of the Swanson home. The house was painted an aggressive blue, as if it were trying to be a Swedish flag without the yellow. The property seemed reasonably well cared for. A late-model black Ford Explorer sat in the drive, so she guessed Swanson was home. Josie took a peek through her binoculars to make sure she could see inside the picture window, then got herself settled in for a few hours of stultifying boredom.

She'd been on plenty of stakeouts. She and Bev often dealt with serial robbers—perps working either on their own or in groups. The thieves usually concentrated on one area of town before moving on to another. It was almost as if they'd mapped their campaign of cat burglary—start in Wrigleyville, hit Lincoln Park, and then invade the Gold Coast. Omaha Beach to Paris.

As Josie grew more manic the previous fall, keeping herself in one spot for any length of time made stakeouts intolerable for both her and Bev. Josie's racing thoughts far outpaced her ability to communicate them, and when deprived of the freedom to move about, she talked constantly. It was impossible for Bev to keep up. No one else saw how ferocious Josie's appetite was for everything, how certain she was she could do anything—catch criminals, pick up women, spend money, drink insatiably, climb Kilimanjaro. Her energy was infinite. Before Bev finally decided to take her concerns to her lieutenant, Josie was suspended for insubordination, in the form of that ill-advised pass in the ladies room. The superior officer in question, Commander Margaret "Tank" O'Neil, could also have played on the front line of the women's professional football team, were she not sixty years old and fifty pounds overweight. The fact Josie tried to pick up O'Neil was her first clue something wasn't right in her head.

During the drive to the suburbs, Josie picked up her phone and called Gabby to ask her to meet. She was a paramedic with the city and worked odd hours. She could meet Josie for an interview the following morning; she sounded like she'd expected the call. Then Josie tried Lauren's office for the umpteenth time and got the same response from the centurion guarding her door—Ms. Wade would not be granting interviews to the press or anyone else. Getting to Lauren would take some stealth on Josie's part. She opened her sandwich and settled back in her seat.

It was close to two hours later when she saw a figure clad in white enter the living room of the Swanson house. Josie grabbed her binoculars and saw a man dressed in martial arts clothing, lifting and moving furniture around to create more space in the center of the room. Too bad she didn't have her camcorder on for that. By the time she'd started the camera and zoomed in, she could see him start exercises of some sort, his arms and legs blazing out from his solid stance. Josie glanced at the photo in the open file she had on Swanson and confirmed it was him. She figured the Bruce Lee imitation alone would do the job for Acme Insurance, but she decided to keep the camera on him a while longer. Swanson walked to the window and reached for the blind.

From the right side of the big window, Josie caught sight of someone entering the room. She swung the camera and saw a woman thirty to thirty-five years old and very attractive, except for the look of terror on her face. Before Josie could swing her camera back on Swanson, his bare foot entered the view and caught the woman square in the chest, throwing her against the wall behind her, where she sank to the floor. Without thinking, Josie threw down the camcorder, grabbed the Glock in her glove box, and ran toward the house. She could see Swanson picking the woman up off the floor as if setting her up for another knock-down blow.

Josie flew to the side door off the driveway and slowed enough to make her entrance as silent as possible. She could hear the woman screaming as Swanson made a loud guttural sound, followed by the thud of another blow finding its mark. She raced through the kitchen, into a short hall, and swung into the living room with her gun in both hands, steadily aimed at Bill Swanson's chest.

"Get down on the floor, hands behind your head. Now!" barked Josie. She could see the incredulous look on Swanson's face. He wasn't able to process what was happening. Josie yelled out her order again and took one step closer. Swanson snarled.

"Who the fuck are you? You can't come into my house."

The woman was creeping backward, taking cover behind Josie.

"If you can get to a phone, call nine-one-one," Josie said, not taking her eyes off Swanson. "And you get on the floor, facedown. I won't ask again."

This time Swanson took a step toward her. Josie moved her gun slightly and shot to his right, exploding a china cabinet full of Hummel figurines. It stopped Swanson in his tracks.

"Down on the ground or next time I won't miss," she said. Swanson quickly assumed the position. As far as she was concerned, he was a deadly weapon once he was close enough to hit her with a foot or hand. If she had to shoot him, she would.

Josie was without a lot of the things that made police work safer than the position she now found herself in. Handcuffs to disable the suspect, a radio, a Taser, and most of all, a partner. She kept her distance from Swanson but made sure his face was to the floor and his hands on his head. Then she glanced toward the door and saw the woman she assumed was Mrs. Swanson standing with a phone in her hand, looking like she was going to throw up. "They're coming," she managed to say before limping down the hall to a bathroom. Josie held her gun on Swanson, listening to her throw up and wondering how long this form of martial art domestic abuse had been going on. Finally, the local police showed up.

The Schaumburg police took her statement as well as her video of Bill Swanson in action, which pissed her off. She'd have to come back with a jump drive to get a copy to submit to Acme. She wanted the money and she wanted them to keep giving her work. There was a ruckus over the fact she'd fired her weapon, but the video confirmed her story, as did Mrs. Swanson. She was licensed to carry a gun, and being an ex-cop didn't hurt. Being a private investigator didn't help, since most cops distrusted them, but eventually they cut her loose.

Josie muttered to herself as she steered her car back to the city. It was midafternoon. Her agency had been open for four days and she'd already been hired in a murder case and discharged her weapon in a routine insurance matter. Greta would have a fit, though Josie had no intention of telling her of the day's events. Nor would she mention how short on sleep she was. It'd been impossible to fall asleep last night, her excited mind moving back and forth between lining up her approach to the entire Lauren Wade case and to the pleasant evening she'd spent with Lucy. She contemplated the word "pleasant," a word she sneered at as boring when in a manic state. Last night, pleasant felt exactly right as she and Lucy talked about their backgrounds, laughed a lot, and moved on to flirting by the end of the night. Josie felt for the first time her life might be more than battling her disease and working.

It wasn't lost on her that this had come about suddenly. Her experience with meeting new women while manic was to have sex as soon as possible. Sometimes over consecutive days with the same woman, but usually only the once. When depressed, she had no interest in women at all. She barely had interest in living. All the talking she and Lucy had done the night before was a first, as far as she could remember. She wanted more of it. She picked up her phone and called.

Lucy picked up after what seemed like forty-nine rings of her phone.

"Hi. It's Josie. I was beginning to think you had the only cell phone in the world without voicemail."

Lucy laughed. "My phone's always as far away from me as possible, or in the bottom of my purse. I set it up to give me a chance to take a call now and then. I would've missed yours."

"I'd have called you back," Josie said. She was drumming the steering wheel as she drove. "I thought I'd check in and thank you for the nice time last night." She cringed. "Nice" always sounded like a backhanded compliment to her.

"It was a great time," Lucy said, with some enthusiasm. "I'm so glad you called."

"It's been a strange day. I got into the middle of a situation and had to fire my gun." She heard a soft gasp, which felt very satisfying.

"Are you okay?" Lucy asked anxiously.

"Yeah, I'm fine. Everyone's fine. It was weird, though. I'll have to tell you about it sometime."

Josie swung onto the Kennedy Expressway toward downtown, which was already clogged with cars. "I'm really sorry your day involved shooting guns. That's not something most people get to say," Lucy said. "Is there anything I can do?"

There was the opening. Josie paused and then said, "I guess I wouldn't mind some company this evening."

"Do you mean my company? It's hard to tell if that was even an invitation." Lucy sounded like she was teasing, but Josie felt a little stung. She was really terrible at this.

"Yes, I meant you. Sorry for putting it so badly. Again."

"Don't be. I'm happy you asked. Let me bring some dinner over and you can tell me all about it," Lucy said.

Bingo. "That would be nice." There was that damn word again.

"Is there anything you don't eat?" Loaded question. A year ago she'd have to say no, based on the fact she was ready to give Tank O'Neil a go.

"Raw oysters," Josie said. "Though it's unlikely you'd be bringing those over."

"Not on the second date, anyway. It's a little too suggestive, don't you think?" Lucy was flirting. Josie was wondering about the concept of being suggestive. She'd never proposed anything as subtly suggestive as raw oysters. A hand up a skirt seemed to get the job done. Also, was this a second date? A horn blared as she absently cut into another lane. *What happens on a second date?*

CHAPTER SIXTEEN

"You're not getting a ten-thousand-dollar advance on a book about towel origami," Lauren said, giving her phone an exasperated look. She listened for a moment. "Okay, seven thousand. But I'm done."

It was at least the fifth difficult negotiation she'd had that day. Her assistant Eva came through the door with a cup of tea in hand. Lauren moved to the sofa and coffee table where Eva put the tea down.

"Eva, does it seem like everyone is a son of a bitch lately?" Lauren kicked off her sensible heels and put her feet up. "I used to love negotiating."

Eva pulled a chair closer to the table. "They're trying to take advantage of your troubles."

Lauren looked worried. "My troubles?"

"Yes, well, the trial, you know. The jail time."

"That's ridiculous. I was acquitted. I've moved on."

"They are businessmen, Miss Wade. They're by nature like wolves."

"So they're testing for weakness," Lauren said, as if she weren't perfectly aware of it. "Bastards."

"Hmm." Eva stood and turned to the door. "You keep doing what you're doing. It'll all blow over eventually."

She left Lauren alone in the office. Sitting on the coffee table was a letter-sized envelope containing a request from the company's board of directors for a public relations plan to minimize the impact of her trial for murder. No one seemed to understand the word "acquittal."

She shut down her computer and got ready to leave for the day. It was five thirty, an absurdly early hour compared to her past schedule, when she loved nothing more than to work late into the evening. As she gathered her things, Eva opened the door.

"That private investigator called again. Third time today." She sounded disgusted, as if she were getting robocalls from the Tea Party.

"You told her no interviews?" Lauren asked.

"Of course I told her no interviews," Eva said, exasperated. "Those have always been your instructions."

Lauren gave her a raised eyebrow but said nothing. She trusted Eva implicitly, but following instructions was perhaps not her strong suit. Eva's devotion to Lauren was her main job skill.

Her VP of operations, David Schofeld, walked in behind Eva. David had been the interim head of the company while Lauren was in jail. He'd seemed relieved when she took the reins back from him. Tim had been VP of operations before Lauren fired him. David had done all of the work and reported to him while Tim took all the credit. Lauren was glad he hadn't left the company before she'd had a chance to promote him. Tim's abuse of his staff was well known, and no threat of Lauren's seemed to make any difference to him. Their parents left the matter completely up to her to manage. They'd refused to intervene when Tim came running to them.

"Lauren, I'm glad I caught you," David said.

"I hope this isn't trouble," she said warily.

"It may be." He looked nervous. David was close to seven feet tall and generally had to bend down to have a conversation.

"Tell me, David. I'm not going to shoot the messenger." If there was one thing she still felt strongly about, it was not alienating David. He was essential to keeping the company running, even with Lauren at her best.

"I just saw Tim leaving the building."

"What?"

"Oh, Christ," Eva muttered.

Tim had been unofficially banned from the premises and until now had stayed away. There was nothing good about his showing up now.

"What was he doing here?" Lauren asked.

David shrugged. "I couldn't tell you. He was heading out the door with a group of women from marketing. You know how they always liked him down there."

Lauren knew only too well. On the few occasions she'd gone

down to the marketing VP's office since firing Tim, she got nothing but daggers from half the women who worked there. In the past year, with half of it spent in the county jail, the company had become a giant eggshell Lauren was forced to walk on, stepping through a confused mess of hurt feelings and strong resentments. Tim was not without his own cadre of supporters.

She stood still, thinking furiously, as David stood inside the door, Eva still behind him.

"That brother of yours is never good news," Eva said. "Maybe you should get a court order to keep him out of here." David nodded agreement.

Lauren picked up her briefcase and started toward the door, knowing that was impossible. "I'll think about that. And if either of you hear anything else about him, be sure to tell me." Lauren intended to talk to Tim about this as soon as she could reach him. She knew his only goal for being on the Wade-Fellows property was to sabotage her in some way or make her more fearful for her parents. He was always full of ideas.

David and Eva parted to let her through. Lauren was at the door of her outer office before she turned and said, "Thank you both. You two are my eyes and ears. Don't think I don't appreciate it."

She saw them smile at each other as she turned into the hallway. She was not herself yet, not automatically polite and approachable. She had to think in order to behave properly. She supposed the jail time did that. She'd become as defensive and guarded there as anyone would. She'd somehow escaped any major difficulties, though the tension there was nearly unbearable. She was worn down with worries—about her parents, Tim, the board of directors, her reputation, Kelly's murder. She tried to pat herself on the back for functioning at all, but she really wasn't a daily affirmations type of person.

And who was that persistent private investigator? She'd been giving some thought to hiring another PI to try to find her parents, but the first time she tried it the tail had been picked up by Tim almost immediately. Her punishment, according to Tim, was to have food withheld from her parents for three days, which she had no reason to doubt he did. She was afraid another attempt would cause even greater harm.

In any event, this new PI had most likely been hired by a magazine to do background for some sort of exposé. She couldn't think who else was interested in keeping the case alive. She climbed into her Lexus and headed home for an evening devoid of any pleasant distractions. Only unpleasant ones.

CHAPTER SEVENTEEN

Lucy arrived at six, bearing two bags of Thai food and a liter of Diet Coke. Now she stood by Josie at the kitchen counter, glopping huge portions of Pad Thai onto their plates. They sat in the dining room and Josie lit a candle in the middle of the table. She wanted to do things right. She liked Lucy, who'd arrived wearing a skirt over a pair of skinny pants, a short jacket over a sweater over a gauzy shirt. Her hair was held up by some hidden structure that pushed her red curls up and out. Josie didn't know what to make of it. Lucy seemed to be wearing every piece of clothing she owned. It would be a formidable challenge to take them all off.

The Grapes of Wrath was the cheery title Josie picked for them to watch. They sat close together on the sofa. The movie had captivated Josie the first time she saw it, but now it seemed interminable. She began thinking of putting her arm around Lucy but she remained paralyzed. She was worried Lucy was bored stiff. She snuck a look and saw her lounging comfortably and watching the movie with apparent interest.

By the time Grandma Joad died, freeing up some space in that overstuffed jalopy of theirs, Josie couldn't stand her anxiety any longer. She hit the pause button on the remote. Lucy turned to her, an expectant look on her face.

"I'm sorry," Josie said. "Is it all right if we stop watching the movie?"

"Of course," Lucy said. Josie was nonplussed by how relaxed Lucy was, how warm her eyes were, how pleasant her smile. Maybe she was on drugs? "Is there any particular reason you want to stop?" Lucy sounded a little coy.

Josie hitched herself a little farther from Lucy. "The movie was boring me. I don't know why I picked it."

"Because you're nervous?"

"I'm not nervous," Josie said. "Not even a bit." They looked at each other and burst out laughing.

"You were ready to shoot someone today, and yet you're nervous now."

"That was nothing. We're trained to handle things like that. I don't think I've been properly trained to handle this."

"Then maybe," Lucy moved a little closer, "maybe you're nervous about our first kiss." She took Josie's hand. "Dinner, a movie, sitting together on the sofa—it's a classic second-date scenario. The only proper thing to do at the end of the movie is to have that first kiss." She'd sidled up to kissing distance.

The laugh had broken some of the tension Josie felt, but she was still fiddling with the drawstrings on her hoodie. "I believe that is much more suggestive than raw oysters," she said.

Lucy laughed, but then seemed to realize Josie was serious. She took her hand. "Oysters imply sex, Josie. I'm talking about a kiss."

Josie recalled a few dates in high school and college when a kiss at the end of the night was the extent of things. Since then, kissing and sex were inextricably bound. Why was she so nervous? She knew how to kiss. She was unlikely to mess that up. Still, she was thinking of excusing herself to get a Klonopin from the bathroom when Lucy leaned over and gently put her lips to Josie's. They lingered there until Josie started to relax and Lucy slowly deepened the kiss.

Josie found her arms moving around Lucy's waist, pulling her closer. Now that the process was under way, she felt more in her element. It had been so long since she'd had sex without being drunk or manic, or, more likely, drunk and manic, it seemed far more frightening than facing down a wife-beating black belt. But nature took hold. She gently pushed Lucy down until she lay partially on top of her and started doing what she did best. It was all automatic. As soon as their tongues met and the heat moved up a notch, she put her hand up Lucy's shirt and brushed it over her breast. She felt Lucy grab her wrist.

"Kissing, not sex," she breathed.

Josie winced. This was so fucking confusing. She pushed herself upright and sat with her head in her hands.

"Is that it?" Lucy said. "No more kissing unless there's sex?"

"What's the point?" Josie said, peeking through her fingers.

"The point? It's called getting to know each other," Lucy said, the frustration coming through her voice. Josie didn't respond. "I know how you're used to operating. But that was last year. You're a different person now." Lucy sat up and put her hand back on Josie's arm, softening her words. "There are other ways to know a person beyond fifteen minutes of talk and then sex."

Josie looked at her. "Fifteen minutes? That's forever." She smiled, a little painfully, when Lucy laughed. "I don't know what I'm doing. You must think I'm a jerk."

"Not a jerk. But I want to know you're spending time with me for something beyond sex."

"This is already a world record for me," Josie said, wondering what "beyond sex" meant. "Doesn't that tell you something?"

"Yes, but we're still not having sex tonight. Though I'm looking forward to when we do."

Lucy started kissing her again and they practiced that for a good while before she said good night. Josie went immediately to her medicine cabinet and downed a Klonopin. Greta had prescribed them for agitation, and Josie had plenty of that.

CHAPTER EIGHTEEN

Tuesday, September 10

Josie's interview with Gabby was at 8:00 in the morning, the end of her overnight shift. Josie had been up for a few hours already, meticulously creating a chart on poster board of all she knew about Kelly's murder and the people closely or tangentially related to the investigation. This involved a lot of circles, squares, arrows, and small writing. When she propped it against the wall, she felt satisfied. In truth, it was no more helpful than a box of rocks.

They met in a diner near the Rogers Park firehouse where Gabby worked. The diner was a grim-looking black and red corner restaurant whose busiest hours were between two and six in the morning. The drunks had cleared out by the time they arrived, but Josie could taste that atmosphere of desperation. Gabby, however, looked like she owned the place.

Gabby's attention was focused on the enormous breakfast in front of her. Josie stuck to coffee.

"I haven't seen you around the bar lately. Where you been?" Gabby poured more ketchup on her potatoes. And her eggs. Josie averted her eyes.

"Think of me as the prodigal daughter of Tilly's. I've come back home."

Gabby grunted. "Ann-Marie tells me you're looking into Kelly Moore's murder."

"I am. I'm curious whether you think they arrested the right person," Josie asked. The server arrived and refilled Gabby's coffee and then overfilled Josie's, leaving a puddle of coffee on the table. There was no apology or offer to clean up the mess, so Josie reached for the napkin dispenser and mopped up the coffee herself. She felt a hot flush to her face, a sign something pissed her off.

"What the fuck," Josie said to no one in particular.

Gabby laughed. "Welcome to the Big M."

"Right. So back to the question: Do you think Lauren Wade killed Kelly?"

Gabby ate for a bit before answering. "I'll put it this way. I was surprised she was acquitted."

"Why?"

"Didn't she have the classic three elements for murder—motive, means, and opportunity?"

"That would explain why she was arrested. It doesn't mean she did it."

Gabby ate and didn't respond.

"You realize, of course, you had the same motive as Lauren," Josie said.

Gabby looked at Josie with a direct gaze. "What motive would I have to kill Kelly? She was Lauren's lover, not mine. If I was going to murder anyone it would have been Ann-Marie."

Josie thought that was amazingly frank. "Did you want to kill Ann-Marie?"

"For a minute." Gabby shrugged. "Kind of like you want to kill the asshole who cuts you off on the expressway or honks at you the second a light turns green. I was furious, but it passed and I realized killing her wasn't what I wanted to do. I love her."

"But you ended the relationship. Your motive for killing Kelly could simply be she ruined what you had with Ann-Marie."

Gabby laughed again and finished her meal, while Josie stared at her and wondered what kind of brain was working in there. She laughed a lot for someone being accused of murder. She looked up at Josie and said, "Isn't this about the biggest dyke drama you've ever heard of? I mean, it's like dyke drama on Broadway."

Josie had to agree that was true. "But what about your motive? Your lover slept with someone else. You had to be furious with Kelly also."

"I was. I was mad at both of them. The reason I ended the

relationship with Ann-Marie was simply a matter of pride, and I don't mind admitting my fucking pride gets in my way a lot. I didn't want to lose Ann-Marie, but I couldn't roll over on infidelity. People would think I'm the biggest wimp around. I figured I'd find out whether Ann-Marie cared for me by how she handled herself after the breakup."

"And?" Josie prompted.

"It was exactly what I thought. Ann-Marie is a lot of things, but she's fucking predictable most of the time. She tried to leave me alone for a few weeks, but then she started calling and apologizing. Then she started showing up at my house and pleading. I strung her along a bit and then took her back. I think it taught us both how much we belonged together."

Josie sipped her coffee, trying to find words that wouldn't offend Gabby. "I'm glad it worked out for you, Gabby. But I have to say I still don't quite see you two together. I mean, Ann-Marie is an art professor and you're, well, a bit earthier than she is."

"There've been stranger matches. I think Ann-Marie has a thing for an old-fashioned butch who wants to take care of her. Call it her sexual preference."

"But Kelly was anything but an old-fashioned butch, and I don't think she'd really take care of anyone. Why would Ann-Marie cheat with her?" Josie asked.

"Kelly was pretty girly, that's for sure. But she also was a woman who was used to getting what she wanted. She probably turned her 'I'll die if I don't have you' eyes on Ann-Marie, and I could see Ann-Marie getting pulled into that. I imagine that's how Kelly got Lauren. I didn't know Lauren before the book club, but she seemed pretty unapproachable to me. That would have been a challenge Kelly couldn't resist. Plus, Lauren has gobs of money," Gabby said.

"And that was Kelly's sexual preference?"

"I'd say it was one of them."

The server tossed a check onto the table and Josie grabbed for it. "I can expense it," she said. "But I do have one more question for you."

"Shoot," Gabby said. She had that supremely confident look on her face again.

"Where were you the evening Kelly was killed?"

Gabby shrugged. "I have no idea. I may have been working."

"I find it hard to believe you wouldn't remember exactly where you were that night. It's not an event that people are likely to forget about."

"If you mean I didn't give it much notice, that's true. I know where I was when Ann-Marie told me she'd been sleeping with Kelly, but really that's the only thing that affected me."

"Can you check back on your schedule and see if you were working?"

Gabby brought her phone out and scrolled and tapped a bit until she got to the previous February. "What night was the murder?"

"February fifteenth."

"There isn't anything on that date." She looked up at Josie. "Does that make me suspect number fucking one?"

Josie slid out of the booth, trying to skirt the sticky parts. "Let's say you now have motive and opportunity." She threw some bills on the table. "Thanks for the chat, Gabby."

She felt Gabby's eyes on her as she walked out the door of the Big M. If nothing else, she now had another solid suspect in the case, though Tim felt more likely than Gabby. She couldn't wait to add it all to her board.

CHAPTER NINETEEN

Lauren saw Ann-Marie standing in front of the Whole Foods on Huron, laden with bags and trying to hail a cab. She should've zoomed by in her Lexus; it made no sense to offer a ride to her lover's lover. But she wasn't feeling confrontational toward Ann-Marie. It was more like curiosity. She pulled over and got out of her car, leaning against the hood as she caught Ann-Marie's attention. Ann-Marie seemed startled.

"Can I give you a lift home?" Lauren asked.

Ann-Marie looked like Lauren had asked if she'd like to take a shuttle to Mars. "I don't understand."

Lauren smiled. "Well, you've got a bunch of groceries and no car, and I have a car and plenty of time to drive you to your place. It's not so hard to understand."

Ann-Marie looked to the street with some faint desperation in her eyes, as if hoping her golden carriage, or at least a Yellow Cab, would materialize before her. Neither did. She turned resignedly to Lauren. "If you're sure…"

"Absolutely. Let's get those bags put away." Lauren popped her trunk open and helped Ann-Marie load the heavy cloth shopping bags. "Was there a sale on rocks in there?"

Ann-Marie smiled despite herself and put a hand on the trunk to help Lauren close it. "I make a great rock soup."

Lauren looked at her appreciatively and opened the passenger door for her.

As Lauren pulled into traffic she noticed how nervous Ann-Marie seemed. "I don't hold anything against you," she said. "Frankly, you could be anyone. It's Kelly's infidelity that was the thing I needed to deal with, not who she was doing it with. God knows I wasn't shocked."

Ann-Marie looked out the passenger window. "It's a little deflating, even in these circumstances, to find out you could be anyone."

"Don't take it personally," Lauren said. "Where's home, by the way?"

"Andersonville. Way out of your way."

"Why are you at this Whole Foods if you live up there?"

Ann-Marie looked away from the window toward Lauren. She seemed to relax with the small talk. "I had to meet with some gallery owners in the area. I made sure I kept the receipt from the store, though."

Lauren looked at her quizzically.

"Not to bring this back to the uncomfortable way we met each other," she continued, "but a PI interviewed me the other day about Kelly's murder. She asked where I was the night it happened and I told her I was at the grocery before coming home to cook dinner. She kept harping on whether I had a receipt or not."

"What PI are you talking about?" Lauren asked.

"The only PI I've ever met. I'm an art teacher. I don't run into PIs very often."

Lauren knew Ann-Marie was more than an art teacher. She had a solid gallery reputation for her work. And she dressed the part. Long-sleeved button-down white shirt with most of the buttons undone to show the grubby T-shirt beneath. Her jeans were worn and had paint splotched on them. She wore boots.

Ann-Marie continued. "Her name was Josie something or other. Kind of cute, obviously lesbian, but definitely all business. It seemed to me she was looking for suspects other than you for Kelly's murder."

"But who would hire a PI to do such a thing?" She pulled up to a small house in the less expensive outer ring of Andersonville. Ann-Marie met Lauren at the back of the car and they both pulled out a bag.

"I don't have the faintest idea. It's not information she was willing to give. But it seems someone wants your name cleared," Ann-Marie said.

"But I was acquitted. What's to clear?"

"Being acquitted and having people convinced you're innocent are two different things, and I know there are a lot of people who still think you did it." Ann-Marie smiled ruefully. "I've heard some talk in the bars, at any rate."

Lauren said a quiet good-bye and climbed back in her car to head downtown to her office. The PI concerned her. She didn't want Tim to think she'd hired another investigator. Tim had noticed the first one right away, and there had been consequences for her parents and for herself. He'd given her another dreadful assignment, this one involving attending a fund-raising gala with Kelly where she was to try to pick up the celebrity guest of honor. In front of Kelly.

She could almost hear Tim laugh in the background at the event, where he'd managed to get hired by the caterer to serve drinks. She and Kelly had arrived together, but soon Kelly was working the room. Lauren had a couple of drinks and summoned the courage to approach the celebrity and flirt with her. When she said something suggestive to her, the celebrity looked at Lauren like she was trying to sell her a moldy mattress and stalked away. Tim immediately swooped by in his catering clothes, holding a tray of champagne. "It's a wonder you've ever gotten laid. Your approach is pitiful." He laughed. "But your assignment's fulfilled. I release you to go deal with your very pissed-off-looking girlfriend." He moved on through the room, looking happy. He'd been happy since the day he kidnapped their parents.

Lauren looked across the room and saw Kelly standing in her beautiful evening gown, her slender arms folded across her chest. She was staring at Lauren, but not with her usual come-hither look. Lauren went hither nonetheless, anxious to explain herself. When Kelly was really pissed about something, there was no peace in their home for days at a time. This pissed Lauren off in turn, creating a vicious cycle that only ended when Lauren caved in and apologized for whatever transgression they both had forgotten by then. It surprised her she'd become so submissive with someone, but Kelly was very good at producing an atmosphere Lauren hated. She knew Lauren would do some groveling to dispel the tension that was unbearable to her. Kelly was good at getting what she wanted.

"What the hell was that?" she asked as Lauren approached her. Several heads turned to stare. "Did you honestly think you were going to seduce Miss D-List celebrity?"

"What makes you think I was trying to seduce her?"

Kelly laughed and drained the rest of her champagne. "To someone who knows you, you couldn't be any more obvious. You never stand that close to anyone. Not to me, and certainly not to a stranger. Whatever incredibly awkward thing you said to Tanya made her look like she'd been offered a pig foot as an appetizer. It was cringe-worthy. Why would you even try?"

"I only tried because Tim dared me to. I couldn't resist."

"Oh, please. That's a little far-fetched, even for Tim. Can't you come up with something better than that?"

"I'm afraid it's the truth." Lauren looked ashamed.

Kelly very slowly relaxed. She rubbed Lauren's arms, as if trying to warm her up. "Why do you keep doing this? Tim's never made a dare you could win."

Lauren looked miserable, and she came by it naturally. "You know what's behind it all. I do better than Tim at everything that matters, and he gets back at me by trying to get me to do things we both know I'm terrible at. I'd rather keep him amused than have him be dangerous."

"I don't understand his hold on you, Lauren. He must have traumatized you as an kid. Maybe you have PTSD."

Lauren smiled. "Maybe, but most of his challenges don't mean anything. I can handle him."

"Not tonight you couldn't. It was a humiliation for me. How would you feel if I tried to pick up a woman in the same room as you?"

Lauren tried to look distressed at the thought, as if she hadn't witnessed exactly that thing happen on numerous occasions. "Yes, I can see how bad this is for you. But if there's one thing I'm sure of, in a seduction contest between you and me, you're the hands-down winner. You'd have had no problem with what's her name."

"You're limiting the contestants to you and me? That's like saying in a boxing match between Muhammad Ali and Woody Allen, Ali would be the clear winner." Kelly sounded a little peeved.

"You're right. How about the world-record-setting National Champion of Flirtation and Seduction?"

Kelly looked thoughtful. "I like the sound of that." More hard thinking. "I bet I could make a fortune teaching people how to flirt. It's amazing how many people are like you."

"I'm sure you could, sweetheart. Now let's go home. You can brainstorm the idea in the car."

Kelly had practically skipped to the parking lot, while Lauren walked sullenly behind. She was so whipped.

Lauren cleared her mind of that memory of Kelly, realizing again how high-maintenance she'd been. She walked into her offices and paused at Eva's desk.

"What can I do for you, Miss Wade?" Lauren had told Eva a thousand times to call her Lauren, but she wouldn't shift her ingrained Southern manners. "You know that woman—the PI who keeps calling here?" Eva nodded. "Get her on the phone and make an appointment for me to see her here at the first opportunity."

Eva looked dumbfounded.

"You do have her number, don't you?"

"Yes, Miss Wade. I'll make the call now."

Lauren went into her office and closed the door. There were so many things that didn't make sense. Who would spend the money to hire a detective to find an alternate killer? Who cared about her that much?

Eva knocked and entered in one motion, making the knock a mere formality. This was another thing Eva never seemed to grasp—that Lauren wanted a little warning before someone entered her office.

"That private investigator, Josie Harper, can be here at eight tomorrow if that's not too early for you. You're booked solid the rest of the day."

"That's fine. You can go on home, Eva."

Lauren slumped in her chair. She had no enthusiasm for her work, which used to be her passion. Now she was consumed with how to get her parents safely released and her own freedom restored. This mission of Josie Harper's was yet another distraction.

CHAPTER TWENTY

Greta rose to greet Josie when she arrived, on time, for her appointment. For a moment she thought Greta was going to hug her and was relieved when she waved Josie to her usual chair. Her office felt as normal as home. At least what she imagined a normal home would feel like.

"I'm wondering," Josie opened, "if we still need to meet twice a week. Isn't it time we cut back?" Josie leaned back in her chair and sipped from her Starbucks cup. "Every child needs to fly from home at some point."

"That's how you're starting our conversation this afternoon?" Greta said. "You know that makes me immediately suspicious." She was wearing an autumn-colored dress and her still-shapely legs were crossed. A high heel dangled from one foot.

"Why would you be suspicious? I've been out of the hospital for a year, I've been a good girl the entire time, and it seems like we go over the same things again and again." Josie also had her legs crossed, but the crossed leg was moving up and down rapidly, restlessly. She grabbed on to her knee.

"Let's back up a bit and you can fill me in on what's been happening since I saw you Friday," Greta said. She picked up a pen and notepad.

What's not been happening? But what to tell Greta?

"I met a nice girl," Josie said, feeling that was innocent enough. "She remembered me from Tillie's, when I was pretty fucked up, and she still hasn't run away screaming. In fact, she seems to like me a lot."

Greta smiled. "That's wonderful, Josie. Tell me about her."

"We've only seen each other a couple of times, but she's supportive and honest and doesn't seem afraid I'm bipolar. She's a social worker, you'll be pleased to know. Despite that, I like her a lot."

Greta seemed to contemplate that for a moment. "Have you slept with her yet?"

Josie feigned shock. "Isn't that a little personal?"

"When I first got to know you, you seemed rather proud to talk about your conquests," Greta said with a smile. "Are you not proud of this one?"

"So you assume we've slept together, though we've only been on two dates."

"Josie, the fact that you've even been on something you call a date is reason enough to assume something is very different, either in you or because of this woman."

"Her name's Lucy. And no, we haven't slept together. We've fooled around; she said that was enough for now."

"Hmm. I think I like her." She jotted something down on her pad.

"I knew you would." Josie looked pleased, as if she'd brought the shiniest apple to the teacher.

"You intend to see her again?" Greta asked.

"Of course," Josie said, "I told you I liked her a lot."

"Yes, but more than two dates might give her the idea you're interested in some form of relationship. Are you ready for that?"

"Why not? Is there some kind of time frame in place before I can start living a normal life? You've said yourself I'm doing much better."

Now Josie was leaning forward as if she were pleading her case. Greta took a slow drink of her tea.

"Let me hear what else has been going on. When we last met, when you walked out of the appointment early, you'd gotten some kind of murder case. How have you been handling that?"

"I haven't been losing sleep over it, if that's what you're asking. I'm interviewing witnesses. Plodding along. That's what this work is, you know. Lots of plodding. Nothing I can't handle." Josie leaned back, but kept hold of her knee.

"Are you any closer to finding what you were hired to find?"

"Not a bit," Josie said. She had no intention of telling Greta about the incident with the black-belt wife beater or that she'd been sleeping very little or frequently forgetting to eat. She was taking her medications mostly every day, though. There was that.

Greta put down her cup and placed her hands on her knees. "This is what I see. In four days' time you've gone from someone stabilized with bipolar I disorder to someone who's feeling pressure to solve a perhaps unsolvable case, who's starting a relationship with a woman unlike any she's been with before, and probably two or three other things you're not telling me. Your speech is rapid and sounds well rehearsed, as if you're trying to keep me from seeing something. You're restless. Your leg is swinging faster and faster, despite all you're doing to contain it. These are signs of a hypomanic state, and that's what we want to avoid."

Damn. There was no getting around this woman. She was the all-knowing Oz, and Josie a humble subject before her.

"What's hypomanic? I know what manic feels like and I'm definitely not that."

"I'd agree. Hypomania is something we see more commonly in bipolar II patients. It's a lesser form of mania—not as dramatic or dangerous. But it can escalate in a bipolar I patient quite easily. You might be distractible, sleeping poorly, shopping or gambling, talking too much. Overworking's a big one. That sort of thing."

"It sounds like when I was manic last year." Josie looked a little worried.

"It is, but in a much milder form. It can feel great—like there's nothing you can't do. And most people won't even notice it in you, including yourself. But right now I see your behavior as not quite the same as when we'd finally found the right medication mix for you."

"When things were boring, you mean."

"That's another sign of hypomania. When you were stabilized, things weren't boring. They were more of a relief."

Josie stayed silent as Greta went over her notes on Josie's medications. "Are you taking the Klonopin?" she asked.

"Yes."

"More than once a day? Only taking it to fall asleep isn't going to help any hypomania symptoms. I'm going to write a new script for the Klonopin and I want you to take it three times a day, with a meal.

It's important you eat regularly. I'm also going to up your Depakote a bit."

"I don't understand this. I feel fine," Josie said.

"You're going to have to trust me again. You're not where you should be and it could lead to real trouble. And you're not the best judge of how you're doing. Has Lucy said anything to you about your disease acting up?"

"No!" Josie said adamantly. "And I don't think it is either."

"Do as I say and it won't."

Josie slumped in her chair, looking grumpy. She didn't look at Greta.

"We have a few minutes left. Are you up to talking about what this new world of dating might look like for you?"

"I guess," Josie mumbled. But the only thing on her mind was how much she hated her disease. Hated it. She'd rather be alcoholic like her parents.

CHAPTER TWENTY-ONE

Josie returned to her office and started spinning in her desk chair, faster and faster, coming to an abrupt halt by grabbing the edge of her desk. That felt good. She'd stopped thinking about her disease for a few moments. She would do anything to not think of herself as uncontrollable. She was controlled and she was making progress on her case. She was enthusiastic, not manic. She thought of the list Greta recited of the symptoms of hypomania. She owned up to three of them, but only to herself—working a lot, racing thoughts, and skimping on sleep. She found it impossible to understand how increasing the amount you worked could be harmful. Wasn't that what being a contributing member of society was about? And if you were lucky enough to not need as much sleep as other people did, you had more time to work. Greta worried entirely too much.

She spun the chair around and focused on the board on the wall behind her desk. It was nearly filled with her meticulous handwriting. The facts as she knew them were written out in black, including her impressions from each of the people she'd interviewed. The possible scenarios for someone other than Lauren killing Kelly were written out in different colors—green for Gabby, blue for Tim Wade, and red for Nikki Moore, Kelly's sister. Josie thought Nikki might have offed her sister out of sheer spite. She seemed truly jealous of how easily things came to Kelly—the lucrative relationship, the great job. Murder had been committed over lesser motives than that.

Tim seemed to have a motive also. There was the long-standing competitive nature of their relationship, with Lauren clearly coming out on top again and again when it came to their parents' approval.

When they made her CEO, she'd won the ultimate sign of their regard. Tim got vice president of operations, a far less prestigious title. That was humiliating enough, but when Lauren fired him six months later, the embarrassment might have put him over the edge. She must have known that was a risk.

But why would Tim kill Lauren's lover and not Lauren herself? With Lauren dead he would have taken over her spot in the company. Perhaps there was a smidgen of brotherly love left and he couldn't bring himself to kill his sister. Killing her lover and framing Lauren for the murder might have seemed like a good alternative.

These were the kinds of thoughts Josie would've bounced off a partner, if she had one. She thought of giving Bev a call, maybe even Stan Waterman. Perhaps hashing it out with them would point her to something more solid. She pinned her hopes on her interview with Lauren. Maybe that would produce something resembling a lead.

She'd started spinning her chair again when her cell phone rang. It was Sarah DeAngeles asking for a progress report. Since she had little in the way of progress to report, she inflated the number of interviews she'd done and told her about receiving the case file from her police source. She made sure to mention her interview with Lauren in the morning.

"You got through to meet with Lauren?" Sarah sounded truly impressed. "When I said you could try to interview her, I didn't think you'd actually be able to."

Josie felt a bloom of pride at Sarah's praise. It didn't take much praise for her to puff up a little. "I'm sure she wants to know what's going on."

"Yes, probably."

"How about I call you right after the interview," Josie said. "I'll give you my impressions."

They hung up with Sarah sounding mollified and Josie feeling a little more secure her job wasn't about to end. She leaned back in her chair. The bright September light flooded the office, but she took little notice. Her brain was galloping along a single groove. Her cell phone rang again.

"Am I speaking to Josie Harper?" a familiar, gravelly voice said.

"Sergeant Lundy?" Josie gripped her cell phone in one hand, while a feeling of dread came over her. "It's been a long time."

"That it has. We all miss you down here," he said. The stationhouse had felt much more like home than did the one she once shared with her parents, like Greta's office did now. That was largely due to people like Sergeant Lundy. Good police. If she weren't so resentful about being taken off the streets because of her diagnosis, she might have had a job like Lundy's, still in the stationhouse, around people she loved. But then she remembered Lundy carried a gun. The reality was she'd probably be shuttled down to the evidence cage.

"What can I do for you, Sergeant?"

"It's about your mother, actually. See, your dad's on his annual fishing trip or we'd have called him. The thing is, your mother got picked up for a DUI and she's here in a cell. It looks like she's still pretty sloshed, if you ask me."

Josie wondered if there'd be no end to the embarrassment she had to endure in front of her former colleagues. There was the unstoppable flow from her father, and there was her own fuckuppery to add to the account. Now even her mother was getting in on it. All three of them were a mess.

"Josie, are you there?" Lundy sounded sympathetic.

"Yeah, I'm here. A little shocked, I guess. It's only four thirty."

"Are you coming down? I don't know who else we can release her to."

"On my way." She hung up and threw her Sharpie across the room, leaving a nice black spot on the opposite white wall. She'd rather do anything other than bail her mother out of jail. Shooting herself in the head seemed an attractive option. Instead, she put her sweatshirt on and headed out the door.

She made a stop at her bank for some bail money before arriving at her old stationhouse. There was Sergeant Lundy, sitting behind the tall counter, guarding his fortress. She pulled up her hoodie and made a beeline to him.

"Sergeant," she whispered. "What's the fastest and least public way I can get my mother out of here?"

The sergeant looked out at the line of people Josie had cut in front of and held up his hand as they started grumbling. He turned to Josie. "She's in the system now, I'm sorry to say. We've got to get bail money or a bond card from you. Then I'll give you your mother and her court date." The sergeant slipped off his high stool and went back into the heart of the station, which Josie knew would be teeming with activity. Uniforms coming and going, detectives at their desks making calls or immersed in the Internet, brass walking from one meeting to the next. She missed it desperately.

Five minutes later, Lundy returned with the paperwork and she forked over the $500 bail. Another five minutes went by before a uniform brought her mother out. It was super fast because she was an ex-cop and her father a detective. She still had a few perks of the job.

Her mom looked like she'd dressed for a ladies' lunch and taken a wrong turn into a grease pit. She must have rolled around on the floor somewhere, because her red suit was smeared with grime. One of her stockings sagged around her ankle, and the heel was off her other shoe, giving her walk a rolling motion that pointed her in only the most general of directions. She clung to the young officer escorting her, who couldn't look more eager to hand her over to Josie.

Josie stepped forward and took her mother's other arm as the officer let go on his side. The transfer caused her mother to sway a good deal, like a willow tree in a stiff wind. Josie was concerned. How could she be this drunk so early in the day? Apparently her special orange juice wasn't simply a jump-starter. Josie knew her mother was an alcoholic, but she'd always been an at-home alcoholic. Life wasn't safe for her beyond those walls. Josie knew all about being in bad or dangerous situations when she was drunk, but she'd always been able to extricate herself from them. Her mother had no such ability.

She took the keys to Elaine's Buick from the baggie of possessions the officer handed her and guided her mom toward the parking lot, using shoulder and hip to stuff her in the passenger seat. Elaine was singing "Bye Bye Blackbird" in a sassy, but thankfully muted voice. Josie gunned the car for the northwest side.

"Mom. Stop singing for a sec. When's Dad coming home?"

Elaine swiveled her head like a ventriloquist's dummy. "What?"

"When's Dad coming home?" Josie tried to keep her patience.

"Few days, that fucking bastard."

"Wow. I've never heard you say anything like that before," Josie said. She snuck a glance at her mom, who was looking straight forward with a sort of drunken determination. "I've always thought he was one," Josie continued. "But, Mom, if you've always thought he's a bastard, which he totally is, why have you stayed married to him?"

She glanced to her side again and saw her mother had passed out cold. Josie had to use a fireman's carry to get her from the garage to the house, thankful it was on a back alley so the spectacle wasn't on view to the neighbors. They were a gossipy bunch. She put her mother down gently and opened the side door. She had to drag Elaine up five stairs to the main level and onto a sofa in the living room. Then she went up and got a nightgown and slippers, as well as wet and dry towels. She somehow got the ruined suit off, wiped away most of the grunge, and pulled a nightgown on her. Bathing her naked mother seemed reasonable punishment for every last bad thing Josie had ever done. She was sweating by the time she was through, while her mom remained entirely oblivious. She got a beer from the fridge downstairs and settled into the La-Z-Boy next to her mother. It was going to be a long night.

CHAPTER TWENTY-TWO

Lauren left the office and ran into David Schofeld in the building's plaza.

"Lauren," he said, drawing up beside her. "Can I walk with you to the garage? There's something I want to tell you."

That couldn't be good news. She sighed and looked up at David. He bent down so he could be close enough to converse quietly. He looked like a very tall Scrooge.

"What is it?" Lauren sighed.

"Earlier today when I said I'd seen Tim in the building, I didn't tell you everything, mostly because Eva was in the room."

"Oh, God. Please don't tell me he abused any of those women."

"No, no. Nothing like that. I suppose it was me he abused. But I'm not saying that as a complaint in any way. I thought you should know."

Lauren kept her face very still. If Tim did anything to drive David away, she might not be able to keep it together any longer. "What did he do?"

"When I saw him in Marketing it looked like he was leading a group of women out the door, probably on their way to lunch. But then he saw me and motioned me over. The others went on without him. Tim led me to the corridor to the men's room. I was worried what he was going to say; I didn't expect anything pleasant. What I didn't anticipate was him turning around and slamming his fist in my belly."

"Jesus!" Lauren said. "Are you okay?"

"I was stunned, of course, but not hurt. He was incredibly fast.

When I didn't go down from the punch, he looked surprised, so I took advantage of that and got him in a headlock. I'm bigger than him, you know. I asked him why he attacked me and he wouldn't say. He kept demanding to let him go or there'd be trouble for me."

"Did you let him go then?" Lauren said, concerned and angry at the same time.

"Yes," David said. "by then I was worried someone might see us, so I pushed him away from me. I don't like being threatened. No one does."

"Well, I'm not surprised you took the high road, though I wish you'd beaten the crap out of him. God knows he deserves it." Lauren took hold of David's arm. "I want you to know there is no way he has any authority to threaten your job with Wade-Fellowes."

"I can't figure out why he'd come after me," David said. "I didn't particularly like working for him, but I did what I was told. There's no reason for him to be upset with me. It's been months since he left the company," David said.

"Since I fired him, you mean."

Lauren decided not to get into the complicated psychology of her brother. Tim was pissed at David because he was a much better operations manager than he was. he didn't like being shown up.

"Thanks for letting me know, David. I'll make sure he doesn't come to the office again. You could press charges, you know."

"Nope. Too much hassle. And my job keeps me awfully busy."

He smiled down at her and they parted at the garage. Lauren was furious, and incredibly frustrated to have no outlet for it. This latest news confirmed for her Tim was losing it. There had to be a way to get out from under his hold on her. She hadn't been successful in any of her prior attempts. After breathing deeply for a few minutes and contemplating her limited options, she gave Cory a call from her car. There were the same bar noises in the background that were there every time Cory answered her phone. This would have given Lauren pause were she considering a relationship with Cory. But she was not. They had a "sex buddy" understanding. Having never had such a thing before, Lauren thought it an excellent arrangement. What it lacked in sincerity it more than made up for with incredibly good sex.

"Hey there!" Cory said, her voice unnecessarily loud, even with the bar noise in the background. So, she'd already had a few. Lauren wasn't interested in having sex with a drunk. "Am I being summoned to come service you?"

"Nothing of the sort. It sounds like you need to get a cab home and climb into bed."

"No way. I was about to get into a fight with someone for inpruning your honor," Cory said proudly.

"Impugning," Lauren said, automatically. She was an editor, after all.

"Right. Anyway, your call just saved this guy a broken nose."

Lauren imagined it was Tim at Tillie's, dressed in his "gay clothes," trying to stir the pot.

"Tell me what's going on." she said.

"There's a guy sitting at the bar telling everyone he has proof you really were the one that killed Kelly." Cory sounded a little more indignant and a little less drunk.

"You don't believe him, do you?" Lauren asked coolly.

"Hell no, I don't believe him. I asked him what proof he supposedly has and he said, get this, he's your brother and knows things the police couldn't possibly have known. When he wouldn't say what they were, people started ignoring him, but I was going to grab him by the collar and punch the daylights out of him. What kind of brother does that?"

Lauren smiled at the idea of Cory physically intimidating Tim. It would have been horrifying for him to be punched by a woman, and Lauren didn't doubt Cory could do it. That woman was built. Humiliation, though, was a real trigger for Tim. It would end in some backlash against Cory, which she didn't want.

"Thank you for being my hero, but it's best if you leave it be. Why don't you come over. I'll make you some coffee. But take a cab, for God's sake."

"I'll be there." Cory laughed. "But I don't promise to behave myself."

By the time Cory arrived, Lauren had showered, slid between the sheets of her bed with her iPad, and made a few moves on Scrabble. It kept her mind quiet and focused for the few minutes a day she allowed herself to play. She'd swept her room for bugs and removed one camera in the bedside table. It was all so ridiculous. Tim put them up, she took them down. Their technologies canceled each other out. When the doorbell rang she slipped on a robe and let Cory in, locking the door behind her but knowing that Tim could get in if he wanted to. She didn't care. If he crept in and saw her making love with Cory, it would irritate him more than her. He wanted her worried every second of every day. She was growing not only tired of it, but less terrified as well. Trying to keep the company thriving and her parents alive was too much.

Cory was a little tipsy, but not distractingly so. Enough for her to take firm control of the situation. She undid the tie of Lauren's robe and slipped her arms inside. "Tonight, Ms. Boss Lady, you're not going to tell me what to do to you. In fact, you're not going to say a thing." Cory put her finger on Lauren's lips. "You're going to be absolutely quiet until I tell you when you can make noise. Do you understand?"

Lauren nodded as a flash of desire rippled through her at the thought of submitting to this unexpected side of Cory. Submit was not a word usually in her vocabulary. Nor was failed, lost, conceded, humbled. At least not until recently. But her arousal grew as Cory pushed her on the bed, raised her knees in the air, and pulled her legs apart, exposing her in a way she'd never been before. She could feel how wet she already was, and Cory wasn't in a teasing mood. She lowered her head to Lauren and used her tongue to make her come in what seemed like a second and a half. Cory flipped her over and arranged her on all fours, spreading her legs once again and entering her from behind, driving into her with two, then three fingers as her other hand snaked around the front and touched her. Lauren cried out in a series of orgasms that were anything but quiet. She slowly came to her senses and turned her head to look back at Cory, smiling wanly.

"I wouldn't feel too smug, my plaything," Cory said. "There's some answering you need to do for not obeying me."

"What?" Lauren looked perplexed.

"I told you to not make any noise until I said you could." Cory stayed behind her.

"That was serious?" Lauren laughed. "You'd have to be dead to not scream during that. Weren't we here in the same room?"

Cory raised her hand over Lauren's ass. "Still, you must answer."

Lauren smiled as she watched Cory's serious face. "I'm afraid you've confused me with some other girlfriend."

"Does that mean no?"

"It means spank me once and you'll regret it," Lauren said teasingly.

"Somehow that doesn't worry me very much. But no is no." Cory lay down and pulled Lauren to her, holding her tight as they fell asleep. Lauren still had a smile on her face.

❖

Josie was bored to distraction. No amount of pacing, cleaning, organizing, or reading could keep her still. She was fairly certain at this point, four hours after being bailed out of jail, her mother wasn't going to aspirate her own vomit and die. In fact, she was sprawled on the sofa in such a way her head hung over the side, face down, as if knowing a bucket was there waiting for her. Still, Josie didn't dare leave the house.

Her father wasn't due back from his fishing trip until Sunday night. The fishing trip, as she learned growing up, involved no bait, no boats, no fish. It was a retreat for some of the detectives her dad worked with. They rented a cabin in Wisconsin for a week, spent their days drinking beer, target shooting, bullshitting, generally acting like fifteen-year-old boys. They'd venture to the nearest roadhouse to drink in a more social setting and try to pick up women. Part of the joy of the trip for her dad was he simply would not answer his phone, so Josie didn't even try to let him know his wife had just been arrested.

She'd been looking forward to her date with Lucy the next night and thought of calling her to see if they could move it up a day. Lucy could hang out with her and her drunken mother. That probably wouldn't increase her chances of successfully seducing Lucy, but maybe her dating code allowed for sex on the third date and Josie wouldn't have to cajole her. Lately she'd noticed her libido making a startling comeback. The meds she was on were libido killers. The fact she'd missed a dose here and there over the past several days was surely not enough for this sort of rebound. It must be Lucy. She picked up her phone and called her.

"Hey there," Josie said.

"Hi!" Lucy sounded surprised to hear from her.

"I'm wondering if you can help me out." She proceeded to tell Lucy what happened and that she could really use the company during her vigil over her mother.

"I'm on my way," Lucy said.

She got there in forty-five minutes, looking freshly scrubbed. Her red hair was loose, the curls reaching up like growing flowers. Josie thought she was amazingly cute, but curiously her desire for her didn't take a jump up upon seeing her. It simply stayed at attention. With the living room occupied by her mother and the basement reeking of her father, she led Lucy upstairs to her old room. "I'm sorry at how this looks," she said. "There isn't anywhere else to hang out except the kitchen."

Lucy looked thoughtful, as if weighing the options. "No, this is good. I want to see the room you grew up in." They went into the middle room in the hallway, still painted the same awful dusty rose color she'd grown up with. It looked like every kid's room—the single bed along one side, the study desk on the other, a few shelves hung to display trophies or cherished objects, neither of which Josie seemed to have. A small bookshelf was stuffed with the kinds of novels you read in English lit in high school and college—from *Silas Marner* to *Jude the Obscure.*

"Were you a lit major in college?" Lucy asked.

"Criminal justice. But I liked the lit classes. I figured I'd read anyway, so why not major in something more practical?"

"Hmm," Lucy said. "There're many layers to Josie Harper, mad seducer of women and lover of Victorian literature."

Josie shrugged.

Lucy went to sit on the twin bed and patted the space by her side for Josie to join her. "Why do you seem so nervous, Josie? Certainly having a woman in your bedroom can't be a strange feeling to you." The teasing was apparent in her voice.

"Well, I usually don't have my mother passed out downstairs. She could wake up at any time."

"Do you really think so?" Lucy said.

"No, I guess not. She was really hammered, more than I've ever seen. She'll be out until morning."

They sat on the narrow bed, slightly angled toward each other, the awkwardness hanging in the air like the fug of cigar smoke. Josie couldn't look at Lucy.

"Josie, are you wondering if it's okay to make love? Because I would really like to."

"You would?" Josie knew she wanted to have sex, but she was

unused to navigating these new rules of courtship. She didn't want to come off as a cad, as the person she was before she got well. But in truth she felt a little like that earlier version of herself, only tamer. If Lucy weren't so adamant about how she wanted to be courted, Josie would have her clothes off by now.

Lucy leaned over and very softly pressed her lips to Josie's. They'd been down this path already and she let Lucy set the pace. And the pace was slow. She kissed Josie for what seemed an eternity before she pulled back and looked Josie in the eye.

"I love kissing you. You're really good at it." Josie thought that had been adequately demonstrated on their second date and moved to pull her T-shirt over her head. Lucy's hand stopped her. "Let me undress you. Please?"

She seemed to be treating Josie like she was a virgin. She drew a deep breath and sought patience, never a strong suit of hers. Lucy stood and brought Josie up with her, and then proceeded to remove every piece of her clothing with what seemed excruciating slowness. By the time Lucy was removing Josie's underwear, she wasn't so much aroused as agitated. She made quick work of removing Lucy's clothes and lowered her to the bed, ready to kiss her way down Lucy's body, which was luscious, much curvier than Josie's, exactly the way she liked it. She was feeling desire again as she trailed Lucy's throat with her tongue, softly nipping at her neck. It felt natural and good and headed in the right direction. Josie made progress down Lucy's neck and was going for her breast when Lucy's hand cupped her chin and looked into her eyes. "Kiss me again, Josie. I want this to last."

Josie thought the Battle of Gettysburg must have felt shorter than this lovemaking with Lucy. She dutifully kissed her, deeply and as soulfully as she could, moving her hand up to cup Lucy's breast, tracing her nipple and moving over to the other. She heard a slight whimper, which was like the first notes from an orchestra pit. Time to get on with the show. But still Lucy would not let go of her lips until Josie feigned breathlessness and broke away.

"I need you now, Lucy. No more teasing." Lucy looked perplexed but lay back at the pleading look in Josie's eyes. The whimpers came more frequently now, but never louder, as Josie did what she knew how to do so well—make a woman come with a shuddering orgasm. Lucy shuddered, but she was so damn quiet. Josie wondered if she'd attended a convent school or something, learning to masturbate as quietly as possible and never losing the habit of muteness. She put "make Lucy scream" on her list of things to do.

Lucy then turned the tables and made love to Josie, who had the same problem she always had when women made love to her. She felt disassociated, not present, and often not able to orgasm. But she made a hell of a lot more noise than Lucy when she finally came. Lucy looked very satisfied and curled up in Josie's arms.

"That was amazing," Lucy said.

"Yeah." Josie could think of no words beyond that. She cared about Lucy. Wanted her. Why did making love with her feel so…boring? If this was what sex was like when she wasn't manic, she wasn't sure she wanted to go on living. Her mind wandered back to her investigation and the upcoming interview with Lauren Wade. Her work, at least, made her feel alive and energetic. She sighed as she pulled Lucy closer to her. She had no answers.

CHAPTER TWENTY-THREE

Wednesday, September 11

When Josie entered Lauren's outer office the following morning, she was greeted with a sour expression from Eva, the protective assistant.

"Are you the private investigator?" Eva said, having reluctantly looked up from her computer screen.

Josie was dressed in her best jeans and blazer, her button-down shirt fresh from the cleaners, her hair under control from the right amount of product. She felt nervous but confident, and not inclined to be treated poorly, especially after her late night. Lucy reluctantly left at one in the morning, Josie insisting it wasn't worth the confusion it would cause Josie's hungover mother if Lucy was there in the morning. Josie didn't fall asleep for hours after, nervous about her interview with Lauren, her thoughts racing with different analyses of what was going on with Lucy, puzzling over the origins of the universe, coveting the new model Dodge she'd love to buy and thinking about what a dick her father was. Now she was operating on two hours of sleep, but felt as fresh as if she'd had a full night's rest.

"I'm Josie Harper. I have an eight o'clock appointment with Ms. Wade."

"Yes, I know," Eva said, crossing something out in a notebook. She pointed to the waiting room chairs. "Take a seat. I'll let her know you're here."

Josie saw Eva was going to take her bloody time letting Lauren know she'd arrived. She clicked over to a news page on the Internet, called the copy room, and printed out a schedule. She finally rose from her desk with the schedule and entered the inner office without knocking. A moment later she came back out and held the door open.

"She'll see you now," Eva said, disapprovingly.

Josie entered the inner office as Lauren came around her desk to greet her. She saw immediately the newspaper photographs she'd seen of Lauren didn't do her the least amount of justice. She was slender like Josie, but so much sleeker and put together she made Josie uncomfortable about her own clothes. She was also gorgeous, with dark eyes and hair, a strong, straight nose, and noticeable cheekbones. She was as tall as Josie, five-eight or so. Lauren walked toward her with her arm extended and gave her a warm shake.

"Thank you for agreeing to come in so early, Ms. Harper. I'm afraid my schedule's full for the rest of the day."

"It's Josie, please, and I'm glad to have gotten in at all. You have quite a gatekeeper out there." Josie had her back to the door and assumed Eva had left. Lauren lifted her eyes to the door and smiled.

"We'll have some coffee, Eva. Thank you." Color bloomed on Josie's face as Lauren turned back to her. "I hope Eva didn't cause you any unnecessary difficulty," she said, pointing to an area of her office with a sofa and side chair. The room was enormous, which shouldn't have surprised Josie but somehow did. Lauren was the CEO of a publishing company—why wouldn't her office be huge and her wardrobe impressive? The room held a very old and beautiful mahogany desk with its back to a view of the famous Chicago skyline—giant skyscrapers poking up between the grand buildings of an earlier era. The light from the windows poured across the room, highlighting portraits of three generations of Wades hanging on the opposite wall. Josie looked around for a coat of arms.

Lauren sat on the chair and gestured Josie to the sofa, which sucked her down low enough she had to look up at Lauren. What a hackneyed move. As if Lauren's dominance in the office weren't obvious already.

"I'm a bit confused about what you've been doing, Josie. I'm hoping we can clear up a few things." Lauren's tone was neutral.

"That's why I'm here."

Eva entered with a silver tray and coffee service, which she placed on the low table before them, and left the office. Lauren poured. She took hers black. Josie stirred in a hefty amount of cream and sugar.

"Perhaps we can start with why you've been so anxious to interview me," Lauren said. "Of all the requests for interviews I've received in the past weeks, none have been from a private investigator. I'm intrigued, of course."

Josie saw the genuine curiosity on Lauren's face. She also saw the beautiful hand holding her coffee cup, the length of leg showing beneath her skirt. She sipped more coffee as she tried to track her thinking back to the business at hand.

"You've been dodging this interview, but there was really no need. My client has hired me to find Kelly's real murderer. Their words, not mine." Josie drank her coffee as she watched Lauren take this in. She looked slightly more annoyed than surprised.

"But that's ridiculous. Why would anyone spend the money to do that? The acquittal speaks for itself. If my reputation's been damaged, isn't that something for me to worry about, not someone else? Who are these clients of yours?" Lauren's voice was steadily escalating.

"I can't tell you that. The fact I've been hired should tell you someone cares about your reputation. I don't think any harm is intended." Josie knew the results of her investigation could influence whether the board fired Lauren or not, but she wasn't going to bring that up. She wanted to stay on her good side.

"Care about me? I find it unsettling someone has been hired to poke around in my life without my knowledge or permission in order to absolve me of something the law has already acquitted me of. Perhaps you could tell your clients I don't feel particularly cared for by their gesture."

Lauren leaned back in her chair, arms crossed, coffee forgotten. Josie sat quietly, pouring more coffee, waiting out the silence like any good detective would. Eventually Lauren spoke. "And you still haven't explained what you want from me."

Josie shrugged. "There's a lot I want to know. You'd make my job a lot easier if you told me you murdered Kelly. The double jeopardy rule applies."

"Yes, but that wouldn't do much for the reputation your clients seem so concerned about."

"Are you saying you didn't kill Kelly?" Josie was reaching for the notebook in her jacket pocket.

"I'm saying I have no reason to say anything to you."

Josie flipped through some pages, as if looking for a particularly damning fact. She was trying to make Lauren nervous, which seemed as likely as Spider-Man appearing outside the thirty-first-floor window. "The thing I haven't been able to figure out is why you remained silent throughout the entire process of being arrested and tried for the murder. Normally a person would aid their defense by offering an alibi or testifying at trial on their own behalf. It's not like you're a loose cannon who could harm your own case should you take the stand. Why the silence?"

Lauren picked up her cup and took a long drink, as if the coffee would have the steadying qualities of a shot of whiskey. "That was the legal strategy my lawyer and I preferred. As the results showed, the evidence was all circumstantial and not convincing to the jury."

"The police seemed most influenced by the fact your own gun was the murder weapon and left on the scene. You would have had plenty of time to get rid of it."

Lauren smiled. "I suppose the jury thought no one could be that stupid."

"Or that clever," Josie said. She saw Lauren's eyes turn to her, appraising her in a new light. "How about an alibi? It must not be a very good one."

"No, it's not," Lauren said. "As I told the police, I was at work until six thirty and then went shopping along Armitage. I didn't buy anything. I was floating down the street, shop to shop, not going in. Window-shopping. I grabbed a bite to eat. The police couldn't find anyone who remembered me."

Lauren leaned toward her. "I'm fortunate to have been acquitted." Lauren paused for a moment, staring at Josie. "It could easily gone the other way, and that would've ruined my life. Compared to that, the idea people may think I actually killed my own lover seems small."

"But you had a motive to kill. Didn't you just find out Kelly had been unfaithful to you?"

Lauren seemed relaxed and leaned back against the chair. "It was a full week before her death that I found out. And it was not the first time we'd been down that road. Kelly had been unfaithful at least once before that I knew about. I don't think it was in her nature to be monogamous. I was spending that week trying to decide if I wanted to end our relationship or not."

"Most people would, don't you think? Fool me once, shame on you, and all that," Josie said. Her brain was running along a double track—the conversation itself and the compelling attraction she was feeling.

"I'm afraid when it comes to my relationship history, I've been quite foolish. My work keeps me so busy I don't give my partners the attention they deserve. I consider Kelly's infidelity to be my fault as much as hers," Lauren said. "But I will admit that it hurt."

"Did it make you angry?" Josie asked.

"Of course. I'm human. Betrayal hurts and the hurt translates into anger." Lauren seemed unconcerned at how that sounded.

"You must have had a very good lawyer. From where I'm sitting, you had the means, motive, and opportunity to kill Kelly."

"Well, it certainly sounds like you're convinced I killed her," Lauren said, still calm.

"You haven't said anything to point me elsewhere. I think leaving the smoking gun at the scene was a ploy."

Lauren shrugged. "As you suggest, I had a very good lawyer."

Josie leaned forward, her senses heightened by how close Lauren was. She didn't want her to be a murderer.

"It almost seems you want me to believe you did it. Why would that be?" Josie asked.

For the first time, Lauren looked conflicted. She paused before saying, "I've already said too much. I can't help how you interpret it."

Josie tried again. "Can you think of anyone else who would have a motive to kill Kelly?"

"I can only think of the obvious people with motives similar to mine."

"Such as?" Josie asked.

"I don't want to point fingers at anyone," Lauren said, as she proceeded to do exactly that. "But I could see Gabby, Ann-Marie's partner, being angry enough to kill. She seems to have an aggressive personality. I don't think she'd kill Ann-Marie and might even have convinced herself Ann-Marie was innocent, that Kelly had lured her into whatever bed it was they were using. And Ann-Marie herself might have a motive because Kelly broke it off so suddenly. At least, that's what Kelly told me—she considered the few times she slept with Ann-

Marie as a mere distraction. It didn't rise to the level of an affair. She said she told Ann-Marie they wouldn't be seeing each other again since I found out about it. I can only assume they would have if I hadn't."

Josie scribbled furiously in her notebook, though there wasn't any new information here. Another arrow pointing at Gabby was interesting, but she'd already concluded the rest of it. What she noted was the monotone of Lauren's speech, as if she were being forced to speculate against her better judgment.

They sat there and looked at each other, the contact lasting a second or two longer than it should between strangers. The hair on Josie's arms stood up and she was glad she'd taken the Klonopin earlier to settle her nerves. Maybe it would keep her from being a fool and kissing Lauren right then. She was tempted, based on the interest she saw in Lauren's eyes. That would make a giant mess of things, but it was exactly what she wanted to do. Damn, this felt good, and she didn't doubt Lauren felt the same. This sort of pull had to be mutual—Lauren was the magnet and Josie the metal shavings. She knew with a few moves she could have her; it had rarely failed her before. Instead, she rose from the sofa and put her notebook away. It wasn't a good sign to feel this good. She took it as a warning.

"I won't take up any more of your time," Josie said. "Though I hope you'll see me again if I have more questions." Josie looked to the right of Lauren's eyes, trying to stay out of trouble.

"Of course, though it seems you're on a pointless mission. Whoever killed Kelly left no evidence at the scene, certainly nothing that points anywhere but at me. The gun had my fingerprints on it."

"I imagine, since it's your own gun. It seems surprising to me you even have one," Josie said.

Lauren shrugged. "My dad gave me and my brother identical Smith and Wesson revolvers one Christmas. He said it was the best thing to have if anyone ever broke in. Simply point and shoot. I can't remember the last time I touched it—probably during the lessons we took to learn how to use it."

Now Josie looked back at her eyes. "So you're saying you didn't commit the murder."

Lauren smiled. "I realized I didn't want you to leave thinking I had."

Josie saw she'd been right; Lauren's body language spoke of interest and her eyes confirmed attraction. Shit.

"And you believe the killer was female?" Josie asked.

"It seems likely, with all of the players being female. And lesbian."

The word "lesbian" seemed to drop on both of them like a cloak, sealing them closer together, the distance now much shorter between curiosity and action. Josie could feel her heart thumping, assumed Lauren could hear it as well. She said a quick good-bye and left, sweeping past Eva without a word. Once down the elevator and out on the building's plaza she concentrated on breathing normally again. She felt revved up, ready to burst. She took another Klonopin. She admitted it was a sign of some mania pushing through that she now wanted Lauren, thought she was every bit the mysterious, dangerous, intelligent, beautiful foil she desired. Her memory of Lucy seemed wispy at best.

She saw streams of people headed toward the entrance to start their workday. A group of them wore messenger bags with "Wade-Fellowes" printed on the side. She stepped in front of them to talk and saw their startled expressions.

"Excuse me for interrupting you," Josie said, making things up on the fly. "I've been interviewing a number of Wade-Fellowes employees recently and would like to ask you a few questions."

"What kind of questions?" said one of the men. He appeared to be a leader of this small group, since they were all looking up to him to do the speaking. He was as tall as a giant.

"I've been hired to gauge the employee attitude to Lauren Wade. She's aware of this. It was a board of directors decision to see how much fallout there's been from Ms. Wade's recent legal troubles." She paused for a moment as they stared at her. "Will you help out?"

"I'm David Schofeld," the tall one said, "the vice president of operations of the company. I work closely with Lauren. It doesn't really matter whether your story is true or complete bullshit because I have no hesitancy in saying Lauren is a fantastic leader, brilliant executive, and the survivor of more crap than anyone should have to go through. If the board's thinking of suggesting she step down, I think they'll have trouble with the rest of the employees."

"That's true," said another, a sharply dressed woman who carried a shiny leather briefcase. "I doubt I'd stick around if Lauren were gone. And I never thought for a moment she was guilty of killing her partner. Someone set her up."

"Why would anyone set her up?" Josie asked. She'd gotten her notebook out. "Especially if she's as good a person as you say."

"The set-up may have come from outside Wade-Fellowes," said another woman, who looked at Josie as if she were a bit thick. "She did have a private life, you know, and I, for one, don't know a thing about it."

Another member of the group, who looked like she was dressed for a shift in the mailroom, hefted her bag awkwardly and looked uncertain. "I don't know if the rest of you have heard, but Tim Wade was in the building yesterday. Someone told me he got in a fight with someone in the hallway to the men's room on thirty. I didn't see it myself."

David Schofeld stepped in as the rest turned to the gossiper and started firing questions at her.

"Hold on a minute." He quieted the group down and sent them in while he stayed behind with Josie. "I don't know exactly what your mission for the board is, if any, but if you do have their ear you should tell them under no circumstances should they consider reinstating Tim Wade to the company. He's very much a disruptive force, and things have run much more smoothly here since Lauren fired him."

"That must have caused some talk in the cubicles," Josie said.

"Sure. Family infighting is something employees are going to gossip about. But I can honestly say that everyone I know is grateful he's gone. I'm afraid that's all I can say."

Josie watched as he strode to the building entrance. She thought he looked a little grim, but clearly he was a popular guy. Everyone waved a good morning to him.

She didn't know if Tim was a mere pain in Lauren's ass or a real threat to her. She decided the only thing she could do to find out more would be to follow Lauren for a while and see what she was up to in her off hours. Did he harass her? Did she interact with him? Did she have women over? She was a little nervous about finding out that last bit. She didn't want Lauren to have a girlfriend. Though why wouldn't she? She was gorgeous and rich. She didn't want any further reason to believe Lauren killed Kelly. What she did want was new leads to surface and a chance to see more of Lauren, even if at a distance. But there were hours to go before she'd come back to watch for Lauren's exit from the building, and she had to find ways to fill the time.

❖

Lauren watched Josie stride out of the office and smiled. She'd been distracted for months, but she wasn't dead. Josie Harper was attractive, in a way similar to Cory—assertive-looking, earnest, slightly boyish. But there was a distinct difference in her response. With Josie it was that *je ne sais quoi* of attraction, impossible to accurately describe to anyone outside its bubble. She thought she saw a spark of interest in Josie's eyes.

But for now she had more pressing things to attend to. Tim had not given her an assignment recently, which made her fearful he was up to something else. His visit to the office yesterday and the truly unhinged act of punching David Schofeld while on the premises signaled something new. He still held the cards, for until Lauren discovered where he was keeping her parents, he had a complete hold over her. But she also felt him losing his grip a little, going outside the established game plan and letting his anger show.

She looked out of her window, down at the sea of people flowing from the commuter stations to the heart of the Loop. When her parents passed leadership of the company to her she'd been thrilled, both at the challenge she faced in running a company and because she beat out Tim. He'd be reporting to her, which she knew would infuriate him. She hadn't guessed how virulent his response to being fired would be.

She punched her intercom and heard Eva pick up. "Would you get my lawyer on the phone, Eva? Nancy Prewitt, not the company lawyer."

"I'll put her through when I reach her. You know how those lawyers are. Usually unreachable," Eva said, in her distinct tone of disapproval.

"Make the call. If I'm in a meeting when she calls back, you can interrupt me."

Two hours later, as she met with her sales and marketing executives at the round table in her office, Eva poked her head in to tell her the call she'd been waiting for was on hold.

"Thank you, Eva." She stood and looked at the group staring up at her. "Would you excuse me for a few moments? We can meet back here in ten minutes." They looked mystified but dutifully pushed back from the table and were out the door in a moment. Lauren sat back down and picked up the phone on the table.

"Nancy?"

"How are you, Lauren? I hope you've been enjoying your freedom."

Nancy Prewitt was a middle-aged, thick-set woman with a super-short haircut and a wardrobe of identical navy blue suits she wore every day in court. Lauren had never seen her in anything else. She wore crisp white shirts with cuff links, of all things. Her only other jewelry was a gaudy engagement ring and gold band on her left hand. Lauren had never quite figured out what kind of life Nancy lived outside of her work, if any, but she knew what a bulldog she was when it came to practicing law. She likely would have been found guilty if it weren't for Nancy convincing the jury there was plenty of reasonable doubt.

"Yes, compared to life in Cook County Jail I've been enjoying myself immensely. But the relief wears off. I'm calling to get a recommendation from you."

Neither woman was much given to chitchat. "What do you need?" Nancy said.

"I'm wondering if your firm uses any private investigators you think highly of."

There was a pause on Nancy's end. "Is there something going on I need to know about?"

"No," Lauren said firmly. "I think our work is done. This is unrelated to the murder case."

"Okay. The firm does contract with a number of PIs, but the guy I've always liked the best is Stan Waterman. He's ex-homicide, old enough to be thoroughly experienced but not so old he's going to crap out on you. He's handled a lot of investigations for us."

"That sounds fine. Can you put me in touch with him?" Lauren said.

"Of course. It's odd you ask. I just got the same request from one of your board members."

Lauren stayed quiet while she tried to figure out what that meant.

Was it the board who'd hired the investigator? The thought made her a little breathless, as if something was squeezing the air out of her lungs.

"Are you still there?" Nancy asked.

"Yes, sorry. If you could tell me how to get in touch with Waterman, I'd appreciate it."

"I'll email his contact info. Tell him I sent you," Nancy said. "And don't be a stranger."

"Frankly, Nancy, I hope to never have to call you again."

"Yeah, I get that a lot. Good luck with whatever you're up to."

They hung up and Lauren stared at the phone. The only way out of this problem with her parents she could see was to try once again to find them herself. Going to the police had led Tim to tie up and gag his parents for three days. He'd made a video to show Lauren, lest she doubt him. The police had been so skeptical of her story of their kidnapping, especially since there were many people saying they were on a trip around the world, that they hardly gave it an effort, except to interview Tim. Either the PI she'd hired after that had been incompetent, or Tim was amazingly eagle-eyed. He'd spotted him right away. She was now willing to take the risk of a second try, and she'd have to trust Stan Waterman to stay under Tim's radar.

CHAPTER TWENTY-FOUR

Josie was back in her car by nine. It would cost her thirty-six dollars to park downtown whether she sat there another few moments or not. She looked around at the other cars, their shininess catching her eye, mesmerizing her for a moment. Her eyes settled on a muscle car and stayed there, staring blindly with lust. Then she looked at her own car and saw a dull, dinged piece of crap whose days were numbered. She decided to drive straight to a suburban Dodge dealer. She had to have that car. Had to. She had an itch to spend some of her money. She had a growing itch for a lot of things.

Her only concrete plan for the day was to stake out Lauren's house later that afternoon. She wanted Lauren as much as she wanted the Dodge, but she also had to wait. She needed to do her job first. And before that, she should see her mother. She hopped on the Kennedy and headed for her parents' house.

As she drove, thoughts tumbled around in her brain. Something wasn't right as far as Gabby and Ann-Marie were concerned, giving her more reason to look into Gabby as a suspect. If Gabby had been abusive toward Ann-Marie, as Kris the bartender said, she found it hard to believe Ann-Marie would put up with that at Tillie's or in the privacy of their home. But the thought of Gabby breaking into Lauren's house, locating her gun, and shooting Kelly seemed too far a stretch, though the possibility couldn't be ignored. It seemed much more likely Tim would have access to the murder weapon, and perhaps a strong motive as well.

She pulled up in front of her parents' house. It was a spectacular autumn day and Josie had a sudden urge to rake all the leaves in the yard and burn the enormous pile of them. She loved doing that and never quite understood why it became illegal. One of the few fond memories she had of her father was him raking up a pile of leaves and watching as she jumped into it over and over again. Then he'd light a match to the dry leaves. They'd both watch as they caught, the fire spreading faster and faster, until the flames were high and the smell of burning leaves swallowed the surrounding air, a smell that could bring her back to that time and place in an instant. Eventually, her dad would head into the house, telling her to stay put and watch until the fire was completely burned out. She'd stand in place, practically at attention, until her job was done. Now they were so estranged, the stars would have to align for them to be civil to one another.

She doubted this visit home would bring the same questions she usually got from her mother, which made Josie think about her medication. She knew she hadn't taken it this morning when she dashed home to change for her interview with Lauren. She wasn't sure about the day before, but was reasonably sure she'd taken it the day before that. She'd be able to tell by her Monday-Sunday pill container, which made her feel eighty years old.

When Josie had left her mother that morning, she was conscious and breathing, but so green in the face she looked more amphibian than human. Josie entered the house without knocking. Ever since she'd moved out years ago, her mother insisted she ring the bell and wait for the door to be answered, probably to prevent Josie from seeing her gulping straight from the vodka bottle.

She found her mother lying on the sofa. She looked like death warmed over. The green cast to her face was still there. Everything about her seemed to be sagging. Josie tried to keep her shock from showing. Her mother's appearance shouldn't have surprised her, really, given how drunk she'd been. But Elaine was one of those drinkers who usually held it together pretty well, or so Josie had thought. She didn't see her mother often enough to really know the state of her drinking.

"Josie," she said, lifting her head up with some effort.

"Sorry I had to leave you for a while, Mom. I had an important meeting."

"What happened to me?" Elaine asked. She pulled the blanket around her shoulders and sat up. She looked shriveled.

"You managed to get a DUI. I don't know where you'd been, but they picked you up at Halsted and Lake. There's nothing good about you being in that neighborhood, Mom."

"I don't remember a thing. Not a thing." She pulled the blanket tighter around her.

Josie went to get the police papers and waved them in front of her mother. If this was her one chance to break through Elaine's denial, she'd take it. "Here's the paperwork. You have to appear in court tomorrow to plead. I'm sure they'll let you come home while you're waiting for trial. I know a good lawyer." She watched as a hundred cascading expressions rolled down Elaine's face.

"But, Josie, I don't remember a thing. How can this all be?"

"I'm surprised you haven't had a blackout before. That's pretty damn lucky. I used to get them all the time. There was this one time…"

"Please do not share your sordid adventures with me. I learned more than I ever cared to hear last fall," Elaine said.

"Mom, I can smell the booze coming through your pores. I don't think you're in a position to make me feel more sordid than you." Elaine pulled the blanket even closer around her. "They're both diseases. I'm bipolar. You're alcoholic. Stop judging."

Josie piled it on by retrieving the red "ladies who lunch" suit, which looked like a rag used to clean up an oil spill. "See, Mom? Yesterday morning you walked out wearing your best suit, going somewhere special, I suppose, and you ended up with both you and the suit covered in whatever this is, pulled over by a cop, and charged with a DUI. That's what your disease looks like."

Elaine looked worried. "Thank God your father's out of town," she said. "I don't want to be here when he finds out."

Josie paused for a bit. "Dad doesn't hit you or anything, does he?" She felt her blood start to boil at the idea of it. If Gabby could be violent, there was no question her father could.

"It depends on what you mean by 'anything.'"

"Tell me," Josie was now down on her knee, looking at her mother at eye level.

Elaine hesitated. "I've never wanted you to know this, Josie, never."

"Tell me," Josie said.

"He doesn't hit me, Josie. I don't want you to worry about that.

But you know how he talks to you like you don't know what you're doing, like you don't have a brain in your head."

Josie grinned ruefully. "Yes, I'm familiar with it."

"That's how he talks to me on a good day. He can be quite… severe at other times."

"And it frightens you," Josie said, as her mother nodded and looked at the floor. She rose and started pacing around the room. "He's such an unmitigated bastard. Why have you stayed married to him all this time?"

This unprecedented conversation with her mother was terminated when Elaine bolted upstairs to the bathroom and slammed the door shut. Josie decided she couldn't really handle this kind of heart-to-heart with her mother now, and clearly her mother couldn't either. She went into the kitchen to put on a pot of coffee and wrote a note before leaving. Her mind spun what she'd heard right out of her head and she trotted to her car to head home. Her fury at her father and frustration with her mother were gone as soon as she shifted to a new line of thought. Her thoughts were starting to ping-pong. She felt a moment of concern.

She took stock of herself. Feeling happy was good, except when it wasn't. She got into her apartment and headed for the bathroom. Her daily pill holder showed she hadn't taken her medication for three days. She hurriedly downed the small handful of pills—some to treat the bipolar disorder, some to treat the side effects of those drugs—and then moved quickly to the kitchen. She hadn't eaten since she had a half sandwich yesterday. Her sleep had been awful the past few nights, but the most worrying part of that was she felt as energized as ever. Greta would be furious with her if she knew all this. No, Greta would worry about her. She had to remember some people, albeit very few, actually cared for her. Even Josie could tell she was hypomanic, but she was convinced she could harness the really good parts of it: feeling fantastic, having boundless energy and brilliant thoughts. Plus she had extra time available when sleep was unnecessary. She could harness it all into finding out just who the hell killed Kelly Moore.

CHAPTER TWENTY-FIVE

Eva raised an eyebrow when Lauren came out of her office and told her to cancel the rest of the morning's appointments.

"But you're meeting with the board at eleven o'clock," she said.

Lauren glanced at her watch. It was a little after ten. "I'll try to be back for that. This shouldn't take too long." She left the office before Eva could ask questions and walked swiftly to the firm's parking lot. She knew Tim had long ago placed a tracking device in the undercarriage of her car and occasionally she removed it, simply out of irritation.

Something made her think the threat to her parents would end soon. She admitted to herself she didn't care if her brother lived, but she'd still do what was necessary to keep her parents alive. She left the tracker on; he would know she was on the way to his house and that was fine. She wasn't interested in surprising him. She was interested in trying to figure out which direction he was headed.

Tim's Lincoln Park place was not far from her own home. Her parents had purchased the house to get him to move out of theirs. Despite his bloated salary at Wade-Fellowes and the amount of stock he owned in the company, he was strangely reluctant to strike out on his own. Finally, at twenty-five, he was kicked right into a million-dollar nineteenth-century brick row house that had three narrow levels, a dank basement, and a two-story coach house in the rear of the yard. She found him in the second story loft of the coach house. This was his project or hobby room. His childhood hobbies often involved dissecting small animals or creating booby traps, one of which nearly killed a neighboring five-year-old. She'd only stepped in this room once or twice before and was chased out on both occasions as Tim tried to hide whatever he was up to. She knew his was a confused sexuality, something she'd be sympathetic to if he'd let her be. But coming upon a collection of art photos of nude men had been a complete surprise to her and a complete mortification to him. He'd thrown a sheet over the table and screamed at her to leave. They never spoke about the photos again. He kept up his metrosexual appearance and occasionally referred to women he was seeing. Lauren went along with it.

Now she opened the door and found him standing at the kitchenette in the rear of the room, making coffee.

"I saw you were coming," he said. "Is regular okay or are you into the decaf part of your day?" He seemed cheerful, which made Lauren more watchful than usual. When he was bitter and resentful she could see what she had to work with. His cheerfulness was unnerving. This time he'd made no effort to hide the spread of documents across his table, and she sat down to look them over. They were autopsy photographs, carefully arranged in rows with their reports neatly squared away beneath them. Kelly's autopsy photo was in the middle of one row of photographs, her body sewn up with the usual Y, her brain opened. Lauren had seen the photo before; her lawyer had insisted she look at it and some of the shock had worn off. But still she drew in a sharp breath at the sight of it. Nothing could make Kelly's death more real than seeing her like this. She thought it seemed excessive to maim her body with a full autopsy when the cause of death was so obvious.

"The human body is endlessly fascinating," Tim said, fussing with cups and creamer. He turned to her. "Don't you think so?"

She looked up at him but said nothing.

"It's extraordinary what it can take." He left the counter to come stand behind her, pointing to one of the photos to her left. "Take this one, for example. This fellow was beaten within an inch of his life, somehow survived, and died two weeks later when a black widow spider bit him. Normally only about five percent of those bitten die. But down went this huge man. Maybe he was weak from the beating." Tim pointed toward the man's ribs. "Isn't it awful what a tire iron can do?"

Lauren knew he wanted to upset her, but she carefully remained neutral. She was trying to gauge his real mood. He pulled a stool up next to her and pushed away the top photo of Kelly, revealing a pile of additional photos from her autopsy.

"And here we have Kelly in the middle of the procedure." He

pulled one from the middle of the pile. He studied the overhead shot of the body opened from throat to pubic bone, clamps of all sorts keeping the cavity open and the organs exposed should the medical examiner chose to remove, weigh, and loosely replace them.

"How strange it must feel to see her like this," he said, almost reverently. "To know her body so well and yet really not at all. Look at how much of her you never got a glimpse of, never got to touch, though I'm sure you got quite a ways up here." He pointed at her uterus.

"Tim, you're an ass, like every other man I know. That's her uterus, not her vagina."

He looked sternly at her, as if she'd ruined the mood he was trying to create. That gave her some pleasure.

She returned his stern look. "I'm surprised you had a chance to stop by the office today when you're so busy here in your House of Horrors. How long have you had all of these?"

"I've been collecting them for years," he said, as pleased as if she'd commented on a display of antique barometers. "I started by going to the county examiner's office and pretending I was a City News Bureau reporter. It seemed the crime reporters could get anything in those days."

Lauren looked around at the photos of scores of dead people on autopsy slabs. Tim was revealing layers of craziness she hadn't known before. Throughout their lives together he'd been simply mean, verging on menacing and sometimes violent. With the kidnapping of their parents he'd tipped into evil, with shades of insanity along with it. Wasn't it insane to think he could keep his parents hidden away ad infinitum?

"A few years ago I dated an autopsy photographer," Tim continued. "I watched who came and went from the examiner's building with camera equipment in hand and saw one young woman who worked there regularly. She fell for me right away and I cajoled her into letting me see her work. Soon I had her transferring photos directly to my computer. It was so easy."

Tim was leaning with elbows on the table, coffee mug in hand. You'd think he was reminiscing about the first time he'd been kissed. "Eventually, I decided to end our relationship. She wasn't that interesting beyond her photography. We have an arrangement now where I pay her handsomely for the autopsy photos of people I select. I don't want thousands of photos of aneurysms or cancer cases. The photos I buy are of unusual deaths, all of them murders. But some murders are much more interesting than others."

Lauren got up and walked around the table, pretending to seriously study his collection. She looked at him. "I imagine the photos of Kelly would be the most interesting to you, if only because you were the one who put that hole in her forehead."

If Josie Harper was looking into other suspects as Kelly's killer, Lauren might be able to put together some real evidence against him, which she could then use as leverage to free her parents. She knew Tim wanted her to think he'd done it.

Tim turned his head back to the photo of Kelly's brain.

"I'm interested in all matter of murder. I find it fascinating to study the look on their face shortly after death." He tapped on a photo of Kelly's head. "Tell me the truth, sis. There wasn't much in this noggin, was there? I mean, you went for her because she was gorgeous, not for her smarts, right?"

"She was smart enough," Lauren said defensively. "And a lovely person. She took good care of me. She wasn't a trophy wife, if that's what you're implying."

"I'm not implying anything. I'm trying to get a rise out of you. Clearly, I'm not the first to question your relationship with Kelly."

This was so tedious. Lauren was made of the same working parts as everyone else. She'd had a strong physical reaction to Kelly. She went for it. Why was that so surprising? She sighed and took a seat across the table from Tim.

"Why did you come to Wade-Fellowes yesterday? You know it's off-limits to you."

Tim didn't seem in the least concerned. "Don't threaten me with a restraining order again. You know who will pay the price."

"We had an agreement you'd stay away. So, I repeat, what were you doing there?"

He shrugged. "I was taking some ladies out to lunch. I have my supporters, you know. A number of people were very happy to see me."

"And you happened to run into David Schofeld and decided to punch him?"

Tim looked dismissive. "That's not what happened. I was leaving with the group for lunch when Schofeld came in the room and pulled me into the corridor. He pushed me against the wall and threatened to call the police if I didn't get out immediately. That guy is huge. When he pushed me again I punched him. Self-defense."

Lauren sat still, observing her own reaction to Tim's explanation. She knew with ninety-nine percent certainty Tim was lying, because that was Tim. And she'd never known David Schofeld to lie. But he could sell anything; for a moment she thought of believing him. He really should have been in the sales end of the company.

"How are Mom and Dad?" she asked.

Tim was straightening Kelly's pile of photos and aligning things precisely. "I was waiting for that question. You're so predictable."

Lauren gave him a withering look. "I have a right to ask how they are, and you're supposed to let me know."

"Says who?" Tim grinned.

"Says anyone who has the least amount of feeling." She knew now he had no feelings, that he was probably a sociopath, that he'd effectively stolen her life from her.

"Well, that might not be me. I seem to have lost all my feelings, if I ever had them to begin with. It's very liberating, sis. You should try it.

"Mom and Dad are doing fine," he continued. "I even brought them a TV and set up cable and bought some new books for them. You don't have to worry."

"Of course I have to worry! I have to put my life on hold for them."

They were both silent for a while. Tim picked his up phone and seemed to be checking email, though she couldn't imagine who he corresponded with. She'd never known him to have a single friend.

"Tim, we have to bring this to an end. You can't kill Mom and Dad. Whether you kill them or let them go, I'd tell the police everything. You'd spend a long time in prison, and I can tell you from personal experience you are not built to survive that kind of life."

"Yes, you could do that. If you were alive. I'd think by now you'd realize I have every angle covered. If you tell the police about this, they will never get the location out of me and Mom and Dad will simply die alone where they're being held. If I get a whiff of you hiring help to find them, like the private investigator that visited me the other day, I'll kill them. If I decide to give up on the kidnapping because it is becoming a bit tedious, you and John and Helen will die. Don't you know by now how smart I am? Also, if I want to go to the office, I'll go to the fucking office."

Lauren's insides churned. "I don't understand why you're doing this. You haven't given me one of your absurd assignments in days. Not that I want one, but that was the motivating factor for you, wasn't it?"

Tim smiled widely. "That was some fun stuff. Seeing you practically suicidal with shame was truly gratifying. But I'm a little over that now. I'm working on something else."

This sent a chill down Lauren's spine. "Are you telling me I won't have a hand in keeping them alive?"

"Yes, you will. But I'm not telling you about it now."

Lauren leaned forward, her hands firmly planted on the photos of two dissected bodies. "You can't drag this out any longer. Tell me what you want from me. Let's get it done. I can't take any more and I'm sure Mom and Dad are at the end of their rope. Do you want me to reinstate you as VP of operations? Would that do the trick?"

Tim rose and headed toward the door, signaling their meeting was at an end. "You don't understand a thing of what's going to happen."

"My gut says this is ending soon," said Lauren, "and not in your favor." She was standing very close to Tim. "If killing me is the ultimate price I have to pay to get them released, then get it over with."

"I'll keep all that in mind," he said, holding the door for her. "Lovely to see you, as always." Then he slammed the door behind her.

Lauren felt like an idiot. Why had it not occurred to her that even if he decided to end the kidnapping, it would be by killing them? And her, too. There was no positive outcome for her parents unless they were rescued. Tim was apparently no longer interested in the strange ransom she'd been paying.

She went to her car and pulled Stan Waterman's number out of her pocket.

CHAPTER TWENTY-SIX

Josie got back on the Kennedy and headed for downtown. She was going to have to start eliminating the suspects she did have: Ann-Marie, Gabby, and Tim. She'd struck Nikki from the list because her alibi seemed sound enough; two friends she said she ate dinner with confirmed her story. The other two had no alibi at all. Gabby wasn't on duty and couldn't remember what she was doing seven months earlier. Ann-Marie's was shaky. Same with Tim. But of all of them, Tim had the strongest motive—hatred of a sister he thought was more loved by their parents than he. Tim was a straight-out weirdo, with his costume changes and general creepiness. She decided to stake out Tim's place for a while and see if it led to anything. Then she'd drive to Lauren's place in the evening for more of the same. The hours this would take didn't faze her. Her only issue was the perennial problem of the solo female on surveillance—how to pee and not miss the very thing you were waiting to see. Maybe she'd stop at Sportmart's camping department and get one of those funnel things.

She exited at Armitage and made her way into the heart of Lincoln Park. Her hackles went up whenever she was in the neighborhood. Armitage itself was beautiful with its vintage greystone buildings and their elaborate, decorated cornices. But it was lined with shops catering to a young generation of wealthy shoppers that made Josie uncomfortable. There were custom-made cosmetics shops, one-of-a-kind clothing stores, and shops with baby clothes you won't find at Babies-R-Us. This was pram country. Women wearing yoga pants pushed monstrous strollers down the sidewalk, giving the evil eye to every car stopped at a stop sign, as if the drivers planned to hit the gas and mow them down. She didn't imagine Lauren would blink at the boutique prices here. Lucy, on the other hand, was a regular at the Howard Brown resale shop. She had a very down-to-earth sensibility and the income of a social worker. Josie thought again of the difference between Lucy and Lauren, which was night and day. She knew Lucy was a good person but she had her doubts about Lauren; there was a veil of mystery where there was only openness from Lucy. Josie felt more excited by and more comfortable with the dark and unknown. Lucy's kindness was more suspect. She didn't trust it.

She found parking far enough down the street from Tim's to be able to see the front door, but not so close that he would see her. She wedged herself behind a Mercedes SUV and in front of a Range Rover. Tim would probably enter and exit his house through the back, where the garage opened onto the alley, but there was no way to be inconspicuous there. No matter where she parked she was in front of someone's garage door, or noticeable simply for parking in the alley. She settled in as best she could for what would probably be a purposeless few hours and thought about investing in a tracking device she could put on Tim's car.

She started doing an Internet search on trackers when she saw a car come up the street and pull into an illegal spot at the end of the block. She sat up straight when she saw Lauren get out of a Lexus. Then she dropped herself lower in her seat to avoid being seen, though there'd be little reason for Lauren to scrutinize a car halfway down the street. Lauren strode to Tim's front door and laid on the door bell, several times, before using the knocker. After a minute without a response, she walked to the gangway on the side of the building and disappeared. Fuck. Josie started her car and tried to get out of its spot as quickly as possible, circling the street to come up the alley to check out Tim's house from behind. She caught sight of Lauren at the top of the coach house stairs, a glimpse of shapely calves walking through the door of the top floor. She'd been studying those legs just a few hours before.

Josie paused in the alley to see if anything was visible through her binoculars. Nothing. The windows were covered with heavily tinted material, like on a drug dealer's car. There were multiple skylights on the roof. Josie wondered what he used the space for. Thoughts of carved-up body parts and gruesome instruments of torture filled her head, but she pulled back on the thoughts like yanking the line of a runaway kite. She knew her thinking often flew away from her, sending her down paths she should never follow. During the height of her mania she'd always followed the flight pattern of her crazy thinking. Now she was aware when she was being misled, at least most of the time.

She stayed in the alley as long as she thought safe, leaving when a man came out with his garbage and gave her a suspicious look. It might have been merely a curious look, but Josie opted for suspicious and drove out of the alley and back in front of the house. There were no parking places open, so she idled by a fire hydrant. She wondered what they were doing. Didn't they hate each other? She spent disagreeable hours with parents she didn't like, but as far as she knew this wasn't a requirement among siblings who hated each other. She was reaching for her coffee when Lauren emerged from the gangway.

Once again, Josie wished she had a partner in the car with her, a team of people behind her. She didn't know whether she should follow Lauren or stay with Tim. She wanted to send orders through a walkie-talkie and hear clipped acknowledgments in return. Instead, she let Lauren go, figuring she would head back to her office. Now that she knew the make, model and license plate number of her car, it would be much easier for her to pick up her tail when Lauren left the office for the day. She circled the alley again, hoping Tim might be leaving as well. When she slowly worked her way up the alley, she saw the garage door opening in his coach house and Tim backing out in a Jeep Wrangler. She could see the other car in the garage was a Porsche.

Two hours later she was following him back from Oak Brook Mall where he'd emerged laden with shopping bags from Nordstrom and Bloomingdale's. She was out of her mind with boredom, frustrated by the traffic on the Eisenhower. She parked on Cleveland to resume watching his house when Lucy called.

"Hey, you," Lucy said. Chipper, as always.

"Hi, Lucy. You sort of caught me in the middle of something," Josie said. She'd gone straight for the exit strategy, not in the mood to talk to Lucy, which felt a little rebellious. She knew she should want to talk to Lucy, to cultivate something with her, that she was good for her. That Greta would approve. All of that now seemed reason enough not to do it.

Lucy's voice was teasing. "I'm sorry. Were you about to make a citizen's arrest? Take down a martial artist?" She waited for a response from Josie, who was scrambling to come up with one. She didn't want to be a bitch.

"No violence yet today," she said, as lightly as she could. "But there's still the night to come."

"That sounds like you plan on working tonight," Lucy said. "I was hoping we could get together."

"I'm on this murder case, you know."

"And it's not nine-to-five. I get it." Lucy didn't sound defensive, or particularly disappointed. This piqued Josie's interest. Lucy seemed so sure of herself she couldn't decide if it was irritating or attractive.

"I'm not sure how long I'll be," Josie said. "But maybe I can come by later? I'd have to call to let you know how things are going."

The case was not going well. The only thing concrete she'd learned that day was how beautiful and smart Lauren was. Josie drifted into a fantasy of making love to her. Then she thought of the same thing with Lucy and her mind stuttered to a stop. Making love with Lucy had been nice. But nice was not a good word.

"That'd be great," Lucy said. "I'm working at the clinic until eight."

They rang off, and Josie felt uneasy. Lucy was like a piece in a jigsaw puzzle. She fit somewhere, but Josie hadn't found where yet.

CHAPTER TWENTY-SEVEN

Lauren got onto Lake Shore Drive to return to her office. She pulled Stan Waterman's number out of her pocket and dialed. He picked up on the first ring.

"Waterman," a distracted voice said. She thought she could hear *Jeopardy* in the background.

"I hope I'm not calling at a bad time," she said.

"Not at all. I'm watching *Celebrity Jeopardy*. Please distract me."

"My name's Lauren Wade. I got your number from Nancy Prewitt."

There was only a slight pause. "I just heard from Nancy. She mentioned you might be calling," he said. "I know who you are, of course."

"I imagine most everyone in Chicago has some idea who I am. Believe me, I don't say that to flatter myself."

"How can I help you, Ms. Wade?"

Lauren liked him. She sensed his honesty and openness. Who would admit to watching *Celebrity Jeopardy*?

"I do need help, right away, actually. I'm wondering if we could get together and discuss the details. Now, if possible."

"Name the place," Stan said.

They arranged to meet at Nookies in Old Town. She called Eva to cancel her meeting with the board, glad of any reason to avoid them. When she arrived at the restaurant, Stan was already seated. He stood as Lauren took a seat, and then she got right to the point.

"Mr. Waterman…"

"Stan, please." She looked at him and felt he was a man she could trust to stay on her side. He was in his fifties and looked it, but he also looked like he didn't care much what people thought of him, very comfortable in his own skin. She wasn't sure the same could be said of her. She hadn't had a day at peace with herself in months.

"Before I begin I need to ask you whether you've been hired by anyone else in regard to my murder trial and acquittal."

He looked confused. "No, I haven't. Is there a reason to think I have?"

"An investigator named Josie Harper asked me some questions today. I want to make sure you don't have a personal relationship with her."

"I know Josie. I know she's working on a murder case."

Lauren took a sip of water and considered this. "Interesting. I still don't know who she's working for. But not really relevant to what I want done."

A server came by and Stan ordered the chicken pot pie. Lauren got a chopped salad. "I'm having a serious problem with my brother and I need your help to resolve it. I'm sure you get a lot of cases involving family disputes, but trust me when I say this is a particularly egregious step taken by my brother."

Stan sipped his coffee, his eyes revealing nothing. "I was a homicide cop for a lot of years. There's not much that's going to take me by surprise."

"First of all, before we move forward, I have to ask for your word you won't reveal this story to anyone, including any associates who work with you. If my brother finds out I've hired private detectives to help me, the ramifications will be horrible."

"Nothing will be done without your okay. Can you live with that?" Stan said.

The food arrived and Stan dug in, prepared to listen to Lauren's story while he obviously enjoyed his food. Lauren merely picked at her salad as she explained how Tim had kidnapped her parents, forced her to perform a series of humiliating stunts, framed her for a murder he committed, and now threatened to change the rules of the game.

"The game?" Stan said.

"Yes, the game he's always played with me, but never before won.

It's the one where he tries to come off looking better than me and claim a victory of some sort. I don't think he's sane. I think it's his way of dealing with our parents clearly favoring me and basically throwing their hands up with him. He was difficult as a child, and he never grew out of it."

"Sounds like he's escalating. He kidnapped your parents? That's a pretty desperate move."

Lauren looked around, as if everyone in the restaurant was leaning in to hear the story. "He kidnapped them eight months ago, and that's when he started having me do all these crazy things. That was his game: if I failed to comply, he'd hurt my parents somehow."

"Why didn't you go to the police?"

"I did and was terrified my parents would end up dead because of it. He very convincingly made it look like they're sailing around the world and impossible to reach. I couldn't convince the police they were missing in the first place. People at their condo building also said they were sailing. I knew there would be a price to pay for contacting the cops. Tim hit me with some of his hardest assignments, and my parents were punished as well. He made it clear if I were to do the same again, he'd kill John and Helen."

"He's not joking around," Stan said.

"Not in the least."

"What about private investigators?"

"I've tried that before, too, and it earned my parents three days without food. Tim quickly picked up on the surveillance by the investigator. It's the reason I'm nervous about hiring you."

"Anything else I should know?" Stan asked. He had the demeanor of a tradesman talking about building a back deck.

"Somehow I feel he's switching tactics and my parents are in greater danger than ever. He's no longer making me carry out those assignments and he's started coming into the office, which he hasn't done in a long time."

"Why?" The server came by and asked if they'd have anything else. Stan ordered blueberry pie. Lauren asked for more black coffee.

"After my parents retired and put me in charge of the company, Tim, who was named vice president of operations, became a real pain in the ass at the office. He was driving our good people away, not doing his work, flirting with our female staff. I had no choice but to fire him.

He seemed to not accept my authority to do so and kept showing up to work. I had to threaten him with a court order to get him to leave."

"And recently he's been showing up again," Stan said.

"He assaulted our new VP of operations, who's everything Tim was not in that position." Lauren paused. "Tim told me the other day he was thinking differently about the whole situation—meaning what to do with our parents—and it made me think he's considering finishing it. It also made me realize he'd never release them alive. I may have been able to amuse Tim for a while. The assignments he gave me were a completely absorbing hobby for him. But now I have no role to play. At least none he's told me about yet. I think he could kill them at any time."

"If he kills them to keep quiet, he'll have to do the same to you."

Lauren had no reaction to this possibility. It didn't seem to matter. "I suppose."

"And everyone thinks they're sailing around the world?"

"Yes," Lauren said.

"How long does that take, do you think? Taking a boat around the world, I mean." Stan was halfway through his pie. Lauren was growing inpatient.

"I suppose about a year, if you don't drown or get captured by Somali pirates."

Stan leaned back and looked her in the eye. "Tell me exactly what you want me to achieve for you."

"First and foremost, find my parents. If we can get Tim charged for their kidnapping, that would take him out of my hair for a good long while. If we could get the evidence we need to get him charged with my partner Kelly's murder, that would put him out of my life for good. That's what I'd like."

Still Stan looked unperturbed. "I think it would be good to pool resources with Josie, to the extent she can. We have a long-standing relationship. I trust her."

"Strangely, so do I," Lauren said. "I have no real objection. These are two distinctly different matters—my parents' kidnapping and the misguided investigation to clear my name. I don't think there's a conflict."

Lauren quite liked the idea. Since their morning interview, her thoughts about Tim had been interrupted often by thoughts of Josie

Harper. Inchoate, but definitely buzzy. She didn't know exactly what to think about her, but she could feel how her body reacted to her.

Lauren drank more coffee as she listened to Stan lay out his initial plan for finding her parents. Any plan would make her nervous as hell. So much could go wrong. As she drove the short distance from Old Town to her office building she answered a call from Tim. The temptation to let it go to voicemail was nearly irresistible, but she forced herself to pick up. Things seemed to be changing rapidly now. She needed whatever information he was willing to give her.

"What do you want?" She didn't hide her displeasure.

"Hello to you, too!" Tim chirped. He sounded triumphant. It reminded her of when he ran cross country in high school, usually one of the boys bringing up the rear. But one day he came in third in a regional race. She'd never seen his face glow as it did when he was announced the bronze medal winner and he ran to his mother to crow about his victory. It was the only time John and Helen had come to one of Tim's events. Then the results were challenged by the parents of another runner and it turned out Tim had cut a hundred yards off his course and a couple of people had witnessed it. The bronze medal was taken out of his hands and his face crumpled into something unrecognizable. Lauren tried to comfort him, but he threw her off. His mother offered no condolence and looked disgusted as he wailed about how unfair it was. Lauren felt something close to sympathy for him. She could imagine how that would feel, though it would never have happened to her, of course. She walked off with the gold in any event she entered, athletic or academic.

"Why do you sound so happy?" Lauren said. "Did you just discover Lincoln's autopsy photos?"

"This is so much better than that, though I would pay a lot for Lincoln's autopsy photos. I wonder if any were taken?" He seemed to be waiting for a reply. When none came, he said, "I discovered something last week that affects both of us. I thought about telling you when you were here earlier today, but I was still contemplating it. It's pretty wild."

Lauren sighed, something she'd done an awful lot of over the past eight months. She anticipated he'd discovered another way to embarrass her. "Give me the bad news," she said.

"I went to the parents' condo last week, as I do every month to let the management know John and Helen are okay and to pay the assessments. While I was in the condo, I spent a little time going through some of their documents, which I hadn't done before. I figured whatever I found would be something favoring you and fucking me over. But I forced myself to open the safe in Dad's study. It took me forever to hack his computer and find the combination. When I got in, I found the usual stuff—bearer bonds, investment account numbers, and their most recent will. And guess what?"

"I don't know. They left me more money than you? I can even it up with you, if that's your problem," Lauren said.

"That's what I thought I'd find, too," Tim said. "But in fact, everything's split down the middle. The big surprise is the recent codicil they added to their will. Recent being right before I kidnapped them. Really, it makes my idea of kidnapping them seem almost prescient. The codicil says if, upon their deaths, the board of directors votes to remove either of us from the company, the shares of both siblings must vote with the board. They laid the groundwork for your removal, basically, since I'm already gone. It's as if they knew you'd be arrested for murder, that your behavior would become erratic, that your numbers would plunge."

Lauren's heart started thumping. She'd parked in her garage spot but continued to sit in her car, waiting to hear how Tim planned to use the new information. The thought of losing the company had never entered her mind. Her job kept her grounded, even if she felt less enthusiasm for it than she had before Tim's blackmail began. It was what she controlled, what she captained, what she did to keep books being published and people employed. Clearly her parents had seen her greater talent for the job when they promoted her upon their retirement. What could make them want to risk someone less competent taking on the title?

Tim stayed silent, again waiting as Lauren processed the information. "I'm a little surprised you aren't waving this away," he said. "You probably never imagined the board wanting anyone but you. But things haven't been normal, have they? You've not exactly been executive of the year potential lately."

"What are you talking about?" Lauren reached into her purse for a cigarette, though she hadn't smoked for ten years. She'd kill for one now.

"Let's look at it from the board's point of view, which I've spent quite a bit of time doing over the last several days. What they see is a formerly effective CEO—that would be you—who has just been released after spending six months in the county jail, and who, on top of that, has been acting very peculiarly. They heard about you dragging your VPs to the Kitten Lounge. And let me say again that your defiant act of switching a strip club for a drag club was brave, but stupid. John and Helen went without food for three days, and believe me, they were furious. Let that be a reminder."

Lauren ignored most of this speech. "Not one board member has complained to me about any of that," Lauren said, defending her crazy actions as if they were her idea and not Tim's doing.

"It's true the board is able to overlook a lot in a family-run business. They pretty much have to. But with John and Helen giving them more power, there's one thing a board is unlikely to overlook," Tim said.

Lauren knew the numbers from the last three quarters were bad. A dip in performance for a quarter or two wasn't cause for panic, but three quarters made everyone extremely nervous. She had a plan she was putting in place to get things back on track, but what if it was too late as far as the board was concerned? She had also assumed when her parents died, she'd have the majority of voting stock; now it appeared Tim's shares would be equal to hers, and their power gutted by the voting power the codicil would give the board. With their death a real possibility now, she saw how she could easily be removed.

Lauren's fidgeting hands froze midair as the realization hit her that Tim might choose now as the time to kill her parents, making it look like they were lost at sea. With more shares left to him in the will than he thought, he wouldn't want them to have the opportunity to change it again.

"What if I were to resign as CEO and persuade the board to put you in charge? Would you let Mom and Dad go?"

Tim scoffed. "Frankly, I haven't decided what to do with them yet. I'm not saying I'm going to kill them, but I'm not saying I'm not either. Same rules apply—if I get wind of any third party knowing about this, trying to pin a kidnapping on me, I will most definitely kill Mom and Dad, either directly or by simply not giving up their location to the authorities should it come to that. Your instructions are to do nothing."

Tim hung up abruptly. Lauren still held the phone to her ear, waiting for him to say what a massively funny one he'd pulled over her. But it wasn't only Tim that had dropped this news on her like a fishnet. It was her parents who'd created the net in the first place. Lauren was shocked to the bone. They wanted to give their son an opportunity, on the off chance he'd become a new man. Or they wanted a mechanism in place in case she became a terrible CEO. Perhaps that was what the board now considered her to be. There was a reason she'd not been made chairman of the board. Lauren knew the danger to her parents had just increased substantially, but she was also deeply hurt. They apparently supported their daughter as long as profits were up. Lauren felt like she'd been dumped.

She backed out of her spot and turned for home, her workday over. She couldn't possibly keep up her act of a competent, take-charge leader today. Eva would see her distress in a second. She called Eva and told her she wouldn't be back and then sped toward home.

Chapter Twenty-eight

Josie was almost out of her mind with boredom. She sat in her car, down the street from Tim Wade's house. Occasionally she'd drive down the alley to see if it still looked like Tim was in the coach house. She had no idea what he was doing up there. All she knew was he was doing something and she was doing nothing.

She took her next reconnaissance on foot and got nothing from it. As she was returning to her car, she saw a blue sedan drive by. She and the driver looked at each other—the driver smiled; Josie frowned. What the hell was Stan Waterman doing here? She jogged to her Toyota as Stan's car continued down the street, not slowing a bit as it passed Tim Wade's house. Before Josie was able to close her door, her phone was ringing. The number was unfamiliar, but she had no doubt who it was.

"Josie, my girl. We're going to have to give you a few lessons. Did I just see you walking from Tim Wade's alley?"

"I didn't know you'd become my training officer." Josie sounded peevish, but she was more embarrassed by her faux pas.

Stan chuckled. "No, those days are over for both of us, I'm afraid. But it looks like we're focusing on the same subject. I'd rather not have you blow my chances of keeping a tail on this guy."

"I don't understand. Why would you be following Tim Wade?"

"Because Lauren Wade hired me to."

Josie clamped her mouth shut and closed her eyes. She felt the sharp sting of rejection, as if it would have made sense for Lauren to hire her instead of Stan. "She told me because you were already involved through your investigation into Kelly Moore's murder, she wouldn't mind if we pooled resources and knowledge. We need to get together to talk."

Now Josie felt the relief of an addict when the needle hits the vein. Maybe she was wanted after all.

She and Stan agreed to meet at Nookies to talk things over. She found him already perusing the sixteen-page menu.

"I'm sick of all the food here," Stan said.

"How's that possible? You could never work your way through that menu, not if you want to stay alive." Stan shrugged and continued to ponder his choices. Josie shifted in her seat.

"I've been looking at Tim as the murderer of Kelly Moore, but from what I can tell, Lauren couldn't have cared less if I'd been looking at the Man in the Moon as a suspect. So why is she suddenly having you keep surveillance on Tim? Did something happen? I mean, you'd think I'd be the first person she'd call if that were the case…"

"Josie. Slow down. I can't tell you if I can't get a word in edgewise."

Josie clamped down on her jaw. Again. She hadn't been aware her racing thoughts were slipping out of her mouth. She wouldn't have stopped talking if Stan hadn't interrupted her. She conducted a quick review: medication—yes. Sleep—no. Tiredness—none at all. Racing thoughts—more so each day. Increase in goal-directed activity—she would hope so. Excessive involvement with pleasurable activity— not so far, but the possibility was presenting itself. Even by her own analysis, Josie could see she was hypomanic. But unlike the full-blown mania of the year before, she wasn't coming off as batshit crazy and she could hide the most obvious of her symptoms. At least she thought she could.

She kept her mouth shut as Stan explained Lauren's dilemma with Tim, the kidnapping of her parents, the efforts to find them. Her mouth dropped open despite herself.

"Stan, you have to let me in on this. I know I can help find the parents and get this guy locked up. Lauren must be going through hell."

"I think he's been tormenting her so long she doesn't remember what normal is," Stan said. "And there was the jail time, too."

"But we can't go about surveillance the way I did today. Even I can see he'd catch on to it, though he seems to spend most of his time in that damn coach house. You'd think Lauren would act more stressed than she does. My guess is she's about to crack," Josie said.

"Agreed," Stan said. "We need another body or two to pull this job off. I've got Tommy looking for a garage or apartment we can use to watch the back of the coach house without Tim seeing us. We'll see him if he goes out back and we'll have a car on the street ready to follow him. The person in the car should see him if he goes out front, but my guess is he nearly always uses the back."

"Who the hell is Tommy?" Josie said.

"My supposed associate. You know, the one who washed out of the department."

Josie scowled. "Two washed-out cops ought to impress Lauren."

"Tommy knows how to keep a watch, Josie. Keep an open mind, that's my watchword for everything in this business."

Stan's phone rang and he spoke a few moments before hanging up.

"That was Tommy," Stan said. "He's just rented a garage apartment across the street. Some kid who's only too glad to crash on a friend's sofa for the dough we offered him."

Josie sat back on the bench. The restaurant was nearly full. A speeding server took their order and then trotted to her next task. Josie kept one eye on her.

"That was fast work of him," she said.

"You'll like Tommy. He's not much of an intuitive thinker but he's a good plodder. We're going to need at least one more to man this properly. I'll work on that."

"All right. What do you think of the kidnapped parents thing?" Josie asked.

"It's tough," Stan said. "There aren't any ransom demands for us to work with. He has the parents very effectively hidden. In eight months they haven't been able to break free. My guess, based on what video Lauren's seen of them, is they're in some crappy, isolated house, somewhere within a couple of hours' distance from here. He has to go out there to replenish their food, make sure they're still there."

"So what we have to do," Josie said, "is be on his tail when he drives out of the city and hope he leads us right to them."

"Yeah. It's not sophisticated, but I can't think of anything better. Feel free to chime in with a plan if you have one."

Josie wished she had a half dozen brilliant ideas to impress Stan with, but she had nothing. Her brain was too active to be that sharp, her need for action too great to put any real thought to the strategic aspects. "No. That sounds best for now," she said confidently. "I'll take first watch."

"No, you won't. You look like shit. I'll take between now and midnight. Tommy can do the overnight, and you be on the job at eight tomorrow morning," Stan said.

"I take it you're the captain of this ship?"

"Let's say I still outrank you. And the client hired me, after all. Now go home and get some rest. Seriously. I don't want you useless on watch."

They paid the bill and headed their separate ways. Josie's first inclination was to find Lauren and reassure her they'd find her parents, especially now she was on the case, but she didn't want to promise anything yet. She was halfway downtown when Sarah DeAngeles called.

"This is Harper."

"Harper? Is that what people call you?" Sarah had a teasing edge to her voice, veering slightly toward flirtatious.

"It's what people called me when I was a cop. Old habit, I guess."

"Well, Harper, I'm afraid I'm calling with bad news." To Josie that could mean only one thing.

"You're calling off the investigation, aren't you?"

"I'm afraid so. The board has been divided on it all along. Now the majority feel it's unnecessary. There are other factors they're considering."

"Like what?" Josie said, trying to sound as professional as she could. "I've only been at this for a week, and I did warn you it might take some time."

"Harper," Sarah said. "I can't tell you anymore than I have, but this has nothing to do with your performance. You worked hard and I appreciate everything you did." Josie again felt relief. Maybe she'd ask Sarah for a testimonial. She needed a brochure and something to put in it.

"Aren't you curious?" Josie asked.

"Not as much as before. Lauren has essentially faded from my life.

Ever since she was released from jail she's been unreachable. Let's say that's slowly dampened my desire to help her out. Also, I'm moving my next book to a new publisher, one that will probably overtake Wade-Fellowes not too far down the road. I'll be resigning from the board."

"I see," Josie said.

"You'll keep the rest of the retainer, of course, and bill me for any expenses you've incurred. That's only right." Josie had nothing to say. She was relieved about the money but pissed off about being fired. "And, Harper, this doesn't have to be good-bye between us. I'd love to meet you for dinner sometime." Josie tried to imagine what that would look like, she and Sarah on a date. She came up blank.

"Maybe I'll run into you sometime," Josie said indifferently. "And thanks for telling me of your decision so we didn't waste any more time." Josie had no intention of stopping her investigation now, but Sarah didn't have to know that.

She pulled into the parking lot of Lauren's building and made straight for her office. She leaned over Eva's desk, looking her straight in the eye. "I need to see Lauren right away. It's extremely important."

Eva must have understood Josie was there to help Lauren, not get something from her.

"Ms. Wade has left for the day. I'm afraid I can't tell you where she's gone."

"Can't or won't?" Josie said.

"Can't. She said she wouldn't be coming back in today." Eva looked a little annoyed, and for once it wasn't at Josie. "She doesn't realize the work I need to do when she disrupts her schedule like that."

"Does she do that a lot?" Josie leaned her hip on the desk and spoke as if they were old mates.

"She has lately. I'm worried about her. If you can do anything to help her, then you have my blessing," Eva said, quite seriously.

Back in her car, Josie twirled down the umpteen levels of parking that would take her back on the street. She was parked in Scotland, level eleven. It was a long way down to the United States at level one, and when she got finally got there she shot onto Madison. She knew where to go. She drove back to Lincoln Park, where Lauren lived on quiet Burling Street, lined with outrageously expensive single-family homes that loomed like cudgels.

She'd found the address by paying for a professional background check, something she'd have to learn to do. Police databases had spoiled her. Lauren's house was among the less ostentatious, but it was on a double-wide lot, with a big extension in the back. Josie didn't want to guess what it was worth. And what did it matter? She was here on the job, not to ponder Lauren's net worth. She pressed on the bell and heard movement inside. She saw Lauren check her out from one of the windows to the side of the castle-sized wooden door. She imagined a soldier opening the door and nodding her into the keep, where servants scuttled about, all in service to the queen. Jesus, where had that come from? She pulled on her jaw as if to reshape her brain and had it back in place by the time Lauren unlocked the dead bolt.

She opened the door and motioned Josie in, as if she weren't at all surprised to see her there. Lauren shut the door quickly behind her. When she turned to look at her, Josie found her expression a jumble. There was frustration, curiosity, and interest. At least that was Josie's observation. Its accuracy was open to question, she knew.

"What are you doing here, Josie?"

Josie met her look with as calm an expression as she could muster, even though the mere proximity of Lauren was doing terrible things to her insides. How had this happened? Physical attraction she was used to, but not this pull she had no defense against. It felt like a whirligig had taken over where her heart used to be. It was fucking uncomfortable. "I thought I should check in with you. There's a lot going on."

Lauren simply nodded and led Josie into the kitchen. "Would you like some coffee?"

"Sure," Josie said. Lauren seemed fine with her being there, which made her happy. Happy? What was that, exactly? When she was in the beginning of mania she felt euphoric. It was the best feeling in the world. But was it happiness? What she felt standing in front of Lauren was different than that revved-up "I can do anything" feeling she now knew was her disease. But she had no time now to tweeze out one feeling from another. She'd go with happy and leave it at that.

"I assume you've talked to Stan Waterman," Lauren said as she started a pot of coffee.

"Stan and I ran into each other near your brother's place. I was there because I'm nearly convinced Tim was Kelly's killer."

"I am also. He's as much as said he did it."

Lauren was leaning against the counter in her big kitchen, the afternoon sun lighting her tired face. She'd changed out of her business suit and into well-worn jeans and a rumpled button-down shirt. She was barefoot and sexy as hell.

Josie stood a few feet from her. "That would have been helpful to know the day I interviewed you about Kelly's murder. But you're not forthcoming about a lot of things."

"I can't afford to be," Lauren said.

"This whole story about Tim keeping your parents hostage and you not able to do anything about it. I wish I'd known that earlier, too."

Lauren smiled at her, as if Josie had just handed her a rose. "Do you think you would have come to my rescue?"

"I know I would've tried." Josie was looking for signs from Lauren there was something more going on. It was ridiculous and selfish, of course, given the two lives at stake, possibly Lauren's life as well, if they didn't rescue John and Helen. The drama of that should have been enough to charge up a conversation between any two people. But she was sure the buzz was something else.

Lauren turned her back on Josie and poured two cups of coffee. Josie could see her hands trembling, not a lot, but enough to be noticeable. She stepped forward and took the mugs to the kitchen table while Lauren brought cream and sugar and watched Josie obliterate her coffee with both.

"I told Stan I'd like you to work with him, if you agree to it. You struck me as very tenacious the first time we met," Lauren said. She drank her coffee and kept her eyes on Josie.

Josie would take "tenacious" as a compliment, though it wasn't the sexiest one she'd ever had. "It turns out your offer is well-timed. I just got fired by my clients."

Lauren looked surprised. "You mean the mysterious client has given up hope?"

Josie hesitated. "I don't know the reason, but I thought you would be glad. I didn't think you were thrilled about me poking around your life. This should be good news for you."

"I wasn't thrilled, that's true. But now anything you have on Tim that I can use as leverage to help free my parents would be welcome. I think he's going to do something soon." Lauren got up and brought the coffeepot over. She looked exhausted enough to drop it and not even notice. Josie took if from her and put it on the table.

"I didn't get any new evidence against him," Josie said. "If Tim had keys to your house, he had access to your gun. I thought his motive could be the resentment he felt about how your parents favored you over him. He told me about it when I interviewed him. Made a point of it. I don't know where he was when Kelly was killed. He didn't give me an alibi."

"No, he wouldn't think that kind of thing applied to him. And yes, he has keys to my house. He insisted."

Josie finished her coffee. "I can't imagine the stress you've been under."

Lauren looked almost amused. "Are you wondering why I'm not more distraught? I am, actually, but you have to remember Tim took them at the beginning of the year. I'm past the hand-wringing stage, but I'm still frightened for them." Lauren continued looking into Josie's eyes. "I don't imagine you've had as strange a homicide case when you were with the police."

Josie returned the gaze. "I never was a homicide detective. I think I had a shot at the promotion, but a bunch of crap happened and I chose to leave the department. It's a long story."

"I'd love to hear it sometime." Lauren smiled. The amusement was replaced with a look that was hard to identify—as if someone was staring at an ordinary object and by doing so began to see all of its interesting properties. Like a bed of moss or a shelf of sedimentary rock. Josie felt she was being intensely examined and a blush started to move up her neck.

Incredibly, she heard herself say, "Maybe when this is all over we can get together for dinner. But now I need to get back with Stan and put our plan in motion."

What she needed was to get away from Lauren. She was aroused and she didn't want it to show in her eyes. But she really wanted to see it in Lauren's. She didn't think she could be wrong that the attraction was mutual, but she'd finally learned to wait a bit before acting on what she thought. That had gotten her into so much trouble before. She stood and Lauren followed her to the door.

"I'm glad you'll be working with Stan. I feel more confident already." They paused at the door and looked at each other silently. "No matter what else happens," Lauren said, "the most important thing is to find my parents. I know you understand that."

"Of course," Josie said. She stepped out the door and turned around. "I—we—won't let you down." She handed Lauren a card. "Here's my cell number. Call me if you need anything. I mean that."

"I know you do. Good-bye, Josie." Lauren gently closed the door and Josie trotted to her car.

Jesus. She was ready for her beer. She headed to Tillie's.

CHAPTER TWENTY-NINE

Josie walked into Tillie's and took a seat in front of the owner, who was tending bar. Tillie was a pre-Stonewall war horse, worn out by activism and content now with looking out for the community that had formed in her bar. She had a mop of gray hair, a sturdy body, and a demeanor that left no doubt who was in charge.

"Hi, Tillie. Been a long time." Josie climbed onto an old bar stool, its back wobbly and the leather worn. "I'll take a draft beer, please."

"I've been here. Where have you been?" Tillie said as she pulled the beer from the tap. She seemed wary, as if knowing that taking that first beer would turn Josie into a totally different person. She'd cut off Josie more than a few times and broken up a few fights, too.

"You think I'll be raising hell again, I can tell," Josie said. "But don't worry. I'm under control these days. One beer a day and that's it."

"Yeah, that's what Lucy told me. She said you were sick for a while but now you're nearly all better." Tillie leaned over the bar to slap her on the shoulder. "I'm glad you're back," she said, before leaving to tend to customers at the end of the bar.

Josie saw red. Jesus H. Christ. What the hell was Lucy doing telling anyone anything about her? That was a deal breaker. She broke up with Lucy in her mind right then. She wasn't even going to tell her they'd broken up. *She'll figure it out.* She felt relief; now she wouldn't have to sort out how she felt about Lucy. No more dates. No more taking things at a glacially slow pace. If her drinking and mania were under control, she didn't need to be with someone as grounded as Lucy. She could branch out a little, have some fun. It wasn't that she wanted to pick anyone up; she simply wanted to know she could if she felt like it. And there was no way she was going to be with someone who gossiped about her.

What she really wanted to do was go back to Lauren and make love to her until she couldn't take any more. Josie could make pleasure last, she was good at that. But it would hardly do for her to seduce her new boss. She should show at least some resistance to it, even though she knew at her core she and Lauren both felt the palpable sexual tension between them. As soon as they had been alone together in her house, Josie could feel the atmosphere change, like walking in a lightning storm when the air seemed to crackle and buzz. She couldn't be making it up.

She sipped her beer and surveyed the room. It was early evening and the bar was filling fast. She saw Ann-Marie and Gabby at one of the tables. Since she was no longer being paid to look for Kelly Moore's killer, whether Gabby was a suspect didn't matter. She had a new job now. She couldn't wait to report for her shift the next morning. She even liked the fact Stan was giving the orders. She knew she had a lot to learn.

Josie looked down the bar and around the room once again, looking for Lucy, with whom she'd just broken up. The whole "who gets the tavern after the breakup" thing worried her. Tillie's was Josie's bar, not Lucy's, for God's sake. She'd fight her hard on that one. Just as she was about to finish her beer and head home, she heard a chair scrape hard across the wooden floor. She turned to see Gabby standing over Ann-Marie, holding on to her upper arm and giving her a good shake until Ann-Marie rose from the table. Gabby kept her vise-like grip on Ann-Marie, who was in obvious discomfort, and pulled her toward the door. Josie didn't think twice before rushing over to help Ann-Marie.

"What the fuck do you think you're doing?" Gabby said. Josie was pulling on her hands trying to free Ann-Marie, but she could tell she wouldn't be able to wrest them away. Gabby was strong, no question, and her fingers were dug so deep into Ann-Marie's thin arm it would take pliers to set her free. Instead, Josie pulled her arm back and punched Gabby square in the face, which hurt her hand like absolute hell. That was more than made up for by seeing Gabby scream in pain as she windmilled backward, crashing into the table of two women drinking chocolate martinis. Gabby was drenched by them, as well as bleeding profusely from her nose.

Josie turned to Ann-Marie. "Do you have your own car here?"

Ann-Marie looked terrified, but she nodded in answer.

"Take your car and go to a friend's house until I call and tell you it's safe to come home."

"But I'm sure she wouldn't harm me," she said, the sobs starting.

"Right. And I'm sure world peace will break out tomorrow." She guided Ann-Marie through the door. "Please do as I say. Quickly."

She saw Ann-Marie leave and turned to watch Gabby struggling to right herself. Blood was still streaming from her nose, but Gabby was tough. She was soon up and barreling straight at Josie. She swung with all she had, a punch Josie barely managed to evade.

"Outside!" Tillie yelled, suddenly right beside them. "Get your asses outside. You know I don't tolerate fighting in my bar!"

Gabby grabbed Josie in a bear hug, pinning her tight as she dragged her out the door Tillie was now holding open.

"I figure you have ten minutes to sort yourselves out before the police come," Tillie said. She shook her head as she walked back in the bar, muttering something about acting like children. Josie had to agree. Breaking Gabby's nose was not something she'd overlook, and Gabby was much more muscular than Josie was. She was a firefighter, Josie a cop. It was well established who was the stronger of the two. Cops were no slouches, but she might be in over her head. As Gabby pulled her onto the sidewalk, Josie saw faces plastered at the windows, eerily illuminated by the neon "Tillie's" sign, eager to watch the fight. There wasn't a single one likely to step out and put a stop to Josie getting her ass kicked.

She started to struggle in Gabby's arms until Gabby suddenly dropped her at her feet. Tillie's was on a quiet street with a small row of commercial properties nestled among brick two- and three-flat buildings. They were all closed for the day. No one was out walking their dog or sharpening their sword or patrolling the neighborhood. No one was there to intervene. Josie wasn't scared, exactly. She simply wanted to avoid getting killed.

"Get up, you coward," Gabby said. She was drunk, same as every time she'd seen her at Tillie's. "Now you're going to pay for messing my face up." Like she was Cate Blanchett or something. No one was going to notice a broken nose on Gabby's face.

Josie managed to get another punch in as she rose from the ground. It was a gut shot and it felt like hitting the heavy bag boxers work out with. It would take about twenty of those stomach punches before Gabby would start to feel it. Gabby moved back and gave them some fighting room, and then came forward with an unexpected left that sent Josie crashing back to the sidewalk. She rolled quickly out of the way when she saw Gabby's boot swing toward her ribs, which pissed Josie off. Fucking firefighters never fought fair. She scrambled to her feet and moved in toward Gabby, who was moving around in a circle. That was when she saw Gabby reach into her leather vest and pull out a switchblade. When she opened the knife it made that *pffft* sound that meant everything was about to go to shit.

"Can we dial this down?" Josie said. "I don't think you want to stab me, do you?"

Josie was circling in counterpoint to Gabby. She considered running away, but she wouldn't give Gabby that satisfaction. They circled around each other like two wrestlers.

"Yeah, I really do," said Gabby, who looked like she'd changed into another person, not unlike the Hulk. Savage, and not necessarily *compos mentis*. "You don't know what I want. You don't know what I can do." She moved in and thrust the knife at Josie, who luckily was more nimble than strong. It was time to put an end to it. She drew the gun holstered at her back and prayed she wouldn't have to use it.

Gabby's eyes fell on the gun. "Now that's cheating,"

"No, it's not. Rock beats scissors." Josie continued walking in the same circle Gabby was, both of her hands wrapped around the Glock. "Don't make me use this, Gabby. All you have to do is put the knife down and we're done. You can beat it before the cops come. They might be a while. I can tell you from experience a fight at a gay bar doesn't have them speeding over with lights and sirens." She saw a flicker of indecision in Gabby's eyes. "So what's it going to be? Are you going to lay the knife down and kick it over to me or am I going to have to shoot you?"

Josie thought Gabby would take some time before deciding how to get out of her fix with the most pride left intact, but as soon as her last word was spoken, Gabby aimed the knife and threw it straight at her. If Josie hadn't turned to her side she'd have a five-inch knife in her gut. Bad news. She swung the gun on Gabby. "Get the hell out of here, now, or I'll shoot you for being a fucking asshole," she said with real disgust. "And if I hear of you hurting Ann-Marie again I'll be back to see you."

Amazingly, Gabby kept coming toward her, toward the barrel of the Glock, putting Josie in the position of possibly shooting an unarmed person. Her training told her no-no. Her thumping heart said yes-yes. When she got within range, Josie flipped the gun in her hand and clubbed Gabby on the side of the head, barely pulling her punch. She really didn't want to kill her. Gabby went down in a heap, yowling.

Josie stood over her. "Now take off, run before the cops come. You have nothing left, Gabby."

Gabby now had blood pouring down her face from a head wound, streaming alongside the blood from her broken nose. She looked like a doomed character in a horror film. She got up and finally turned tail. She disappeared down one of the residential streets, and Josie did the same as she heard the first sirens coming their way. She ran in the opposite direction and stopped running when she reached a tot lot a couple blocks away from Tillie's. What the fuck was that about? She knew Gabby was a hothead, but she saw something lethal in her eyes, and something crazy. She knew she'd have to deal with Gabby at some point, if only to keep Ann-Marie safe. If she were still looking for alternative killers, Gabby would be back to number one on the list.

After enough time had passed for Tillie to get rid of the cops, Josie walked back through the door and returned to her seat at the bar. Tillie came over and glared at her.

"Sorry. But I couldn't let Gabby manhandle Ann-Marie like that. It isn't right."

"No, it isn't right. I'm glad you stepped in, but I had to throw you out anyway. You know how it is." Tillie poured another beer and placed it in front of Josie. "I think you've earned this one."

Josie stared at the beer, seriously considering drinking a second one for the first time since she got out of the hospital. Greta would be livid. She was totally against Josie having even one beer a day. She said it made the meds less effective. Clearly, Greta didn't know everything.

She was picking up the mug of beer when she felt her phone vibrate in the back pocket of her jeans. She pulled it out. The number wasn't recognizable, but Josie had no doubt who it was and her heart began to thump, more than it had when she was being threatened with a knife minutes before. The text simply said, "Get back here."

❖

Lauren flung the door open immediately after it rang. She wasn't interested in being coy. She wanted Josie as soon as possible. Josie stood on the doorstep, a little rumpled, her cheeks flushed, her eyes searching Lauren's for a signal. Without speaking, Lauren reached out for Josie's arm and pulled her into the house, kicking the door shut as she put her arms around Josie's neck. Josie turned and pushed Lauren against the door and kissed her for all she was worth. Lauren felt invaded by the kiss, filled by it, breathless from it. She broke the contact and stared into Josie's somewhat dazed eyes.

"So you've done this before?" Lauren said, smiling.

"Once or twice."

"Kissed a girl for the first time like that?"

Josie hesitated. "Sure. But I don't remember it ever feeling this way."

"What way?" Lauren was teasing her, hooking her fingers through Josie's belt loops and pulling her closer.

"Like I want to rip your clothes off."

Lauren saw the pure desire in Josie's eyes. "What are you waiting for, then?" She'd changed into a tunic length T-shirt and slim stretch pants after she'd called Josie, wanting the minimum of fumbling. She'd imagined the scene almost exactly as it was playing out.

Josie kissed her again as intensely, before pulling Lauren's shirt over her head and pushing her pants down to her ankles. Lauren kicked them away. She stood naked against the door and watched as Josie looked at her from an arm's length away.

"You're beautiful," Josie whispered.

Lauren didn't say a word. Standing before her, fully clothed, Josie was gorgeous. Her hair was wildly swirling around her head from Lauren gripping and tugging and running her fingers through it. Her lips looked plumper, pinker than before the bruising kisses. Lauren crooked her finger and summoned Josie, who did not need much direction.

"Don't mess around," Lauren said, pushing Josie to her knees. Josie kissed an inner thigh as she placed Lauren's leg over her shoulder. That was the end of the teasing kisses. Josie brought her mouth to her and hit the exact right spot with her tongue on the first try, making Lauren squirm and moan above her. Lauren gripped the door frame, trying to keep herself upright as Josie devoured her. She tried to hold out, but she'd been speeding toward orgasm from the moment she opened her door. There was no holding it at bay now. She gripped Josie's head and screamed her bloody head off. Before she went completely limp, she felt Josie's arm come around her waist to support her.

Lauren's head still rested against the door and she took some time to recover before opening her eyes and looking at Josie. "Upstairs," she said.

Josie took her hand and led her up the old banistered stairway, both of them weaving slightly as if they were drunk. Lauren pointed toward her bedroom, where they shut themselves away for the night. Everything had played out as she'd imagined, but she hadn't anticipated her emotional reaction to it. She'd never been as aroused before, not with Kelly or any other woman. All of her past lovers had been beautiful—this wasn't simply a physical reaction. She'd been expecting something like her experience with Cory—light, fun, and very satisfying. But her reaction to Josie was so far beyond that.

Love was not something she needed right now.

Holy shit. Josie lay on her stomach, trying to recover. She'd just had six orgasms. Six. That was about six more than she normally had with her sex partners. She'd blamed that on her drinking. She'd been numb from the waist down for a long time. She never suspected it might have to do with her disconnection from the women she was fucking. She felt foolish to discover what sex could be at her age, but it was a stunning revelation. She felt she could go on all day and into the night and never come up for air.

She rolled onto her back and drew Lauren over her, like a blanket. Their slack bodies molded to each other's curves like one of those foam mattresses she'd tried out at the store. Shockingly expensive. She was surprised Lauren didn't have one. The room they were in was large and luxurious. She'd visited the master bath once and was rendered mute. The shower was on the other side of the room from the bathtub, not in the bathtub. The toilet was closed off in its own little room. It had a control pad installed next to the toilet with icons of people sitting on the can. Water was shooting at their privates from a variety of angles. Your choice. Josie was completely bewildered. Everything was complicated when it came to Lauren, even her toilet.

The solid but relaxed way they were now cleaved together felt better than any postcoital feeling she'd ever had. Of course, six orgasms would account for much of that, but it was her openness to Lauren that allowed those orgasms to happen. The way Lauren gave herself to Josie, the way she was so immodest and wild, so accepting. It was glorious and probably disastrous.

"Do you think we've had enough for one night?" Lauren whispered. She lay on top of Josie with the slack weight of a sleeping baby.

Josie looked at the nightstand clock. It was four in the morning and she had to report for her shift at eight. For the first time in a week she felt she could sleep a whole night.

"Possibly not," Josie said, rubbing Lauren's back. "But I think it's all I can do. You practically killed me."

Lauren raised her head and smiled smugly. "I'll take that as a compliment."

"It was. You have exceptional gifts," Josie said.

Josie kissed the top of Lauren's head and instantly went to sleep.

CHAPTER THIRTY

Thursday, September 12

It was seven in the morning and Josie was trying to get out of Lauren's house and to a coffee shop before her shift. Lauren kept dragging her back into bed. Josie squirmed around to face her, seeing the glint in Lauren's eyes, the satisfied look on her face.

"You look like you've been well and truly laid," Josie said. She might have to work on her romantic lines, not having had much practice with them.

Lauren smiled, and then yawned and drew Josie even closer. "Like I've never been before. I want to fall back asleep, but I'm afraid if I do you'll skedaddle out of here."

Josie leaned on an elbow and traced a line down Lauren's jaw. "Well, boss. If you remember, I'm on a team trying to track down your parents. Don't you think it's a good idea to let me go?"

Lauren looked contrite. "Of course. Maybe sex like that is the only thing that keeps them from my mind." She looked teasingly at Josie. "Perhaps I've hired you for the wrong job."

Josie looked down at her. She knew she was teasing, but she also knew how desperate Lauren was to lessen the pressure she'd been under for months. She was warm and pliable now. It must feel like heaven. Josie could relate. She felt slack also, as if her legs wouldn't hold her up once she stood. She was used to bounding out of the bed of whoever she'd just had sex with and escaping as quickly as possible. Reluctantly, she extricated herself from Lauren and slid out of the giant bed.

"I really have to go. I have to meet Stan in an hour and I still have coffee to get for the crew. He'll be pissed if I'm late," Josie said.

Lauren watched as Josie put on her clothes. She looked regretful. "This won't be the last time for us," she said. This was a declaration, not a question. She was out of bed, wrapping a green silk robe around her. It clung to her body and Josie couldn't take her eyes off her.

"No, not the last time," Josie said. "But first things first. I'm heading out to find your parents. That's the priority."

Josie led the way downstairs. They kissed good-bye before Lauren closed the door on her. She climbed into her car, her mind as jumbled as her body was relaxed. Did she just spend the night with Lauren? It barely felt real.

❖

Josie made a quick run home to change clothes, take her meds, and stop at Kopi for coffee. Two extra-large cups went into her thermos, and she added a few to-go cups for the others on duty at Tim's. She wore her comfiest jeans and a few layers of shirts. The September weather was starting to feel cooler, but sitting in a car in the sun could be hot. There was really nothing comfortable about doing surveillance.

As she turned from the counter to leave the coffee shop, Lucy walked in. Josie felt a mixture of annoyance and guilt. She wanted to feel as if she'd been wronged, but she knew she was about to be a gigantic ass. Lucy beamed a smile and walked straight toward her.

"Finally!" she said. "I thought you'd been swallowed whole by this case you're working on." Lucy was dressed in slim trousers and a green button-down shirt with a rakish scarf around her neck. She looked fantastic. Still, Josie stiffened as she remembered Lucy had gossiped about her.

"Good morning," Josie said. She was holding her thermos and a cardboard tray as she tried to take a step around Lucy.

Lucy frowned. "What's going on? You're acting like I have the plague."

"Sorry," Josie said, as she got through the door and onto Clark Street. The air was brisk, but the sun shone brightly in that peculiar way it does in September, the blues almost as bright as the sun itself. Josie slipped her sunglasses down from the top of her head. Lucy was right behind her and touched Josie's elbow to get her to stop. Josie kept walking toward her car, which was parked in front of Cas Hardware, a derelict mom-and-pop hardware store wedged between a Homemade Pizza and a do-it-yourself yogurt shop. Ancient merchandise slid into a pool in the front window of the shop. It felt sad. Josie worried about small businesses. She felt bad for the owners when they were forced out of business. Their dreams had been somehow short-circuited, something Josie related to.

Lucy strode beside her, looking at Josie's stony face. "Josie, aren't you the woman I slept with a couple nights ago? What's happened? Have I done something you're upset about?"

Lucy seemed confident enough to hear what she had to say, unlike Josie, who would never ask that question for fear of what the answer might be. She stopped at her car and put the coffee on the roof to unlock the door. She actually had to insert a key and turn it. There were no fobs involved.

"There's one thing I can't stand, Lucy, and that's gossip about me. I was at Tillie's last night and Tillie told me you'd been talking to her about my illness. As far as I'm concerned, we're done."

Lucy looked stunned. And then indignant. "Had it ever occurred to you to ask me about this before you decided to break things off? One thing I can't stand is a unilateral decision on what happens in a relationship. We hardly know each other yet, but still I think I'm owed that courtesy."

Josie looked at her across the roof of the car, trying to disguise her dismay. Lucy was right. She set the coffees carefully on the front seat and turned back to her. "Are you saying you didn't talk to Tillie about me?"

"Not in the way you think," Lucy said. "Tillie said she'd heard you were back in the bar and chatting me up. She wanted to know where you've been for so long, especially since you used to practically live there. I simply replied you'd been ill and hadn't been out much the last few months. She asked me what you were sick from and I told her I had no idea. Is that what you're breaking up with me about?"

Josie hesitated. She probably would have easily relented to Lucy's very reasonable explanation, but now there was Lauren to consider. Why were lesbians so awful about seeing more than one person at a time? She couldn't see trying to keep up both budding relationships, especially with two such different people. All she could manage was a shrug. "I'm sorry, Lucy. I'm sure you didn't mean anything by it, but I still think an 'I don't know' would have been a better answer to Tillie's question." She got in her car and rolled the passenger window down, leaning over to talk to Lucy. "It changed the way I feel about you. That's undoubtedly more about me than you."

She rolled the window up quickly as she saw Lucy's mouth open in further protest. As Josie drove away, feeling like a complete asshole, she watched in the rearview mirror as Lucy stared after her. What a fucking cad she was. She liked Lucy a lot, but she loved the spark between her and Lauren. It was like a drug. Lucy was like treatment. Right now, Josie chose the drug.

She drove down Lake Shore Drive to get to Lincoln Park as quickly as possible, passing the lagoon with the early morning rowers out, and then west on Fullerton and south on Stockton to drive through the heart of the park itself, where the zoo was spread across the greenery and she could hear a lion roar. She drove on another minute and pulled up at the end of Tim's street just as her phone rang.

"Good morning, Stan."

"You're barely on time." He didn't sound happy.

"True. But I brought coffee for everyone," Josie said.

"Park on Hudson and bring it to the observation post. You're on duty up here today." He hung up. That was very good news. Sitting in a car was becoming almost intolerable for her, her need to move around had become so great. Plus, she felt slightly aroused every time she thought about her night with Lauren. Sitting still would only double the torture. She made her way to Hudson and squeezed into a parking space. Then she walked to the alley that took her behind Tim's house and climbed the stairs to the garage apartment Tommy had rented the day before. Tommy answered her knock, a two-day growth of beard on his face and slight rings around his eyes where they'd been glued to a set of binoculars. She hadn't met Tommy before and they sized each other up. They knew each had left the police department in less-than-ideal circumstances, which gave them a natural bond, of sorts. Josie was relieved to see he was doing his job while on duty, and when he showed her the hourly log he'd drawn up, she liked him all the more.

"Where's Stan?" she asked.

"He ran off right after he called you. There's been nothing to report

since one in the morning. Tim moved from the coach house to the main
house, where our man in the car out front was on watch."

"Who did we have in the car?" Josie said.

"That would be Nigel," Tommy said.

"Nigel? What, is he with MI5?" Josie moved over to the window
and picked up the binoculars from the table placed next to the chair. "Is
he English?"

"No," Tommy said. "Well, English-American, I guess. He has
passports for both. He talks like an American, though."

"Where'd Stan find him?" She turned briefly to Tommy, who
was yawning and putting on his jacket. He stuffed his iPhone and
headphones in his pocket.

"I think Nigel was a sheriff's detective. He got demoted from
detective to patrol, so he quit."

"We're like a team of misfit cops," Josie said. She liked the idea.

"True. Anyway, Nigel relieves you at 1800. Stan's set up some
ten-hour rotations as he recruits a few more guys." Josie looked up. "Or
girls. Women." Tommy winced.

"So no movement in the coach house or the garage since you've
been here?"

"He took the garbage into the alley at one, after he locked up the
coach house. It's in the log."

"Why don't you walk by his garbage can on your way out and take
the top bag out. Maybe we'll find something useful."

Tommy looked doubtful. "Don't you think it's possible he might
see me and we'll blow the whole thing?"

Josie was already calling Stan. He was parked on Cleveland in a
panel van for a basement sealing company. "Anything going on?" he
answered.

"Nothing. I had an idea."

"God save us all," Stan said.

"Shut up, Stan," Josie said firmly. "You sound like my dad."

Stan paused and then said, "You're right. Sorry. What's the
idea?"

"Tommy says Tim took his garbage out at 0100 and the lights in
the back of the house went out shortly after. When did the lights go out
in front?"

"Let me look." Josie could hear Stan rummaging around for

something. "Nigel's log says at about three in the morning. The guy's a night owl."

"Right," Josie said excitedly. "I thought it'd be a good idea for Tommy to grab the top bag in Tim's garbage can. It's early yet for someone up that late, and I don't see any lights in the kitchen. He's asleep for sure."

"Do it. I'll drive to the end of the alley and take it from him."

"Cool," Josie said and disconnected. She turned to Tommy. "Get going, Dumpster Dan. Grab the top bag and deliver it to Stan. He's coming around to the end of the alley to pick it up from you."

Tommy didn't look happy, but he did as told and soon had the white garbage bag in hand, walking casually toward the panel truck that appeared at the T of the alley. He tossed it in the back of the truck and then walked the other way. You'd think they were on a CIA mission.

Josie set herself up to watch the coach house. She had a clear view of the gangway and the stairs leading up to the second floor. She could also see most of the back of the house and all of the yard. With her binoculars she could see more detail in the kitchen and family room, but unfortunately they did not penetrate the dark covering on the coach house windows. Still, they had good coverage of Tim's property. The problem was Tim didn't seem to go out much.

Having nothing active to do was dangerous in her increasingly ramped-up state. She couldn't think of anything to take the edge off. Alcohol, certainly, but that had miraculously lost its appeal. Her body craved to move, to siphon off the great amount of energy she had. There was no correlation between how little sleep she got and how buzzed she felt. She'd made sure she took all her medication that morning, but missing those few days seemed to have fucked her up.

She shot up from the chair and started pacing and daydreaming, mostly about the incredible sex of the night before. And Lauren. She hadn't been able to focus on the experience with Lucy, who had the unenviable task of satisfying someone who wasn't fully present. Her gentleness fed Josie's impatience. Lauren, though, wasn't particularly nice in bed. She was aggressive and demanded satisfaction in a way that had Josie jumping to pleasure her. She'd been so excited Lauren barely touched her before she'd exploded. She didn't think her therapist would choose Lauren as the person to teach Josie what love was. But what did Greta know? If the sex was that good, it had to be love.

All of this was flying through her head as she returned to her post. She'd been gone for less than a minute. She saw Tim's garage door closing and the Jeep nearly to the end of the alley. "Fuck!" Josie yelled and dived for her phone. Stan picked up at first ring.

"Subject's on the move," Josie said. "He turned right toward Hudson."

"Turned? You mean he's already on his way?"

"Yeah. He's in the Jeep, probably headed toward the Drive."

"Goddammit, Josie." She could hear him take a big breath. "We'll be lucky to pick him up." Josie could hear him put the old van in gear as he pursued. "Nigel and Tommy might still be in the area. I'll let them know my position." He disconnected.

Josie let the phone dangle from her hand, her head dropped. This was not like a reprimand from her father, which she'd learned to ignore because it was usually bullshit. This was like being dressed down by your favorite uncle, the one who was always nice and made you feel special and taught you to do unusual things, like shoot a bow and arrow or fly a radio-controlled airplane. She didn't have an uncle like that, but Stan was as close to one as you could get. They'd lost touch over the years as Josie grew up and her relationship with her father became more strained. When she was young, she always wanted to impress him, to feel favored by him. And now she looked like a complete fuckup in his eyes. Tommy must look like Sam Spade in comparison. Well, hell. She'd only been away from the window for a minute. What if she'd gone to the bathroom and missed something? Should she feel guilty then? You can't expect eyes on the subject at all times.

She picked up when Stan called ten minutes later.

"I have him," Stan said. "It looks like he's headed into the Loop, so I don't think we need to call in the troops. Not yet, anyway."

"Is he headed toward Lauren's building?"

"Hold on," he said. A couple of minutes went by. "Looks like he's going into a garage a block away from her building. I'm going to find a place to perch and keep watch. Maybe I can follow him on foot. Goddamned parking in the Loop. If I were still a cop I could pull up in front of the mayor's office and no one would say a word. I'll report back."

Josie caught him before he could hang up. "Stan, I'm sorry I messed up. He left just as I turned my head for something. That's all

I can figure." She wasn't ready to be honest enough to say she was pacing and thinking of sex. It scared her too much. "I'm really sorry," she said contritely.

Stan sighed. "Don't worry about it, kid. This is why most surveillance teams have two sets of eyes from every position. We're not robots. Keep watch for him coming back in case I lose him. If I do lose him, I'm going to go into the garage and put a tracker on his Jeep."

He rang off and Josie sank into a chair with relief. She reached for a Klonopin, hoping that calming her hyper state would keep her more vigilant. She wanted to be perfect.

Stan called twenty minutes later. "He went in to the garage, but he hasn't come out."

"Does the garage have a couple of exits?"

"No, only the one onto Madison," he said. "And Tim Wade has not walked out of it. I'm kind of hovering across the street in a tow zone. Unless he's dressed in costume, I haven't seen the man walk out of there."

"A costume is not out of the question with him," Josie said.

"I'll stay here awhile longer, but keep your eyes peeled for him coming back."

"Copy that," Josie said, feeling strangely like she was in a cop movie and not, in fact, dealing with a real lunatic. She dialed Lauren at her office and was eventually put through by Eva.

"I thought you were on guard duty, or whatever you call it," Lauren said with a teasing tone. "Are you allowed to talk?"

"Only if it's about sex," Josie said.

Lauren laughed. "Then we're in good shape. That's all that's on my mind."

Josie paused. She was ready to have phone sex. The sound of Lauren's low voice got her going. But she shook it off and got serious. "Tim's on the move. I want you to get some of your security guards posted close to your office and on the lookout for him."

"Where's Tim now?"

"He's somewhere near your office. He went into a parking garage on Madison and we haven't seen him exit. Stay alert, okay?" Josie said. "I think he's crazy and I think he's after you."

"It won't be the first time. He's been coming after me since I was a kid," Lauren said.

"You know what I mean. This is serious. I think he's certifiable."

Lauren put her on hold for a minute. "There, I've put two gigantic security men in my outer office. Eva will love it. Now can we talk about last night?"

"Is your door closed?" Josie asked.

"Closed and locked."

Josie made herself comfortable in front of the window and kept her eyes on Tim's garage, the coach house, the alley. "By all means," she said. "Let's talk about last night."

CHAPTER THIRTY-ONE

Tim didn't show up at the office. Lauren was mildly distracted wondering what he was up to, and thoroughly distracted thinking of her night with Josie. She decided to take the unusually spontaneous step of surprising Josie during her shift at the observation post. It was late in the afternoon and Josie would be getting off work soon. She found the address Stan had given her when he rented the apartment and she set off on foot down the alley to the entrance. She drew up the hood of her jacket as she neared Tim's coach house and trotted up the stairs to the garage flat across the alley. The look on Josie's face when she opened the door to her knock was almost amusing. She flashed surprise, happiness, and suspicion, one after another, like a fast-moving slide show.

"I don't know what you're planning," Josie said, waving Lauren in, "but we're not doing it here."

Josie went back to the window overlooking Tim's and peered out. She seemed satisfied with what she saw and glanced over her shoulder at Lauren. "What are you doing here? This isn't a good idea." Josie seemed stern. Her hair was held back by a red bandana to keep it out of her eyes. She looked like she worked in a food co-op.

"Since you called me every half hour, you know Tim didn't come to my office," Lauren said. "Any idea what he was doing?" Her tone was businesslike, but a smile twitched at the side of her mouth.

"None," Josie said. "Stan couldn't find Tim to follow him, not until he pulled out of a parking garage a couple of hours after he entered it." Josie looked at Lauren. "So what are you doing here?"

Lauren looked around the darkened room. "What do you think?" she said. "All I can think about is last night." She moved closer to Josie, backing her toward the window.

Josie reached out and took her hand. "You look beautiful. Lighter somehow."

"I'll attribute that to the amazing sex. It took my mind off everything. Maybe it erased a wrinkle or two." Lauren grinned. They sat on the folding chairs in front of the window.

"Don't get anything in mind," Josie said. "I'm working here and it's important."

"Of course," Lauren said, smiling.

An orange crate sat between them. It was littered with binoculars, empty coffee cups, and fast food wrappers. "I refuse to pick up after these boys," Josie said. "Though I may cave in any time. It's a health hazard here."

Lauren turned to face Josie. She had ideas on how to fill the time before the end of the shift, despite Josie's warning.

"I can't look at you." Josie said. She picked up the binoculars and stared at the coach house.

"Hmm. More opportunity to study you." Lauren took Josie's left hand and cradled it.

Josie held on to the binoculars with her right hand and threaded the fingers of her left through Lauren's. "You should probably know something if we're going to see more of each other."

Lauren looked at her sharply. "Is there someone else? Of course there probably is. How foolish of me." She sat up and pulled her hand from Josie's. She stared straight ahead, trying to calm her whirling brain. She and Josie had been together one day. One night of sex, which could easily mean nothing, but she'd hoped Josie felt there was something. It had been so long since she'd felt so fine.

Josie reached for her arm. "Hold on. You're going down the wrong road here. I was seeing someone recently, but that's ended."

Lauren relaxed a little. "What could you need to tell me, then?"

Josie turned back to the window. "I have an illness," she said. She was nearly whispering. "My doctor says it's something I'll have to deal with the rest of my life. I think it's a good idea to tell you in case it changes your mind about seeing me."

"I can't imagine you have anything that would keep me from wanting to see you, with the possible exception of leprosy." She gently turned Josie's head to look at her and tried out a grin.

"It may be worse than leprosy. I'm bipolar. I went off the rails with it last year and had to be hospitalized." She took a deep breath. "Now you know the worst thing about me."

"If that's the worst thing about you, you're a saint compared to most of the people I know," Lauren said.

"I'm no saint, that's for sure. I'm afraid I racked up quite a reputation while I was at my most manic. You should know if we're going to be seen together. People have long memories."

Lauren reached into her large tote bag and pulled out a bottle of wine and two plastic glasses. She took a corkscrew to the bottle and had it opened in a moment. "Let's drink to the fact you're not seeing someone else. Your illness doesn't worry me."

"I'm not drinking," Josie said, as Lauren tried to hand her a glass. "One beer a day, that's the limit. I'm also supposed to sleep the same hours every night, eat meals at the same time every day, exercise like I'm training for a marathon, and generally do everything I've never done."

Lauren brought the glass to her lips. "Are you saying this to scare me off?"

Josie smiled. "No. For that I save the big guns. Like the fact I make my condition worse each time I have a manic episode. Or how the depressions that follow the mania are even worse. I can't function at all. Then there's how I act when I'm manic—sleeping around, buying shit I don't need, talking your ear off. The list goes on." Josie met Lauren's eyes. "How am I doing scaring you off?"

"You're failing miserably." She put her glass down and kissed Josie slowly, not with the passion of the night before, but reassuringly, lovingly. She kissed her again and heard Josie's breath catch. The sweet kiss quickly became heated until Josie moaned and broke away, her eyes returning to the view on Tim's coach house.

"I can't do this. I'm on the job, remember? Tim, your parents?"

Lauren sat up straight. "Of course," she said, straightening her jacket. "You make my thinking fuzzy." She saw Josie grin as she put the binoculars to her eyes.

"It's okay if you stay," Josie said. "But I have to stay alert."

Lauren hesitated only a moment before sliding gracefully to the floor and between Josie's legs. Josie lowered the binoculars.

"Keep your eyes forward," Lauren said. "I wouldn't want you to miss anything." Her hand reached for Josie's belt.

"You can't." Josie grabbed Lauren's hand, which was busy unzipping her fly. Lauren looked up at her and saw only desire. Her resistance was purely for show. She moved Josie's hand away and yanked at the top of her jeans.

"Lift up your butt." Josie complied, her eyes on Lauren. "And keep your eyes on the target." Lauren drew the pants down until they pooled around Josie's ankles. She pulled off a tennis shoe and freed one leg from constraint, spreading her thighs.

Josie moaned again as Lauren's tongue traced one thigh and then the other, skipping right over where she wanted it most. She peeked and saw Josie with her head back, her eyes closed. She smiled and brought her mouth to Josie, who cried out and bucked against the flimsy chair.

"Oh, God," Josie gasped. Lauren dispensed with any lingering exploration and quickly brought Josie to the brink. She could see her straining against the back of the chair, her eyes squeezed shut.

"Josie, look out the window."

Josie said something incomprehensibly guttural and opened her eyes. Looking dazed, she tried to lean forward and peer out the window and have an orgasm all at the same time.

"Fuck!" Josie shot to her feet and reached for her pants.

"What is it?" Lauren said. She was sprawled on the floor.

"Tim's on the move."

CHAPTER THIRTY-TWO

Josie scrambled to pull up her pants and grab her jacket and bag. She'd installed an app on her iPad to track Tim's car after Stan got a tracker placed. She threw it into her bag, all traces of arousal gone. This was what she'd been waiting for; the action, the chance to prove herself. She felt focused and on fire.

"You can see yourself out," Josie said to Lauren, who was standing in the middle of the room, perfectly composed.

"Not so fast," Lauren said. "Do you think Tim's on his way to his hideaway?"

"It's possible, but I don't know. This is how we find out." Josie opened the door.

"Let's go, then. I'm coming with."

"Absolutely not. It might be dangerous." She certainly hoped it would be. She left the room and trotted down the stairs, pausing at the bottom to take out her gun and check the magazine, as if there was going to be a shootout in the alley.

Lauren ran down the stairs behind her. "I'm coming with. We can take the Lexus."

"We can't take the Lexus. And you're not coming with."

"Why can't we take my car?" Lauren asked.

She followed Josie into the alley. Tim's Jeep had already disappeared. Josie was moving fast, not caring if Lauren kept up.

"We can't take your Lexus because your brother knows the car and we're more likely to be spotted."

"Of course. I hadn't thought about that." They turned the corner onto the street. "What kind of car do you drive?"

Josie tried to remember what shape her car was in. Last year it would likely have underwear and empties strewn about, but those days seemed to be over. She stopped outside her car and looked at Lauren.

"It's right here." Josie unlocked the passenger door of the Corolla and threw fast food bags off the passenger seat.

Lauren looked surprised at the car, as if Josie should have been driving an Aston Martin.

"You really can't come, and I have no time to argue about it," Josie said, knowing she'd already lost the argument.

Lauren climbed into the car as Josie got into her seat. "Then let's go. I'm paying the bills, I decide whether to go or not."

Josie rubbed her face briskly. Things were feeling a little twirly in her head, with too many thoughts rushing forward. It didn't help she'd been three seconds away from orgasm not five minutes before. She felt like she could literally jump out of her skin.

"This car is nondescript. Perfect for following someone," she said.

"I stand corrected," Lauren said. Josie thought she detected a brief smile before Lauren looked politely at her.

Josie frowned when she pulled her cell phone and iPad out of her bag. "Why the hell didn't my phone ring? I've got two messages on it." She listened to the first before starting the car and pulling out into traffic. "Fucking Nigel."

"What do you mean?" Lauren said. Josie was keeping one eye on the road while punching something up on the iPad.

"Nigel's in the car that was parked in front. He relieved Stan midday. Now he's behind Tim. I'm going to pull him off." A map displayed on the tablet showed Tim's car. It was stationary. "Looks like Tim's pulled into the 7-Eleven on Clybourn."

"Why would you call him back? Isn't he doing what he's supposed to?"

Josie hesitated. Nigel was doing what he was supposed to be doing, but he wasn't doing what Josie wanted him to be doing. She hadn't called him from the observation post when Tim pulled out of his garage, so he must have seen him leave on his computer. She hoped he hadn't yet called Stan.

"I need to take the lead on this," she said, looking squarely at Lauren before turning back to the road. "And I need for you to be behind me. I'm concerned what will happen if multiple cars show up where Tim's holding your parents. It's better for him to form up with Stan and we decide how to proceed."

Lauren looked at her skeptically. "Doesn't it make sense to have more people there? What if Tim goes berserk?"

"We don't even know he's going to where your parents are. He might be picking up beer and some nachos for another night at the coach house. Can I count on you?"

Lauren nodded. Josie stabbed at her phone.

"Nigel. It's Harper. Where are you?"

"Parked behind the subject at the 7-Eleven." Nigel had a high, squeaky voice that annoyed the hell out of her. She'd met him briefly earlier in the day. He was sturdy, almost plump, with a five o'clock shadow at noon. The squeaky voice seemed to come from a ventriloquist.

"Good job," Josie said. "I'm a couple of blocks away and have him up on the computer."

"I have him on the pad as well." Nigel sounded a little defensive.

"Yeah? Well, I need you to head back to the post. I'll get Stan and Tommy there and Stan can tell you what to do. We need to organize this, Nigel. I'll stay on him until I hear from Stan."

"That doesn't sound right," he said.

Josie became impatient. "Doing what I say is what sounds right. Plus, I've got the client here with me." Lauren gave her a regal smile and nod.

Nigel hesitated before saying, "Okay. But if he's headed out of town, don't do anything stupid. I'll call Stan now."

"You do that, buddy. Harper out."

Lauren raised an eyebrow. "Harper out?"

"That's the way we talk." Lauren seemed determined to keep irritating her. It seemed she was damned good at it. "Get used to it."

Josie was coming up on Tim's location when she saw his Jeep pull out of the 7-Eleven and drive north. She fell back so there were at least two cars between them.

"I think he's headed out of town," Lauren said.

"Has he been strange like this his whole life?" Josie had

compassion for Lauren because of her own fucked-up family. But as bad as her father was, Tim Wade was worse.

"He made my life hell when I was young," Lauren said, still staring out her window. "But his behavior never reached this level of crazy. Putting me through the paces with all those embarrassing assignments was very much his style. But kidnapping? Cutting off my father's finger? I've never seen him like this."

Josie stayed on Tim as he headed north on Clybourn and turned toward the expressway entrance on Fullerton. She watched with one eye as the tracker fed his location to her pad.

"This might be it," Josie said, her voice tinged with excitement. "I think he's getting on the Kennedy."

"Shouldn't you call Stan?" Lauren asked.

Josie's phone rang as Lauren spoke. It was Stan. She wondered how much trouble Nigel was in. Or her, for that matter.

"Harper, what the fuck are you doing? You're like your old man with this Lone Wolf crap."

"I'm on the tail of our subject, Stan. I'd call that doing my job. And it's a good thing I am. It looks like he's headed out of the city."

"Fuck me," Stan said. He sounded stressed again. She hoped he wasn't going to have a heart attack. "Okay, we're on our way. Nigel's fifteen minutes behind you, instead of ahead of you like he should have been. I'm coming from home, Tommy was sound asleep. He'll bring up the rear."

Stan disconnected. Comparing her to her father was a low blow. They should be thankful she was on the job. She tried to focus on tracking Tim, but she didn't feel entirely in control of her emotions. But who cared? She had people to save. This was what she lived for.

She glanced down at the tracker and saw Tim entering the expressway. She felt another pump of adrenaline enter her system. She picked up her pace as she followed him onto the ramp, less concerned he'd notice her in the sea of cars on the Kennedy. He crossed over to the left lanes to stay on the interstate going northwest, headed toward the airport.

"Do you have any guesses as to where he might be headed?" Josie asked. "He could be going to rural Illinois, maybe up to Wisconsin."

Lauren turned to her. "No, we don't have any special family spots in the Midwest. Our vacations mostly consisted of me and Tim being sent to expensive camps while my parents snuck away on their own. They were inseparable."

Josie looked at her perfectly composed face. She felt hypersensitive, as if she could feel everything around her; the straining engine, the wind whistling through a gap in her window, her own undiluted energy and racing thoughts. It was visceral. Lauren kept her thoughts to herself, but Josie was about to explode. She couldn't not talk.

"Are you okay?" she said, taking Lauren's hand and giving it a squeeze. "I know you want this over with. We'll take care of it, I promise you." Lauren didn't respond, but Josie hardly paused before her compressed thoughts came tumbling out.

"You've got a great team working for you. I thought Tommy and Nigel were wimps, but they're not. I shouldn't assume anything about anyone. You, for example. A person might think you were a bit uptight and reserved until they got to know you better. Then they'd see what I see—a beautiful, sensuous woman who is anything but reserved."

Lauren looked at her sideways, a puzzled look on her face.

"And me. I know a lot of people think I'm deranged because of the way I acted last fall. But I'm not insane, I'm ill. That's what my doctor keeps saying, anyway. You should meet her sometime. Her name's Greta and she's like a grandmother with an Austrian accent, very nice and nurturing until *bang!* She hits me over the head with something that makes me cry. Did I just say that out loud? I don't like to cry. As a general rule I'm against crying, though I know a lot of people are all for it. For me it's a nuisance. I think crying is highly overrated."

Josie was hunched over the steering wheel. She paused for the briefest of moments.

"I see Greta twice a week because my illness needs to be 'managed,' a term I really hate. There's about a hundred things I'm supposed to be doing at all times to manage it. It's impossible to keep up."

"You're not doing any of them, are you?" Lauren said.

"Not true! I'm in good shape. My thinking's sharp, my energy strong." She looked at Lauren, who was staring out the window again. "I can see you're worried. That's why I didn't want you to come. I mean, it might be dangerous, sure, but all the anticipation, the worry, that's the hard part. I remember once when I was on the gang squad, before I made detective, and we were staked out waiting for a big drug deal to happen on the West Side. There was all kinds of backup in place, but I was getting sick with worry about how I would perform. Once the thing itself happened, I slipped into automatic pilot and did what I was trained to do. But you're not trained, which is why you'll be staying in the car, no argument."

Lauren turned and gave her a thin smile before turning back to the passenger window. Josie looked at a passing mileage sign. "We're headed toward Rockford. I'm surprised your brother took them out this far. I thought he had them in some nondescript 'burb. My dad's very thorough and he's not a nice guy either. But I have to say, he hasn't kidnapped or maimed anyone, at least to my knowledge. He's a run-of-the mill racist, narrow-minded, homophobic bastard. A cop's cop. I can't believe I used to look up to him, that I followed him into law enforcement. Though truth be told, I never wanted to do anything else. I still don't. Having to leave the department was the worst thing that ever happened to me."

Josie continued to talk until Lauren finally told her to shut up. She bounced in her seat instead. They'd long since cleared city traffic and fallen back, keeping a close eye on the tracker. Stan periodically checked in. They were in western Illinois, where the flat Midwestern land gave way to rolling hills, dairy farms, and more cornfields. When they pulled off the interstate onto State Highway 20, Stan called again.

"Josie, we're two-lane now. You have to fall back farther."

"Copy that. How far back are you?"

"Ten to fifteen minutes. Use caution if he turns into a driveway or dirt road or whatever. Drive by and then circle back. If the tracker says he's stopped, hold your position until we arrive."

"Acknowledged." Josie disconnected and glanced at the tracker. Tim was a steady hundred yards ahead of her, his car lights occasionally visible as they traveled the twisting roads and surprisingly steep hills. It was fully dark out. She was going out of her mind sitting in the car.

"Looks like he's turned off 20," Lauren said.

Josie could see he'd turned onto a county road. She stayed far back as she followed him.

Josie handed the iPad to Lauren. "Keep on eye on this and tell me if he turns or stops."

"What, do you think I'd keep that information to myself?" Lauren asked. She seemed a bit insulted.

"Don't be sensitive." Josie said. "We don't have time for sensitive." She put her foot harder on the accelerator.

Lauren appeared pensive. "Did I tell you Tim was arrested for animal cruelty when he was a kid? It's such a classic marker for a disturbed personality, but my parents refused to see it."

Josie looked at Lauren. She couldn't sense any resentment or anger.

"Didn't your parents do anything about Tim beating you?"

Lauren's cocked her head to one side. "Did I say he beat me? That makes it sound like a chronic thing. Really, it was a couple of times when he was wound up and out of control. It wasn't that bad."

"Is that what your parents told you?"

"What?" Lauren said.

"That it wasn't that bad," Josie said. "Children will believe that and you know it's bullshit."

Lauren handed the iPad back to her. "Something's happening."

Josie could see Tim had turned north on what looked like a very small road. A moment later the tracker stopped.

Josie took the coordinates from the iPad and transferred them to the GPS screen stuck to her dashboard with a suction cup. She wanted to be sure of the route.

"Continue one hundred yards west," the computer said. She sounded like Judi Dench.

Josie slowed as she drew close, peering out the window for a dirt road to come into range of her headlights. She was almost upon it before she could see it. "You have arrived at your destination," Judi said.

"What are we going to do?" Lauren said. "Has Stan told you yet?"

Josie grabbed a flashlight and handcuffs from the glove compartment and took her gun out of its holster. She had the door open and one leg on the ground. "I don't know what Stan's going to do. I'm going to go find your parents." She started to get out. "And if you don't stay in the car, I'll shoot you."

Lauren looked frustrated. "You can't go up there on your own. I don't think you should go up there at all."

"What?" Josie said. "Why?"

"I don't think you're entirely well," she said.

Josie closed her door with a soft but emphatic push. "I'm fine. Stay in the car. You can tell Stan where I am when he gets here."

She trotted toward the dirt road, her heart pounding. The dark was nearly absolute, something she never saw in the city. Never dark, never quiet. She could hear her own rapid breathing. The narrow road climbed and Josie followed it as best she could in the pitch black. She could sense the trees on either side, and twice she found herself headed into a ditch as the road curved. She didn't dare use the flashlight for fear Tim would see.

After a five-minute hike the road leveled off. Her breath now sounded labored. She took a moment to rest and assess what she was seeing. Straight ahead was a small house, with light leaking out around the frames of the windows. There was no sign of Tim's Jeep. Josie approached the house as silently as possible, holding her gun in front of her. As she got closer she could see the windows were boarded up, the light pushing past where the plywood didn't quite meet the frame. It was enough light for Josie to see where she was going if she stayed close to the house. She crept to the rear to see what the exit situation was. Tim's Jeep was parked on the scrabbly lawn behind the house. There was a door and two windows in the back of the house. These windows were also boarded up, but the door hung open. She could see a huge padlock dangling open at the door, used, no doubt, to lock the house from the outside. A weak light fell upon the lawn. Josie crouched and peeked through a slice of the window not covered by plywood.

She tried to control her breathing, which sounded like ocean surf in her ears. She could see the enclosed back porch and beyond that a brightly lit kitchen. John and Helen Wade sat at the kitchen table while Tim poured them a cup of coffee and sat down to join them. It looked like they were settling in for a long chat, but for the frightened look on John's and Helen's sallow faces.

Josie thought she had about fifteen minutes or so to make things happen before Stan and company arrived. She stepped back and scooped up a handful of gravel that had settled around the base of the house and threw it against the screen door. Then she flattened herself behind the door that was open.

She heard the scrape of a chair and a clumping step approaching. The screen opened outward, and as soon as Tim cleared it Josie stepped out and raised her gun.

"Stop right there, Mr. Wade. Don't move an inch or I'll shoot you."

Tim turned to her. Josie thought she'd never seen such a shocked look on a face. But a half second later he closed the distance between them and kicked her in the ribs. He was wearing heavy boots. She hadn't even seen him start his move. The pain was unbelievable and Josie fell to the ground, clutching her side. She raised her gun hand to hold him off, but he pounced on her before she could aim, landing flat on top of her, crushing her rib and holding her gun arm to the ground. For a slender guy he felt dense, strong. Josie struggled beneath him, unable to move enough to fight. As he reached for the gun, lifting enough off her to give her room, she brought her knee up hard and caught him square in the balls. Tim cried out and rolled off her, grabbing himself in the classic pose of man at his most vulnerable. Josie didn't let the opportunity pass. Her head was pounding from the great flood of adrenaline rushing through her, but she felt as sharp as she'd ever been. She grabbed her gun and paid him back with a solid kick in the ribs. There was no way she'd lose to Tim. It wasn't possible.

While he was curled on his side, Josie trained her gun on him. "Get on your knees and put your hands on top of your head. Now."

Tim hesitated before shakily rising to his knees. Josie took her handcuffs out of her pocket and tossed them in front of him. "Put a cuff on one wrist and your hands behind your head." Tim didn't move. "Now, Mr. Wade. I'm not famous for my restraint."

"I suppose my sister put you up to this. You're a fool if you believe anything she's said to you."

"Cuff on. Now."

Tim reached for the cuffs and shut one on his left wrist. Then he put his hands behind his head. "She's a pathological liar. My entire life has been shit because of the lies she's told about me. About everything. You should be warned."

"I'll take it under advisement," Josie said. She approached from behind and put the gun to the back of Tim's head. "Don't move a muscle. I can't miss at this range." As she reached for the cuffs to secure his wrists, his leg shot out again, a swift backward kick that took Josie's legs out from under her, landing her on elbows and knees. She couldn't believe how fast he was. Faster than that Swanson jerk. He whipped around and slugged her in the face, snapping her head back and sending her sprawling. Still she kept hold of the gun and now aimed it with the full intent of wounding him, but knowing if she killed him it would be a mistake she could live with. She fired at his shoulder and watched as he fell, the shock returning to his face. He screamed bloody murder as he held his hand to his upper arm. Josie sensed the screaming wasn't all about the pain. It was like he was having a temper tantrum, furious that he'd been spanked, that his toy was being taken away. Josie walked over and held the gun on him once again, but the fight seemed to have drained out of him.

"I see that got your attention," she said, tapping her boot against his ribs. She figured it was the most effective bullet she'd ever fired. It scared the shit out of him. "Over on your stomach or I'll put a bullet in the other arm." Tim rolled over and Josie yanked his wrists together and secured the handcuffs.

"I need a doctor," Tim moaned. "I'm going to bleed to death."

Josie ignored him and dug out her phone. Her face was throbbing and her left eye was already closing. There was a stabbing pain from her lower ribs every time she moved. She'd never felt more alive.

"Stan. It's me. I've secured the suspect."

"What? Don't tell me you went in without waiting."

"Okay. I won't tell you."

"Goddamn it, Josie," Stan barked. He was too stressed out. He didn't handle the action the way he used to. He was old. "Is anyone hurt?"

"You mean aside from me?" she asked. "Wade has some lead in his shoulder, but he'll live." She saw Tim looking up at her. "More's the pity."

"Have you called nine-one-one yet?"

"No. I was about to," Josie said. She put her foot on Tim's back as he started to squirm. As soon as he felt it he stopped.

"Let me handle the local cops. We'll get an ambulance out there, too," Stan said. "I'll be there in ten."

"Okay. Harper out."

Josie thought about Lauren and her parents for the first time. She saw the three of them lined up outside the house, watching her. It looked creepy, like they were watching a public hanging. She wasn't surprised to see Lauren there. It would have been a surprise if she'd stayed in the car. But she wondered why they hadn't come out to try to help her and felt a little disappointed in them.

She waved her hand and indicated they should come over. Lauren led her parents to Josie. She stared down at Tim, and from the look on her face Josie wondered if Lauren was going to kick him herself.

"Don't worry," Josie said. "The police will be here to arrest him."

"Did you shoot him?"

"In the arm. He's not badly hurt."

"That's too bad," Lauren said. Her parents stood behind her. "Josie, these are my parents, John and Helen." They both nodded to Josie but didn't say anything. They looked unhappy with everyone around her.

"Glad to see you in one piece," Josie said. Shouldn't they be jumping up and down with joy? Everyone seemed so glum. Perhaps more angry than glum, and who could blame them? "Why don't you go into the house and wait for us there? We've got help coming any minute."

Lauren stayed behind as they watched John and Helen walk back to the house.

"Clearly you plan to never do anything I say. I'll have to keep that in mind," Josie said. She was trying to make a joke, but Lauren didn't even smile. "How did you get in the house, anyway?"

"The door wasn't locked. Tim must have come in that way when he arrived," Lauren said. She looked dazed.

Tim was now lying in perfect stillness on the ground. Josie's gun dangled loosely from her hand; she wasn't worried about him, but she'd be glad when Stan arrived to relieve her. It was going to be a hassle and a half with the cops; she'd shot someone, after all. She hoped the Wades would provide the self-defense evidence, since it seemed they'd been watching the whole fight. But she didn't feel entirely confident. She looked back at Lauren.

"Did you see the whole fight?" Josie wouldn't mind a little recognition of her heroics.

"I saw it."

Josie felt deflated. She didn't need a ticker tape parade, just an appreciative word from her lover would do. Lauren didn't say anything.

"How're your parents? They seem pretty subdued," Josie said.

"I suppose if you were held captive for eight months you'd feel subdued yourself," Lauren said coolly.

"True. But you seem the same way. Aren't you happy to see them?"

Lauren's expression remained cool, removed. "I couldn't describe to you how I'm feeling. And what would be the point?"

Josie was beginning to understand the Wades were truly a fucked-up family. Granted, hers wasn't much better, but she'd probably be able to rustle up a look of relief if her parents had been pulled back from the brink of death. Lauren went back in the house without a word.

Stan arrived a minute ahead of the police and ambulance and the scene was soon crowded and noisy. He briefed the officer in charge while the ambulance took Tim away with a police escort. Another ambulance took Lauren and her parents to the hospital after they were briefly interviewed, and Josie promised to meet them there as soon as she could.

Josie sat on the ground. She wasn't feeling great. It was like coming down from a high. She hurt physically, but her mood was the thing going downhill. She realized how amped up she'd been.

Stan walked over to her. "You need to get to the hospital yourself." He leaned over and offered his hand. Josie allowed herself to be pulled up.

"Don't the police want me?"

"You'll have to give a statement. They're sending someone to the hospital to do that. But you're in the clear. Our victims gave a pretty good account of you acting in self-defense. Personally, I wish they'd lock you up for a few days, maybe teach you some sense."

"Hey. I got the job done," Josie still had a modicum of hubris, despite her plummeting mood. Why should she be reprimanded for saving the day?

Stan looked at her, his face a mixture of amusement and frustration. He took Josie by the elbow and started toward the front of the house.

"Come on. I'll drive your car to the hospital. Nigel can meet us there." Josie didn't argue. Her ribs hurt like hell.

By the time they got to the small, rural hospital, John and Helen were being transferred from the ER to a room. Josie found Lauren in the empty waiting area. If anything, she looked grimmer than before.

"How are your folks?"

"The doctors insist on keeping them overnight," Lauren said. "I don't think there's a thing wrong with them, but that's the situation."

"That's okay. We can stay and drive them back tomorrow. I've got to get patched up anyway. We'll find a motel."

Lauren didn't respond. There was no sense of the vibrant person she'd made love with such a short time ago.

Stan had decamped to the police station and reported that Tim would be kept in the lockup over the next day or two, but would most likely be transferred to Cook County for prosecution. Josie had already forgotten about Tim. After she got her ribs wrapped and the cut over her eye taken care of, she found Lauren in the same chair in the waiting room, staring straight in front of her as if she were having a stare-down contest with someone, only no one else was there. Lauren turned to Josie.

"We're going back to Chicago. I'll have a car pick up my parents tomorrow."

"Are you sure you don't want to find a local motel? It's a good two-hour drive back to the city," Josie said. Her ribs were sore. She'd prefer the motel.

Lauren's eyes narrowed. "I really need to get out of here, if it's all the same to you. I'll drive. It looks like your eye's swollen shut." She stood, gathering her things.

Josie didn't want any hassle with Lauren. There was something going on with her. Maybe she could get to the bottom of it and this icy, removed woman would give way to the one she'd been having so much fun with.

They got into the Corolla, Lauren at the wheel. It was pitch black as soon as they cleared the town. Highway 20 snaked through miles of farmland, interrupted occasionally by another hamlet-sized town. Their headlights picked up the corn crops edging close to the side of the road. Inky blackness lay beyond them. It looked eerie, like a black-and-white scene from a Hitchcock film, where a deranged killer burst through the towering corn stalks.

"What's going on, Lauren? That was the grimmest reunion I've ever seen. It was like you didn't know each other."

Lauren was quiet. "We don't."

"What do you mean?"

Lauren gave a short bark of a laugh, the first sign of animation she'd shown for hours. "At this moment I wish Tim had killed them. The result would have been better than this."

Josie put a neutral look on her face. She was getting a very bad feeling. Time seemed to have slowed. Where everything had been rushing by up to the fight with Tim, now she had a good look at Lauren. There was something off. "What result?"

Lauren glanced at Josie. Her lips were pursed as she looked back at the road. The silence stretched on.

"Lauren? There's something going on I don't know about. You're not making any sense."

She glanced at Josie once more. "You can't possibly know how important my company is to me, can you?"

Josie was having a hard time focusing. Her head was throbbing. "No?"

"That's right. No one can, except for my parents." Lauren's voice took on a bitter tone. "And they just fired me."

"What?" Josie snapped to attention. "I'm not following. What does your company have to do with your parents' kidnapping? Why are they firing you?"

Lauren looked at her as if she was a little slow, and truth be told she felt a bit dense at the moment. She tried to stay focused on what Lauren was saying, but she felt awful and her mood was in free fall. That probably signaled the end of whatever mania she had. It hadn't been so bad. She hadn't slept with anyone's girlfriend, or spent days at the Horseshoe Casino, or even talked too much, too often. She'd saved two people, for God's sake. But now her thoughts kept drifting.

"Everything that happens in my family has to do with the company," Lauren said. "Tim kidnapped my parents because they belittled him his whole life. He hates them. But another reason was to make me look foolish to my employees and the board of directors by forcing me to act like a buffoon. He hates me, too."

Josie was shifting around in her seat, trying to get comfortable. The pain pill she'd taken was making her drowsy. "So Tim hates your parents, you hate Tim, or at least I assume you do. But why would they fire you?"

Lauren remained quiet. A vertical line ran up her forehead, giving her a fierce appearance.

"My parents and I declared a truce when I first started to work as an editor at the company. I would say relations before then were strained. They expected a lot from me, mostly because I shone compared to Tim. They were deeply disappointed whenever I failed to meet their expectations, though they seldom explained to me what those expectations were. We fought a lot. They weren't around often, but when they were it was uncomfortable. Still, it was always assumed I'd work at the company and make my way up the ranks, and I wanted that. I understood that one day the place would be mine. I'd risen nearly to the top by the time they retired, while Tim showed only a shaky understanding of the business. But I learned recently that Tim and I would have equal shares upon their death. All of my hard work made no impression on them."

"I still don't see why they fired you. And don't you think they'd strip the shares from Tim because of the kidnapping? I mean, who wouldn't?"

Lauren gripped the steering wheel tighter. Josie could see veins starting to bulge on the top of her hands. They were barreling down the highway; she didn't want Lauren to get more upset. "They think I should have rescued them sooner. They're furious with me. That's what we talked about when I first saw him. They didn't even say hello." She was speaking through her teeth.

Josie roused herself. "Are you telling me they've taken your job away because you couldn't do the impossible? What bastards."

Lauren seemed to be growing angrier by the minute. "Like I said, I seldom know what their expectations are. They're higher than I thought."

Josie thought the Borgias were a more loving family than this lot. She noticed the speed of the Corolla inch up.

"What my parents feel is always dependent on how the company's doing," Lauren said. She didn't seem to be talking to Josie. It was more like she was recording something for the record, for posterity. "I've had declining profits for three consecutive quarters, which is the most significant transgression. The board has complained about my unusual behavior, which of course my parents knew about. Tim reported all of this to them. He probably showed them video of me singing karaoke with the women in accounting. They aren't happy with that or the fact that I stood trial for murder, despite the acquittal. But all they said to me was I failed to rescue them and couldn't be trusted." Lauren took a shuddering breath. "I suppose I should have seen this coming."

"Wow." Josie was struggling with how to respond; the situation was well beyond her experience. At least her parents were a case of "what you see is what you get." Granted, what you got wasn't much, but at least they didn't operate at a Machiavellian level. She felt sorry for Lauren.

Josie was fighting sleep. "I don't understand why your parents weren't grateful to you. It was you who kept them alive and rescued them," she said. "I'd think that would be worth a thank you and few extra shares." Shares being the coinage of love in the Wade family. She tried to think of what it would be in her own family, but beer was all that came to mind.

Lauren increased her speed; the cropland was flashing by even faster. "After everything I've done for the last eight months to keep them alive, and they can't rely on me. I wish Tim had killed them."

The engine had to be reaching its limit. She peeked at the speedometer, which showed ninety miles per hour. She hadn't known the Corolla had it in her.

Lauren seethed. "The shit I've been through this year is unbelievable. First with Kelly, then with Tim, now with my parents." She hit the steering wheel hard with the base of her palm; the car jiggered a little, crossing the median line. Josie sat up. "The relationship with Kelly was mostly a joke," Lauren said. "I stayed with her to show I was in a stable relationship, something my parents and the board demanded, though no one was crazy about my partner being a woman. Fuck all of them."

Josie shifted again in her seat. It felt surreal to fly down the empty highway with a madwoman at the wheel. She tried to revert to her training, to stay calm and, hopefully, alive. Asking questions wasn't the smart thing to do, but she couldn't help herself.

"Does that mean you didn't care when you found out Kelly was sleeping with Ann-Marie?"

Lauren stayed silent. A look of resignation and a certain stillness in her body came over her. Another five miles per hour showed on the speedometer.

"I wasn't surprised. Not by Kelly or my parents or Tim. It's always been a matter of how much crap I was willing to take. I'm not willing to take any more."

With a flash, Josie knew Lauren had reached the end of her rope, just as Lauren yanked the steering wheel hard to the right, plunging them to the side of the road. She saw the corn stalks bathed in a sepulchral light before the car hit the ditch and flipped over. And then over again. It was the last she knew.

CHAPTER THIRTY-THREE

Josie opened her eyes. Her head felt like a wrecking ball was swinging back and forth in her brain. She didn't understand where she was or what had happened. All she could tell was the law of gravity was working against her. Her head was where her feet should be.

She took stock. She was upside down in her car, her head held inches from the roof by a straining seat belt. Her ribs were a mess. The one that Tim kicked was probably broken, along with a few others. There was something wrong with her leg; she tried to move and screamed in pain. Broken. Blood dripped downward from a cut on her forehead. When she tilted her head she could see a puddle of it pooling in the roof of the car.

In slow dribs and drabs, more came back to her. Lauren and all she'd said, Lauren and her suicidal crash into the side of the road. She turned her head carefully toward the driver's seat, half expecting to see Lauren dead at the wheel. Instead she saw an empty seat and a wide-open door. She might be lying next to the car, injured. Josie felt upward toward her seat belt, fumbling with slick, bloody hands to release it. It was hard with all her weight straining against it, holding her up like a parachute harness. When she finally snapped it open, she fell down to the roof, her brain lighting up like fireworks when her head hit the surface. She lay still for a minute, long enough to convince herself to move again.

The passenger door was smashed shut. She inched over to the driver's side and crawled out the door, landing on the corn stalks as she slithered to the ground. Her leg shot arrows of pain up her body, but it was the tibia, maybe the fibula, that was broken, not the femur. She could cope with it. But her inventory of injuries was growing. Her knee seemed to be pointing somewhere off center. From the blood now dripping down her face she knew she had two gashes, not one. None of it would kill her. She pushed herself up and tried to look around the immediate area. Her leg held, but it hurt like hell. It was so dark she could barely see the corn rising up all around the car. The headlights were off, the engine no doubt ruined.

She almost immediately tripped over Lauren and fell partly on top of her, but there was no response from the body beneath. Josie knew she was dead. She could see the rag-doll way her body lay. She rotated her until she could feel for a pulse in her neck. She couldn't find one.

Josie slowly stood up again, her pounding head making it hard to process what it all meant. She'd thought she'd found something with Lauren. She remembered that. The attraction, the physical connection, the sharp mind that seemed to see through Josie in a way most didn't. But something came apart. She began to recall the car ride—the bitter tone to Lauren's voice, the screwed-up perspective that showed itself more with every mile they raced down the highway. Her sudden certainty Lauren had killed Kelly after all. And then the suicidal crash. Apparently it meant nothing to Lauren that Josie could also have been killed.

Josie eased her hand into her jacket pocket. Her phone was there, thankfully intact. She dialed 911 and looked at the compass on her phone to give the dispatcher her GPS coordinates. Then she dragged herself through the trampled corn to the road and sat down to wait. She speed-dialed Stan.

"Waterman." Stan's voice sounded groggy. He was wisely getting some sleep in a motel before coming back to Chicago.

"You're not going to believe what's happened."

"Probably not."

"Lauren drove us off the road and we flipped at least twice. She's dead." She noticed her voice getting shaky.

"I'm on my way. Give me your location," Stan said, sounding wide-awake. It made Josie feel better, safer, that Stan was coming to help her. If he were in front of her at the moment, she might very well have allowed him to wrap her up in his arms and pat her back.

Josie gave him the coordinates and rang off. Soon she heard the sound of sirens. The town of Elizabeth was two miles behind them. She waved down the cop car and ambulance and almost cried when they pulled over to save her.

CHAPTER THIRTY-FOUR

Monday, September 16

Josie had been banged up before, but she had to admit this was bad. Her ribs were the worst. It was hard to breathe, hard to move around. Her sofa, the one that felt so comfy during Bears games and long naps, now felt like upholstered rocks. Her head still hurt four days after having it knocked around in the Corolla. The most inconvenient injury was the dislocated kneecap and broken tibia. Her right leg was in a cast up to the thigh. That meant driving was impossible for a while. It also meant going to the bathroom was an Olympic event.

Her headache seemed to grow worse as her mother sat by the sofa, determined to be helpful. She slept in Josie's bed at night, hovered about during the day, and drove Josie perilously close to insanity. She intended to stay until Josie could get around on her own, so Josie put forth a Herculean effort to start moving about the apartment as if it wasn't painful in the least.

"I'm getting along fine, Mom. You should head up to Aunt Mona's," Josie said, laying back on the sofa.

"Not until you're better. You're still an invalid."

"Invalid? Aunt Mary's an invalid, Mom. I'm going to be fine. In fact, I'm perfectly capable of taking care of myself. My neighbor can come in if I need anything. Besides, I think you should get out of here before Dad tries to find you."

"I still can't believe I've left your father. I can't thank you enough for making me see the light, Josie."

Josie's father wasn't yet aware his wife had actually left him and wasn't simply camped out with Josie. Her mother's sudden eagerness to help wasn't the only change Josie noticed. She'd been with her for four days and hadn't seen her once take a drink. If she was seeing the light, it was probably from thinking clearly for the first time in years.

"Mom, aren't you dying for a drink? I don't think I've seen you with one since you've been here." Elaine didn't look up from the *Oprah* magazine she was flipping through.

"I've given it up," she said.

"Just like that?"

"Yes. It's been four days."

Jose looked at her skeptically. "Have you been sneaking off to AA meetings?"

"Oh, there's no need for any of that. It's a simple matter. You decide you aren't going to have a cocktail anymore and that's it."

"Maybe being sober a few of days helped you realize what an ass Dad is. I'm glad you're trying, Mom."

Josie adjusted herself on the sofa again, moving the discomfort from one spot to the next. She knew her mom would be in an AA meeting by next week. Her aunt Mona had been sober thirty years and would be dragging Elaine in first thing. She hoped it worked, though she doubted it would.

The buzzer downstairs interrupted Josie's meal of frozen enchiladas, part of the plethora of frozen meals her mother had brought to the apartment. These were a definite improvement over the Swanson fried chicken dinners her mom served when she was a kid. Every meal went from box to oven to table. Microwaves were the technology miracle of Elaine's lifetime. She hadn't turned on an oven since they were invented. The buzzer rang again and Elaine sighed as she walked to the old wall unit that buzzed people in. "Who is it?" she screamed, unable to believe her voice would make it down the three floors of the apartment building. "I swear to God, Josie, it's like you're the queen of England; it's been one person after another through here."

"That'll be Stan, Mom. You can buzz him in."

Elaine looked alarmed. "You don't think he'll tell your father anything, do you?"

"If I did, I wouldn't let him in. Anyway, Dad knows you're here. You're supposed to be looking after me. It's when you're up at Aunt Mona's he'll figure it out." Elaine looked alarmed, as if the idea of her husband looking for her hadn't crossed her mind. "You're going to have to be strong, like we talked about. If he shows up here, I'll talk to him. Let Aunt Mona do the talking if he comes up to Madison. She'll kick his ass."

The thought cheered Josie. Aunt Mona had always been her hero. She took crap from no one, raised hell about every social justice issue that crossed her path, and never married. She was the family iconoclast. Mona had been living with a woman's studies professor in Madison for nearly thirty years. It didn't take much of a detective to figure out what was going on there.

Elaine was putting on her coat when Stan knocked on the open door. The two had never been friendly, even if Stan kept her husband out of more trouble than Elaine would ever know. Stan nodded at her as he took a chair by the couch and handed Josie a cup of coffee. He looked over his shoulder when he heard the front door close.

"How's she doing?"

"I can't begin to explain, Stan. But I'll say her new mother act is close to driving me crazy."

Josie shifted around until she was propped up with pillows and could look Stan straight in the face. "What's up?"

"You ready to hear more about Lauren Wade?"

"Not really," Josie said. She felt guilty and embarrassed she hadn't seen through the woman. Really, all she'd seen was how hot she was. Her mind had fallen into that slot grooved so deeply during the past years of impulsive behavior.

"I don't have much to add. So far the police have found bupkis in her house or office that would further explain anything—why she committed suicide or why she killed Kelly Moore, which I'm pretty sure she did. They were looking for a note, I guess."

Josie didn't say anything. Given the insane way Lauren acted just before the crash, there was no reason to think she hadn't killed Kelly. It was ridiculous to think she'd left behind a suicide note. Josie closed her eyes. She'd not only been taken in by Lauren, she'd almost been killed by her. The thought of Lucy came to mind, making her squirm even more. She groaned when her sore ribs protested. She groaned when she thought of the way she'd treated Lucy.

"Are you okay?" Stan asked anxiously.

"Yeah, I'm fine. These ribs are killing me."

"Well, I'll get out of here so you can rest," Stan said.

Josie opened one eye. "No, stay for a bit."

He shrugged out of his jacket and took a bag out of its pocket. He passed it over to Josie. "Gummy bears."

Josie had to admit it was hard not to love a man who remembered your childhood devotion to gummy bears.

"I even took the green ones out," he said.

Josie let a tear slide down her cheek. She didn't have the energy to fight it. "Thanks, Stan."

"Your father's a real bastard, you know? He hasn't been here to see you yet, has he?"

"No, and I don't want him to. I don't even consider him a father, Stan. Let's forget about him."

Stan looked at her thoughtfully. "Done."

"What'd you find out about Lauren?" Josie asked.

Stan paused a moment. "The police didn't do much. As far as they were concerned, the suicide simply confirmed Lauren had been guilty of Kelly's murder. They don't give a shit about anything else, especially when it's a suicide. If she hadn't died it would be a different matter. They could charge her with attempted vehicular homicide because you were in the car. But you can't charge the dead."

Josie stared at him.

"And I talked to a few people at her company and on the board and even to those creepy parents of hers. It looked like Lauren's career with the family biz was just about over. That's about it." Stan shifted in his chair and took a sip of the coffee he'd brought in. "There's something else I wanted to talk to you about," Stan continued.

Josie looked at him warily. She held up her hand to stop him while she took a painkiller. "What is it?"

"It seems to me you'll be a pretty sharp private investigator, despite your tendency to go your own way. Why don't we join into one firm? Waterman and Harper Investigations. It has a ring to it, don't you think?"

"Why would you want to do that?" Josie asked. "I nearly fucked up this entire thing. I could have gotten the Wades killed. I could have prevented Lauren being killed." She reached for the bottle of pills to take another, but Stan caught her wrist.

"Or you could say you did exactly what you'd been hired to do.

You found out who killed Kelly Moore and you freed Lauren's parents. What more do you want from yourself?"

Josie stared at the ceiling a moment. "I wanted it to be more satisfying."

"Satisfying? What, like sex?" Stan was helping himself to the gummy bears.

Josie shot him a look. "No, not like sex. Sheesh. More like having the ends neatly tied together."

"Like in *Law and Order*," Stan said. "Don't worry about that. It never happens."

They stayed silent for a while. It wasn't uncomfortable.

"As I was saying," Stan said. "Waterman and Harper Investigations sounds good, doesn't it?"

"Drop the ampersand and I'm in. Waterman Harper has a better ring to it. More professional."

Stan slapped his hands together. "Excellent! We'll be a great team."

Josie thought so, too. "When can I start?"

Stan laughed. "Given the looks of you, I think it's going to be a few weeks yet. But I'll get your stuff moved into that second office of mine and you'll be ready to go. Getting out of that lease will save you a lot of money. Plus I'll have you to yell at. It's a win-win."

Josie didn't think Stan would do much yelling, but she could stand it if he did. She knew very well how easily she could make mistakes, how much she could learn from him. When her eyes grew heavy again she heard Stan quietly let himself out. She woke sometime later to the sound of the buzzer again.

"Fucking A," Josie muttered, as she reached for her crutches and hobbled over to the intercom. She didn't bother to ask who it was. She buzzed them in, then headed to the bathroom since she was already upright. When she finally made her way from the bathroom back to the living room, she saw Bev sitting in the visitor chair.

"I feel like I'm in an episode of *Friends*," Josie said. "Everyone I know is coming by."

Bev rolled her eyes, which she often did in front of Josie. "Honey, you're once again under the impression that the center of the universe is you. And you look like shit. How long since you changed those clothes?"

Josie eased herself back on the sofa. There was a film of sweat on her brow and she was panting. "Don't start on me, Bev. I really almost died this time."

"You're like a cockroach. Practically nothing can kill you. How're you feeling?"

"Let's leave it at bad. The details require too much energy." There was a coffee table pulled up next to the sofa holding everything she needed: remote control, water, a bag of Chex Mix, *Jane Eyre*, her laptop, and her phone. If she didn't have to pee, she'd never get up.

Bev took a handful of Chex Mix before reaching into her bag for a folder. "I come bearing presents. I finally got Nicholson's notes on the Kelly Moore murder. I don't know enough about it to tell whether there's anything significant in there but thought you might pass some time taking a look. A copy's in the folder."

Josie felt only mildly interested. Finding out who killed Kelly Moore seemed like the concern of another life, another person. And it seemed a sure thing it was Lauren. Who cared at this point? "Leave it on the table. Please. I think I'm going to pass out for a while."

Bev looked down at her with a frown. "Are you here alone? That doesn't seem right."

"Believe me, I'd prefer it to my mother being here. But she should be back any minute."

"Okay. Let's stay in touch." She kissed the top of Josie's head and left, moving in the swift, sure way that was very much Bev.

At four o'clock the following morning, in keeping with her completely messed-up sleep schedule, Josie lay wide-awake staring at the ceiling. By some miracle she was neither depressed nor manic. Greta said the same thing when she made a house call shortly after the accident. But she was bored nearly out of her head. A streetlight kept the room from total darkness. She reached over to the table to get her sippy cup of water and saw the file left behind by Bev. She scooched up to read, turning on the floor lamp next to the sofa. The file was thin, containing two pieces of regular eight-by-eleven sheets of paper on which the pages from a small notebook had been copied. There were four notebook pages in all. The first seemed to be a series of codes, probably notations on upcoming horse races. The fourth page was a grocery list most likely dictated to him by his wife. There were too many fruits and vegetables for it to be Nicholson's creation. That left the two in the middle related to the murder of Kelly Moore.

The second page noted aspects of the murder scene that were later officially recorded by the forensics team. There was Nicholson's description of Lauren Wade. She was sitting at the breakfast bar when Nicholson arrived on the scene. He described her as shaken but not greatly so, kind of like a witness to a bad car crash. The only words she spoke were to identify herself, Kelly, and the gun. Beyond that she remained silent. Nicholson took her upstairs to have her show him where the gun had been kept. She led the way to the master bedroom suite. The middle drawer of the nightstand on the right side of the bed was open, with a handful of bullets in the drawer. She was then taken into custody.

The third page of notes was made during the brief investigation into the murder. Mostly they consisted of comments about the people being interviewed. Kelly's parents seemed nearly catatonic, the sister eager to tell them of Kelly's infidelity and Lauren's discovery of it. Gabby was described as belligerent, but she didn't feel right for the murder of her lover's lover. Nicholson felt it much more likely she'd punish Ann-Marie somehow. Ann-Marie's interview related her alibi— that she went straight home from work on the day of the murder. Home at that time was her sister's place, where she'd been staying since Gabby threw her out. Nicholson noted that she sounded "tentative." Josie's brain went from hazy to sharp in an instant. Her own notebook was across the room in her bag. She threw off the comforter and reached for her crutches. It had been hours since her last pain pill, but she didn't want one. The walk across the room was a struggle, compounded by a trip to the bathroom. By the time she got back to the sofa with her notebook, she was exhausted. She got herself situated again and reread Nicholson's notes. Then she started paging through her own. There was something about the alibi Ann-Marie gave Nicholson that didn't jibe with the one she gave Josie.

She found the page and saw Ann-Marie had told her she'd stopped at a Mariano's on her way home but didn't have a receipt to show what time she was there or whether she was there at all. She was staying with her sister and cooked dinner for the family that night. Why tell Nicholson she'd gone straight home? No mention of the grocery store, no mention of cooking for the family. It was possible the lazy bastard didn't write everything down and that Ann-Marie had told him the same thing. Josie fell asleep before she could think things through.

When she woke again she saw her mother sitting on the chair, a large suitcase at her side. Her coat was draped over her arm.

"Oh, you're awake. Good. I wanted to talk with you before I left for Mona's. I thought it over and I think you're right that it's best to get out of Chicago for the time being. But I feel terrible leaving you here."

"Don't worry about it, Mom. I'll be fine. I'm getting my ass off this sofa today. I have people who can stop in if I need help." This didn't seem an entire certainty, but she wanted her mother on her way. She had things to do.

After her mother took another fifteen minutes to say good-bye, Josie headed to her bedroom and put on some fresh sweatpants. She matched them with a hoodie and made her way slowly to her dining room table. She spread out her notebook and other documents on the case and suddenly felt a surge of energy. Josie wasn't as sanguine about leaving a case with loose threads as Stan was.

She pulled out every reference she had to Ann-Marie and tried to figure out what the discrepancy in her alibi meant. It wasn't unusual for a witness to be rattled and misspeak, but it was equally likely the witness would speak the truth in the immediate wake of an event. She'd been interviewed the day after the murder. Nicholson said she was tentative when saying she went directly from the school of the Art Institute to her sister's place in the West Loop. Why would she change that to include a stop at the grocery store? There were two reasons Josie could think of—she'd simply forgotten to mention it when first interviewed by Bill Nicholson, or she needed to avoid her sister saying something different should she be interviewed. Their stories needed to coincide. As it turned out, the sister was never interviewed, though her name and number appeared on Nicholson's notes.

Josie swore as she clumped her way to the living room for her phone and then back to the dining room. A growing sense of excitement was keeping her upright, but she still felt like hell. Her pounding headache and steady diet of pain pills made her feel dull. But it couldn't feel any worse if she called the sister with a few simple questions. Her number was in Nicholson's notes.

"Hello?"

"Is this Mrs. Sexton?" Josie noticed the harried hello and the sound of children racing around the background. "My name's Josie Harper of Waterman Harper Investigations. I'm looking into the death of Kelly Moore." She liked the sound of the new agency name.

There was a silence on the line, which meant Ann-Marie's sister was uncomfortable. Josie wondered if she knew her sister had been sleeping with a murder victim.

"Yes, this is she. You can call me Clarissa."

"If you have a moment I'd like to ask you a couple of questions." Josie sounded very mellow, which she attributed to the hydrocodone. She tried to find a comfortable position on her rigid wood chair; there was none.

"I'm calling to corroborate Ann-Marie's movements on the night of Kelly's death," she continued. "Do you recall when she got to your place from work that night?"

There was another pause before Clarissa said, "As I recall it, Ann-Marie came home from work, changed out of her painting clothes, and planned to go out to the grocery store to get food for dinner. She was going to cook for me and the kids."

"What time was that?"

"I don't know. Maybe four o'clock? We were leaving to see Gina's dance recital. We agreed to meet at home at seven, and Ann-Marie was just getting back when we arrived."

"What about the rest of the evening? Did Ann-Marie go out?"

There was silence on the line. Finally, Clarissa said, "I don't know for sure."

"What do you mean?" Josie felt like a bird dog on point.

"Jim and the kids and I were downstairs watching a movie. Ann-Marie said she was spending the rest of the evening in her room. It's possible she went out without us knowing."

"That lines up with what Ann-Marie told both the police and me. Thank you."

An uproar could be heard coming from her end. "I've got to go," Clarissa said and hung up.

Josie added this new account of Ann-Marie's movements to her list. How could it be the police didn't confirm Ann-Marie's alibi with her sister? The different alibis didn't mean much in themselves. The murder itself happened later than the dinner she shared with her sister's family. It was the fact that her story changed, now with a third version, that piqued her interest. Now there was also the distinct possibility Ann-Marie didn't stay in the whole evening. She leaned back in her chair, wondering if she'd ever get any good at this stuff. She should have thought to interview the sister. Waterman Harper might become simply Waterman in pretty short order. She picked up the phone again and called Ann-Marie and Gabby's house. No answer. She called each of their cell numbers. No answer. It was a Friday, so Ann-Marie could be at school. She called the Art Institute, but no one could tell her if she had been away from the school for an unusually long time. The department secretary told her she'd been there for her Wednesday class but she hadn't seen her since.

Next Josie called the fire house and talked to Gabby's lieutenant.

"Gabby missed a shift yesterday, which is very unlike her. She's a wild thing, always getting into trouble, but when it comes to her job she's dedicated. We're giving her until next shift, which is midnight tonight, before we call the cops. We can't get her on the phone so the betting is she's shacked up with someone."

Josie was convinced that wasn't the case. She had to get to Ann-Marie. There was either nothing to the confusion in her alibi—maybe she was simply an absentminded artist—or there could be something very big about it. Her gut told her it was big. She picked up the phone again.

"Hi, Bev. It's Josie again. Yeah, I miss you, too. Listen, something popped in those notes of Nicholson's and I need your help to see it through."

"I'm listening," Bev said. Josie could hear sounds of the station behind her. She told Bev about the discrepancies in Ann-Marie's alibi and the fact that both Ann-Marie and Gabby seemed to be missing in action.

"Give me their address. I'll take a ride over there," Bev said.

"Oh, no. Not without picking me up first. If I start now I'll be at the bottom of the stairs before you pull up."

"Josie, there's no way you're going with me. You're not well enough, number one, and you're not authorized, number two."

"I say bullshit to both. I'm getting around fine, and you wouldn't even know about this if I hadn't told you. I'll see you in fifteen."

Josie could hear Bev swear as she disconnected, but knew she'd be heading to her car to come get her. She hurriedly put a thick sock over the toes of her plaster-encased foot and a sneaker on the other. She never knew she had such contortionist abilities. The pain was bad and she thought about taking a pill. But she was going to have to gut it out. She stuck her gun and her burglar's tools in the kangaroo pocket of her sweatshirt. The worst bit would be getting down the three flights of stairs. It took almost the full fifteen minutes to get out on the street, but it was worth every moment of agony. The fresh air felt glorious. There was color touching the leaves of the trees lining her block and it was still warm enough for a light jacket. The air dried the sweat from her face, hiding the effort it had taken to get this far. She wanted to look strong for Bev.

CHAPTER THIRTY-FIVE

Bev didn't offer to help Josie into the car. She probably was assessing her abilities. Josie pulled her casted leg into the car with a smile on her face and said, "1752 Olive Street, James, and make it snappy."

Bev snorted and hit the gas, following a series of one way streets until she pulled up in front of an old frame two-story house on Olive, near the commuter train tracks. The blinds were all drawn.

"So this is what I was thinking," Josie said. "We'll both go to the front door and say we're checking in on everyone involved in the investigation of Kelly Moore's murder, in light of Lauren Wade's recent suicide."

"Why would that make any difference to them?" Bev asked.

"It probably wouldn't. It's a nonsense question. Go with me on this. Once we have them in a conversation, even though you're a cop and that's usually a conversation stopper now that I think of it…"

"Josie," Bev warned.

"I'll ask Ann-Marie if Lauren's suicide makes her think any differently about who killed Kelly. Does it seem more likely now Lauren did kill her? Then I'll ask her about her alibi again." Josie seemed satisfied.

"I think once Ann-Marie hears the word 'alibi,' she'll clam up," Bev said.

"Then we'll know it's a touchy point for her. That's good information. Come on."

Josie pulled herself out of the car and trailed Bev to the front door. She pushed the doorbell and got no response.

"Maybe they're both working," Bev said.

"No. Remember I called both their work places? I wonder if their car is here?"

Bev trotted down the gangway to the garage in the rear and was back in moments. "There are two cars in the garage."

Josie rang again. After they waited another five minutes, Josie said, "I have a very bad feeling about this. I want to get in."

"I can't go in there, Josie. There's no probable cause."

Josie dug into her jacket pocket for her set of burglar tools. She'd taken them from a man she'd arrested for a series of burglaries in Lincoln Park. She shouldn't have taken them, but he had two sets. No sense letting one go to waste. "You're such a stick in the mud, Bev. There aren't many rules when you're a private cop. You know how I feel about rules," she said as she tinkered around with the pick and the lock. Suddenly the sound of a gunshot exploded from above them. Josie stepped away and looked at Bev. "There's your probable cause."

Josie stepped back farther as Bev drew her gun and blew open the lock. She flew up the stairs that were to the right of the doorway, leaving Josie in a jumble of door, screen door, and crutches. She freed herself quickly and then heard a bloodcurdling scream.

"You shot me, you stupid motherfucker." It was Gabby and she continued swearing until everything suddenly went silent again. Josie guessed Bev had just entered the room.

"Put your gun down and your hands in the air," she heard Bev say. Shit. A Metra train came by, a long rush-hour commuter that masked the sound of Josie's crutches. Josie was on the fifth of ten steps, her knee screaming. She picked up her pace, unable to imagine what trouble Bev might be in. Gabby had recommenced her cries of outrage, which told Josie she wasn't gravely injured. She heard nothing from Ann-Marie.

She finally reached the top of the steps just as the train passed and saw Bev was in the bedroom straight ahead. There were four bedrooms laid out in a square. She put down her crutches and lay flat, crawling her way toward the room. She had to pull her gun from her pocket so it wouldn't scrape along the wood floor. She could see part of Bev standing in a shooter's pose. From the direction she was pointing, it looked like Ann-Marie and Gabby were near the west wall of the room.

"Put the gun down," Bev said. "It's the last time I'll warn you."

"You can stop your bluffing, Detective. If you shoot me, I'll shoot Gabby, which you can see I have no problem with. If you don't mind that blood on your hands, do what you have to."

"What will it take to let Gabby go? We need to get her to the hospital, Ann-Marie," Bev said, cool as she could be.

Bev stepped back so Josie could see her whole body. She knew Bev was aware of her and carefully not letting on. "Tell me what you need, Ann-Marie."

"I need people to treat me better." Ann-Marie's voice was harsh, bitter. Josie could barely recognize her.

"That's probably true," Bev said. "But killing Gabby isn't likely to help you there. What's something I can give you in exchange for Gabby?"

Josie could tell from their voices they were sitting along the west wall of the room, with Ann-Marie on the left side, probably holding her gun on Gabby. She crawled to the edge of the door. Bev moved toward the north wall, drawing Ann-Marie's eyes away from the door.

"Stop moving or I'll shoot her," Ann-Marie said.

"Calm down. I'm not doing anything. This way we have a better look at each other."

Gabby let out a moan. "I'm not kidding. I'm bleeding out here."

Bev's voice took on new urgency. "Ann-Marie, we can't mess around anymore. I need you to pull yourself together so no one else gets hurt. You don't want that, do you? Now I'm going to hold my gun flat in the palms of my hands like this. See? I'm offering my gun to you in exchange for Gabby."

"How does that help me?" Ann-Marie asked.

"Simple. I'll take Gabby to the hospital and you walk away. There aren't any other cops here. I won't tell what's happened here."

"I'm supposed to believe that?" Ann-Marie said.

"I'm only interested in getting Gabby to a hospital. I'm getting to my knees now, Ann-Marie. See, my gun's not even pointed at you. I'm going to put it on the ground like this, and when I count to three I'll shove it over to you."

Josie was poised at the doorway; she could see Ann-Marie and Gabby. She held her gun in a two-handed grip and hoped she wouldn't have to fire it. If her shot was less than totally debilitating, Ann-Marie could fire at Gabby or Bev. Probably Bev. If Josie shot at her gun arm, she'd likely miss. If she went for the hip or leg area there was a chance Ann-Marie would hold on to the gun and fire. Anything less than a certain removal of the gun from Ann-Marie's hand put them in danger.

"One," Bev said, her voice steady. Josie got in position, exposing herself a bit. Ann-Marie's eyes were glued on Bev.

"Two," Bev said. "Remember, I'm sliding this to you. That's giving you all the power, Ann-Marie. I don't want you shooting me because I'm shoving a gun your way. Understand?"

Ann-Marie remained silent, but she could see her tighten her grip on Gabby.

"Three."

The gun skidded across the hardwood as Ann-Marie turned her gun on Bev. Josie brought her arm around the door and shot. The only shot she could take. The shot she was trained to take at the academy. Shoot the middle. Ann-Marie slumped and didn't move. Josie pulled herself into the room and managed to prop herself against a wall. She was panting and sweating. Bev gave her a concerned look before checking Ann-Marie's pulse. She looked at Josie and shook her head. Then she frisked Gabby.

"You've gotta be fucking kidding me," Gabby roared. "I've got a bullet in my leg, for Christ's sake. Call an ambulance!"

Bev stood and turned away from Gabby. She pulled her radio out and called in the scene before finding a towel to press to Gabby's wound.

"Hold this and shut up," she said to Gabby. Then she walked over to Josie and sat next to her.

"Crap. Now I'll never know if Ann-Marie killed Kelly," Josie said. "I think she did, don't you?"

"Oh, yeah."

"I bet between Gabby abusing her and Kelly dumping her, she kind of snapped," Josie said.

They were silent for a while, watching Gabby push herself away from Ann-Marie's body. She didn't look heartbroken.

"Thanks, by the way," Bev said.

"No problem."

"I owe you one."

"No, you really don't," Josie said. "It felt good to be a partner."

Bev turned to Josie, who felt only a little better than death warmed over. "You were always a good partner, Josie."

Josie put her arm around Bev's shoulder as they waited for the cops to get there. They came too quickly as far as Josie was concerned.

Chapter Thirty-six

Thursday, September 19

Josie thought she'd proved herself capable of any sort of physical endeavor with her cast on. Her head didn't hurt anymore, and her ribs were less sore every day. It was time to get out of the apartment. She clunked her way down the three flights of steps and got out into the fresh air. It felt cathartic. The air was crisp, the breeze light. She felt as if she'd never noticed these things before.

Even on crutches it took her only a few minutes to get to Kopi. As she reached the corner of Clark and Summerdale she stopped to rest for a minute on one of the benches set along the corner. The sky was a brilliant blue. She put her sunglasses on, propped her leg on the bench, and stared out into the street. She'd found sitting and staring wasn't as boring as she once thought it was. She didn't always think about anything in particular, and she wasn't anxious about anything either. This was fairly delusional, she knew, since she had plenty to think and be anxious about. But she'd enjoy it while she could.

Lucy lived a block away from where she sat. She thought about Lucy when she did all that staring into space. She remembered how much she liked her, how safe she felt with her, how adorable she was. Other times she felt only remorse, embarrassment, and shame for treating her so badly. Would Lucy ever understand that it was the beginnings of a mania, the excitement of a case, that made her see everything through such a skewed lens? Probably not. Now, on the bench, she thought of what might have been as she stared onto Clark Street.

She felt a hand on her shoulder and her left leg went to the ground as she tried to look behind her. She saw it was Lucy, who was gently pushing her shoulder down so she'd stay where she was. She sat on the edge of Josie's bench. Her crazy hair was tied in a knot of top of her head. Her hoodie had a large recycling logo on it.

"Is it okay if we talk?" Lucy said.

Josie felt alarmed. Her heart rate had picked up noticeably. "Of course. I was hoping we'd be able to talk again. I didn't know if you'd ever agree to." Josie arranged herself to sit more comfortably and looked at Lucy, who gazed back at her.

"I think I saw the Josie from last year, the part of you that's ill."

"Ill perhaps, but the symptoms are remarkably similar to assholitis."

Lucy laughed. "Yes. I was confused for a bit over the diagnosis. What happened to you?" she asked, pointing at Josie's cast.

Josie dropped her head to examine the frayed straps on her backpack. "I'm fine."

"You're not going to tell me?"

"Not yet," Josie said. "I want to try to apologize first."

Lucy was silent for a while. "I was pissed off at the way you broke things off with us," she said.

"Who could blame you?" Josie was still fiddling with her backpack.

"Look at me, Josie."

Josie lifted her head. It weighed at least a ton. "I don't really know how I can apologize for that. Everything I say will sound like a ridiculous excuse. I was a jerk."

"Hmm. I can begin to work with that, I think. All I need is for you to turn that into a simple 'I'm sorry,' and we may be at square one."

Josie looked at her in confusion. Square one was them starting to date. Was that where Lucy wanted to go?

"I'm truly sorry," Josie said. "There was no reason to stop seeing you other than I was out of my mind."

"Okay," Lucy said.

"Okay?"

Lucy stood and smiled down at Josie. "Okay. As soon as you feel like getting together, give me a call. You've got my number."

Lucy walked off toward Alamo Shoes and even stopped to window-shop as Josie watched. Soon she was out of sight. Josie pulled her phone out of her pocket and sent a text. "I feel like seeing you now. You?" Minutes later Lucy was back and helped Josie up from the bench. They hobbled their way halfway down Summerdale, when Josie stopped and leaned on her crutches.

"I have two questions for you," she said.

"All right." Lucy looked at her curiously.

"First—may I kiss you?"

Lucy answered by bringing her lips to Josie's. This kiss felt nothing like the kisses they'd shared before. Josie could feel the electricity move through her body and out her crutches. The lingering kiss ended and Lucy held Josie's eyes.

"And the second question?" she asked.

"What floor is your apartment on?"

"First."

"You really are an angel," Josie said. "Let's go."

About the Author

Anne Laughlin is the author of *Veritas* and *Runaway* with Bold Strokes Books. *Sometimes Quickly*, an edited version of her first novel, will be published in 2014 by BSB. She is a three-time Goldie Award winner and has twice been shortlisted for a Lambda Literary Award. Her story, "It Only Occurred to Me Later," was a finalist in the 2013 Saints & Sinners Short Fiction Contest. In 2008, Anne was named a Lambda Literary Foundation Emerging Writer. She's been accepted into residencies at Ragdale and the Vermont Studio for the Arts. She lives in Chicago with Linda Braasch.

Books Available From Bold Strokes Books

Because of You by Julie Cannon. What would you do for the woman you were forced to leave behind? (978-1-62639-199-4)

The Job by Jove Belle. Sera always dreamed that she would one day reunite with Tor. She just didn't think it would involve terrorists, firearms, and hostages. (978-1-62639-200-7)

Making Time by C.J. Harte. Two women going in different directions meet after fifteen years and struggle to reconnect in spite of the past that separated them. (978-1-62639-201-4)

Once The Clouds Have Gone by KE Payne. Overwhelmed by the dark clouds of her past, Tag Grainger is lost until the intriguing and spirited Freddie Metcalfe unexpectedly forces her to reevaluate her life. (978-1-62639-202-1)

The Acquittal by Anne Laughlin. Chicago private investigator Josie Harper searches for the real killer of a woman whose lover has been acquitted of the crime. (978-1-62639-203-8)

An American Queer: The Amazon Trail by Lee Lynch. Lee Lynch's heartening and heart-rending history of gay life from the turbulence of the late 1900s to the triumphs of the early 2000s are recorded in this selection of her columns. (978-1-62639-204-5)

Stick McLaughlin by CF Frizzell. Corruption in 1918 cost Stick her lover, her freedom, and her identity, but a very special flapper and the family bond of her own gang could help win them back—even if it means outwitting the Boston Mob. (978-1-62639-205-2)

Rest Home Runaways by Clifford Henderson. Baby boomer Morgan Ronzio's troubled marriage is the least of her worries when she gets the call that her addled, eighty-six-year-old, half-blind dad has escaped the rest home. (978-1-62639-169-7)

Charm City by Mason Dixon. Raq Overstreet's loyalty to her drug kingpin boss is put to the test when she begins to fall for Bathsheba Morris, the undercover cop assigned to bring him down. (978-1-62639-198-7)

Edge of Awareness by C.A. Popovich. When Maria, a woman in the middle of her third divorce, meets Dana, an out lesbian, awareness of her feelings bring up reservations about the teachings of her church. (978-1-62639-188-8)

Taken by Storm by Kim Baldwin. Lives depend on two women when a train derails high in the remote Alps, but an unforgiving mountain, avalanches, crevasses, and other perils stand between them and safety. (978-1-62639-189-5)

The Common Thread by Jaime Maddox. Dr. Nicole Coussart's life is falling apart, but fortunately, DEA Attorney Rae Rhodes is there to pick up the pieces and help Nic put them back together. (978-1-62639-190-1)

Jolt by Kris Bryant. Mystery writer Bethany Lange wasn't prepared for the twisting emotions that left her breathless the moment she laid eyes on folk singer sensation Ali Hart. (978-1-62639-191-8)

Searching For Forever by Emily Smith. Dr. Natalie Jenner's life has always been about saving others, until young paramedic Charlie Thompson comes along and shows her maybe she's the one who needs saving. (978-1-62639-186-4)

Blindsided by Karis Walsh. Blindsided by love, guide dog trainer Lenae McIntyre and media personality Cara Bradley learn to trust what they see with their hearts. (978-1-62639-078-2)

Blue Water Dreams by Dena Hankins. Lania Marchiol keeps her wary sailor's gaze trained on the horizon until Oly Rassmussen, a wickedly handsome trans man, sends her trusty compass spinning off course. (978-1-62639-192-5)

Let the Lover Be by Sheree Greer. Kiana Lewis, a functional alcoholic on the verge of destruction, finally faces the demons of her past while finding love and earning redemption in New Orleans. (978-1-62639-077-5)

About Face by VK Powell. Forensic artist Macy Sheridan and Detective Leigh Monroe work on a case that has troubled them both for years, but they're hampered by the past and their unlikely yet undeniable attraction. (978-1-62639-079-9)

Blackstone by Shea Godfrey. For Darry and Jessa, the chance at a life of freedom is stolen by the arrival of war and an ancient prophecy that just might destroy their love. (978-1-62639-080-5)

Out of This World by Maggie Morton. Iris decided to cross an ocean to get over her ex. But instead, she ends up traveling much farther, all the way to another world. Once she's there, only a mysterious, sexy, and magical woman can help her return home. (978-1-62639-083-6)

Kiss The Girl by Melissa Brayden. Sleeping with the enemy has never been so complicated. Brooklyn Campbell and Jessica Lennox face off in love and advertising in fast-paced New York City. (978-1-62639-071-3)

Taking Fire: A First Responders Novel by Radclyffe. Hunted by extremists and under siege by nature's most virulent weapons, Navy medic Max de Milles and Red Cross worker Rachel Winslow join forces to survive and discover something far more lasting. (978-1-62639-072-0)

First Tango in Paris by Shelley Thrasher. When French law student Eva Laroche meets American call girl Brigitte Green in 1970s Paris, they have no idea how their pasts and futures will intersect. (978-1-62639-073-7)